TWINS FOR THE COWBOY DAD

LISA CHILDS

Recycling programs for this product may not exist in your area.

ISBN-13: 978-1-335-46039-4

Twins for the Cowboy Dad

For questions and comments about the quality of this book, please contact us at CustomerService@Harlequin.com.

Harlequin Enterprises ULC
22 Adelaide St. West, 41st Floor
Toronto, Ontario M5H 4E3, Canada
www.Harlequin.com

HarperCollins Publishers
Macken House, 39/40 Mayor Street Upper,
Dublin 1, D01 C9W8, Ireland
www.HarperCollins.com

Printed in U.S.A.

Strong hands gripped her arms, steadying her.

"Are you all right?" that deep voice asked, gruff now with concern.

Trish nodded as the wave of dizziness passed. Keeping her eyes closed, she smelled the familiar scents of hay and horses and leather and a trace of sweet smoke. These were the scents she'd always associated with home. But when she opened her eyes, she couldn't see the house or the ranch; she could see only the man who stood in front of her, holding her. The glow from the yard lights illuminated his dark eyes and his square jaw, shadowed with dark-auburn stubble.

But Brett Lemmon could *not* be home to her. He was a stranger, albeit a very good looking one. And she couldn't make the mistakes she had in the past of trusting the wrong people. Trish pressed her hand over her belly. Not when she was about to have the family she'd wanted for so long...

Dear Reader,

Welcome back to Willow Creek, Wyoming! I'm happy to share another Bachelor Cowboys book with you. I love the Haven/Cassidy/Lemmon family, probably because I come from a large family myself and I also married into one. "Family first" is my mantra, like it is for Sadie March Haven-Lemmon, the matriarch of this extended family. She'll do anything to make sure her and her new husband Lem Lemmon's family finds happiness.

That hasn't been easy with Lem's grandsons because their recent inheritance of the Four Corners ranch is being contested, and they might lose their livelihoods and their home. But what the Lemmon brothers keep losing are their hearts! Liam lost his to a baby left in the barn and the CPS investigator assigned to little Lucy's case. Then Blake lost his to the lawyer who wrote up the will being contested. Brett, the oldest brother, vowed he would never lose his. But he just may have met his match when Trish Dempsey shows up at the ranch—pregnant with *twins*!

I hope you enjoy this book with all the family and ranch animals as much as I enjoyed writing it. And rest assured that this is not the last book. Octogenarians Sadie and Lem aren't done matchmaking yet.

Happy Reading!

Lisa

New York Times and *USA TODAY* bestselling, award-winning author **Lisa Childs** has written more than one hundred books. Published in twenty countries, she's also appeared on the *Publishers Weekly*, Barnes & Noble and Nielsen Top 100 bestseller lists. Lisa writes contemporary romance, romantic suspense, and paranormal and women's fiction. She's a wife, mom, bonus mom, avid reader and less avid runner. Readers can reach her through Facebook or her website, lisachilds.com.

Books by Lisa Childs

Harlequin Heartwarming

Bachelor Cowboys

The Cowboy's Unlikely Match
The Bronc Rider's Twin Surprise
The Cowboy's Ranch Rescue
The Firefighter's Family Secret
The Doc's Instant Family
The Rancher's Reunion
A Match for the Sheriff
The Cowboy's Baby Surprise
The Cowboy's Claim

Visit the Author Profile page at Harlequin.com for more titles.

With great appreciation for every member of my incredible review team, Lisa's Bookies!

Thanks for all your support!

CHAPTER ONE

THE PARTY WAS OVER…a couple of hours ago. The birthday boy, Brett Lemmon's grandfather Lem, was probably asleep by now. Brett should have been, as well, but he was too on edge after what had transpired that day. So he paced the dark paneled den at the Four Corners Ranch and ruminated on everything that had happened.

His grandfather had turned eighty-one today, and his wife had thrown him a wonderful party with all their enormous family gathered around him at Ranch Haven, an hour away from the town of Willow Creek, Wyoming, and an hour away from the Four Corners Ranch. Lem should have been the focus of the day, but as usual, *she* had disrupted it. Talk of her. Thoughts of her. And then she'd sent that strange text message: I am on my way to Willow Creek. Alone. Divorce is finally final. I will explain everything when I get to the Four Corners.

How could she possibly explain what she'd done?

Brett couldn't think of any excuse good enough

to justify her not being here when her dad had been hurt and lying in a coma in a hospital bed. What reason could she possibly have had for not coming home to attend her own father's funeral? And how could she justify contesting his will, fighting his final wishes?

Brett didn't care that she'd been going through a divorce. He didn't care about anything except honoring his late boss and friend, Frank Dempsey. Frank's daughter, Patricia "Trish" Dempsey-Trent, obviously hadn't cared about her father. But Brett had. He'd admired, respected and loved Frank. And he would do everything within his power to make sure that Frank's wishes were carried out.

When he'd been alive, Frank had been denied his most fervent wish. He'd wanted a relationship with his only child, but Frank had told Brett that once Trish had been too old for enforcement of the custody agreement between him and his ex-wife, she had stopped spending summer and school holidays with him. He'd only seen her sporadically over the years.

And he'd missed her so much.

After pacing around the leather couch, Brett headed toward Frank's massive oak desk. Brett and his brothers, Blake and Liam, who helped him run the ranch, hadn't been able to bring themselves to sit in Frank's chair yet. They couldn't imagine anyone else sitting in the big chair that Frank had used so often the leather had worn thin on the armrests. Brett and his brothers hadn't touched the desk either; it still had the things on it that had mattered most to Frank: a box of expensive cigars, a metal shoe from his favorite horse and pictures of his *girls*, or as he'd called them, Frank's angels—his daughter, Trish, and her cousin Frankie, who Frank had raised after her parents died, and their best friend, Maci Bluff.

One of the photographs was about eight or nine years old, from the last summer before their senior year of high school, so they were all about seventeen. Their faces were sunburned, their smiles bright and the love and affection they felt for each other was so clear in their expressions and in the way that their arms were wrapped tightly around each other.

Frankie looked the same now as she had in the picture, with her wild, unruly brown curls. Maci had changed quite a bit. Her short pixie cut had grown out, so her blond hair was longer now and her freckles must have faded away.

And Trish…

Brett had no idea if she still looked the same. He hadn't seen her in the five years that he'd worked at the Four Corners Ranch. In the photograph, she looked a lot like Frankie with the same delicate features, but her face was fuller, rounder. And her eyes were a lighter brown than Frankie's, more like topaz. She had curly hair, too, but it was shorter and kind of frizzy. There were other pictures of her, too, but she was even younger in those. In one, she was a baby, and Frank was holding her up over his head, and she was smiling down at him.

Frank looked so happy in the picture that Brett's heart ached for him, for how much he'd loved his daughter. But he'd lost her. He'd blamed his vindictive ex-wife and cautioned Brett to never get married. But Brett didn't only blame Frank's ex for breaking his heart; his daughter had done the most damage to him. And she still continued to disrespect him by disrespecting his wishes, by fighting the will in which Frank had laid out how he wanted to divide his estate.

Frank hadn't wanted just his daughter to inherit it, or even just his daughter and Frankie. Frank had wanted his estate split equally between Trish, Frankie, and Brett and his brothers. And Maci, as the executor of his will as well as the lawyer who'd drawn it up, would receive a percentage of the value of it. Brett hadn't expected Frank to include him, let alone his brothers. But in those first couple of lean years when Brett had rarely drawn a salary, Frank had promised that he would make it up to Brett in the end. And Frank had always kept his promises.

Headlights suddenly shone through the blinds over the window in the den that faced the driveway. Brett glanced at his watch. It was after midnight. While her text had said she was on her way to Willow Creek, he'd assumed that meant she would show up tomorrow or the day after, not tonight.

And definitely not when he was the only one awake in the house. Even his niece, Lucy, was sleeping, and Brett had recently wondered if the baby ever closed her eyes. He loved the little girl, but he certainly didn't want any kids of his own. They were more work than the ranch was.

He preferred to be out riding fences than walking the floor with a fussy infant. He intended to take his late friend's advice to heart and never give his heart to anyone. Focus on doing what he loved instead of falling in love. That was his plan.

His matchmaking grandpa Lem and his new wife, Sadie March Haven, weren't going to like that, but he didn't care. He was going to protect himself and, most importantly, he was going to protect his heart.

TRISH SHOULD HAVE stopped for the night in Willow Creek; there were hotels there, bed-and-breakfasts that would have been open still. She could have checked in and rested before coming out to the ranch in the morning. But knowing she was only an hour away had pushed her to keep driving. She'd been gone so long that she hadn't wanted to wait a minute longer, let alone a day, to see the ranch again. Maybe it was better that she arrived at night since she was unlikely to see anyone else. Surely the Lemmons slept in the bunkhouse where the ranch hands always had, so it would only be her cousin Frankie in the house. And her room, the one her father had promised to always keep for her, should be just as she'd left it years ago.

Now that she was here, she couldn't wait to get out of the truck where she'd been confined for too long without moving. That wasn't good for her. Or for them…

She pressed her hand over her swollen belly. First one foot kicked, and then another. She smiled. They were letting her know that they were okay. After losing other babies, she needed this reassurance more than anything.

She pushed open the driver door, maneuvered her pregnant belly from beneath the steering wheel and stepped out onto the gravel driveway.

"This is *home*, babies," she whispered. This was the place she'd been the happiest in her life, with the people who'd meant the most to her. But one of them wasn't here any longer.

If only she could see her father again…

It was too late for that now. He was gone. And she hadn't even been able to say goodbye. Tears stung her eyes, but she blinked them away and focused on the house she'd always loved so much. Yard lights illuminated the long, one-story ranch house, and another light glowed in one of the front windows and spilled onto the porch that ran the entire length of the house.

Despite not having visited for years, she knew which window that was: her father's den. That light had been on so often late into the night like it was now, while her father had pored over the ranch books.

Had he been struggling to keep the business afloat like Maci Bluff had told her?

She and Maci had once been so close back when Trish had spent every summer at the Four Corners Ranch. Those summers had been the best experiences of her entire life, hanging out with her best friends and playing with animals outside all day long. She wished she'd never stopped spending her summers, or even more of her time, at the ranch. She wished she'd listened to her father about her ex, because then Harold Trent would have been her ex-fiancé instead of ex-husband. She wished she'd listened to her father about everything else as well, all the advice he'd given her over the years, like being self-sufficient and not letting her mother get in her head, but it was too late now. The mistakes had been made, and he was gone.

What she wouldn't give to hear his voice one more time…

"Who's out there?"

The voice was deep, gruff and very male. A man was standing on the porch, the front door open behind him. He wore a cowboy hat and boots, but with the light behind him, his face was in shadows.

"Who are you?" she asked. Goose bumps rose on the skin of her bare arms, making her shiver. She had truly expected that only Frankie would be living inside the house.

"Brett Lemmon," he replied.

She sucked in a breath. This was one of the brothers who'd worked for her father and had somehow convinced Frank to put them in his will.

"And you're Patricia Dempsey-Trent?" he asked, as if he couldn't believe it.

"Trish Dempsey," she corrected him. She'd worked hard to drop *Trent*. The divorce had dragged on for far too long. But it had finally been settled, leaving her free to come home at last. And she didn't have to worry about her ex getting any part of the ranch. She just had to worry about Brett Lemmon and his brothers getting it.

Her lawyer had been fighting that, too, just as he'd fought her ex for her freedom. But after Trish had talked to Maci and her cousin Frankie, she wasn't sure that contesting the will was the right thing to do anymore. Maci and Frankie were upset with her for not honoring her father's final wishes.

But what if her lawyer's suspicions were founded, and the Lemmon brothers had conned her father and her friends?

She had to be careful. She couldn't make the

mistake of trusting the wrong people again. If only she'd listened to her dad instead of her mother…

She pressed her hand over her belly. Everything she'd done had led her to where she was now—about to have the family she'd wanted for so long. These babies were just *her* babies, not her ex's. Harold Trent had lied to her about wanting kids, just as he'd lied about so much else. But after a couple of years of denying herself what she wanted, she'd realized their marriage would never last. They didn't really love each other. She wasn't sure they'd even liked each other.

And so, she'd started the divorce proceedings and the IVF treatments because she'd realized that the smartest and safest thing for her was to be a single parent. Then she would never have to share custody if things didn't work out. Her kids would never be shuffled back and forth between two homes, fought over and poisoned against another parent. They could just be kids, confident in the love of the one parent they had, and happy.

She knew they would be happy here at the Four Corners Ranch. But she hadn't considered that she might not be happy here now, without her dad, and with these Lemmon men living on the ranch, too. She'd figured that if they stayed at the Four Corners, they would be living in the bunkhouse, not the main house, and she would have some distance from them. And if her lawyer was right about them, they wouldn't necessarily be here for long. But what if Nolan Stokes was wrong?

"You were in the den?" she asked. "When I saw the light..." For a moment she'd imagined her dad was still here, waiting up for her like he used to when she and Maci and Frankie had gone into town on one of those long-ago summer nights.

He nodded. "Yeah."

"And you live in the house?" she asked. She really didn't want to share it or the ranch with anyone but her family. But if it was truly what her father had wanted, which was what Maci and Frankie claimed, then she might have to share.

"Yes," he said. "My brothers and I live here."

"What happened to the bunkhouse?" she asked. That was where the ranch hands used to stay back when she spent her summers with her father. One of those ranch hands had once dated her but had really just wanted to get closer to her father and, behind her back, to Frankie. After that experience, she never should have dated—let alone married—a man who'd worked for her mother's new husband. She should have known that *she* wasn't what he'd really wanted.

"The bunkhouse needs plumbing and electrical updates, and Frank wanted us in the house with him," Brett Lemmon said, his voice suddenly as chilly as the late spring wind that swirled around her. "He was lonely."

She wasn't sure if there was recrimination in

his tone, but she flinched as if he was blaming her for that loneliness. She already blamed herself, and that guilt weighed heavily on her shoulders, which were physically aching from the long drive. Overwhelmed with exhaustion and guilt, she closed her eyes to hold back tears that threatened to fall, and as she closed her eyes, she swayed on her feet from a sudden rush of dizziness.

Before she could steady herself, strong hands gripped her arms, holding her. “Are you all right?” That deep voice was tinged now with concern.

She nodded and, keeping her eyes closed, drew in a deep breath that smelled faintly of hay and horses and leather and a trace of sweet smoke. These were the scents she’d always associated with home. But when she opened her eyes, she couldn’t see the house or the ranch; she could only see the man who stood in front of her, holding her.

He could not be *home* to her; he was a stranger, albeit a very good-looking one. The glow from the yard lights illuminated his dark eyes and his square jaw that was highlighted with dark auburn stubble.

“You must have been driving for hours,” he said.

Nearly too exhausted to speak, she nodded again.

“You should get some sleep,” he said. “Let me help you into the house, and then I’ll come back and grab whatever you need from your vehicle.”

The quad cab truck was full of her stuff, as was the trailer that she'd pulled behind it. She'd packed everything she owned to come home, because that was what the Four Corners had always felt like to her even though she'd spent more time at her mother and stepfather's estate in the city. Her father had always made certain that she'd felt that way, too, that the ranch was hers and would always be hers.

But was this really her home anymore or had the Lemmon brothers completely taken it over?

"Do I…is anyone using my room?" she asked.

"Uh…" He grimaced slightly as if he was uncomfortable. "Frankie moved into your old room when she gave hers up to Liam and Elise and the baby since her room was bigger," he said.

Since Frankie had lived full-time at the ranch after her own parents died, she'd had the bigger bedroom with the en suite bathroom. It wouldn't have made sense for Trish, who'd only visited for the summer and holidays, to have that room. But Dad had insisted she decorate hers as she'd wanted it to look, and he'd said that it would always be there for her whenever she wanted to use it.

"We didn't realize you were coming tonight, or she could have taken my room," Brett said.

"You weren't waiting up for me?" she asked. Not that she was under any illusion that he'd intended to welcome her home. In fact, she was surprised that he was trying to help her. After realizing he was staying in the house, she'd half expected him to bar her from entering the ranch.

He shook his head. "I couldn't sleep."

"That's why I kept driving," she said. After she'd sent the text to Maci that she was finally coming home, she'd been so excited and sleep had seemed impossible. But now that she was here, she was exhausted. She certainly didn't have the energy to deal with Brett Lemmon, especially now that he was being kind to her.

The text she'd sent Maci hadn't given an exact time that she would arrive at the ranch. "I should have called to let Frankie know that I was going to drive straight through, but I didn't want to wake her up this late." She'd thought she would just be able to let herself into the house, with the key she'd kept all these years, and into her bedroom without waking anyone up. But things had changed at the Four Corners, maybe even the locks.

"You can take my bed," he said. "I'll sleep on one of the couches."

He was willing to give up his bed for her. Would he give up his share of the ranch? Would he let her have the one thing she had left of her father for just herself and her family? She wanted to ask him, but first she had to talk to Maci.

She had to learn what her father really wanted. And she had to respect that, just as she wished people had respected her wishes for what she'd wanted out of her own life. “Thank you,” she said. “I have an overnight bag on the passenger seat. That’s all I need for tonight.”

Tomorrow, after getting some rest, she would figure out what she would do with the rest of her stuff and how to carry out her plan for what to do with the rest of her life.

THE SOUND OF voices woke Frankie up, not that she’d been sleeping all that deeply. Since learning that her cousin was coming home, she’d been on edge. From a distance, Trish had been causing so much trouble. What would happen when she was here, presumably staying under the same roof with Frankie and the Lemmon brothers?

But it wasn’t just the guys now. Liam was married to Elise, and they had baby Lucy. So Frankie had given them her room, and she slept in Trish’s now, which was exactly as she’d left it all those years ago like a shrine Uncle Frank had kept of his daughter. Maybe Frankie should have moved out when they’d returned from the party at Ranch Haven. But Trish hadn’t said that she was coming tonight. And it had already been so late that Frankie hadn’t believed that she would arrive tonight or maybe at all.

She recognized the voices she heard coming from the living room. One was Brett’s. She wasn’t surprised that he was still awake; he’d been even more on edge than she was. While all the Lemmons loved the ranch, Brett was the most invested in it.

He'd come to work here first, and then when he'd seen how much trouble the Four Corners was in, he'd enlisted his brothers to help. And maybe he was most invested in the ranch because it was all he had, unlike his brothers, who'd found love.

Not that Brett wanted love any more than Frankie wanted it. She wanted to go back to her band and life on the road. But she couldn't do that until she made certain that her uncle's wishes were carried out. For everything that Uncle Frank had done for Frankie, she owed him that, as well as her life.

The other voice belonged to her cousin Trish: the reason that Frank's wishes hadn't been carried out yet. And now she was here.

Frankie rolled out of bed and pulled open the door. Then she hurried down the short hall to the living room. Brett blocked Trish from her view. A bag dangled from one of his hands as he argued with her cousin. "You can't sleep on the couch in your condition. Take my bed."

"Condition?" Frankie asked with concern. Trish was more than a cousin to her. After Frankie had lost her parents, her uncle had become her guardian and Trish had become her sister and her best friend. What was wrong with her?

Brett turned toward Frankie, and as he did, Trish stepped out from behind him. It had been a few years since they'd last seen each other, but Trish didn't look any older. In fact, with her dark hair curling around her heart-shaped face, she looked younger. She must have finally given up trying to straighten it like she used to. The only thing giving away her age, or at least her stress, was the dark circles beneath her eyes. Frankie's gaze skimmed below her cousin's face to see that she wore leggings with a shirt over them that was stretched tight across her belly. A gasp slipped through Frankie's lips. "You're pregnant?"

Of all the things Frankie had been thinking about Trish lately, the fact that she could be pregnant had never crossed her mind.

Trish nodded, and a faint smile curved her lips as she patted her burgeoning belly. "With twins."

"But…you said in your text that you're divorced?"

Trish nodded again. "These aren't Harold's babies."

Frankie gasped again.

Trish laughed and shook her head. "I don't mean it like that. I mean that I did this alone, through IVF and a sperm donor. They're just mine."

Brett sucked in a breath, probably over the possessiveness in Trish's voice. Was she just that way about her babies or was she being possessive of the ranch, too, wanting it all for herself?

But Frankie suddenly realized that maybe Trish

wasn't thinking only of herself, but also of these babies that she looked like she was about to deliver any minute.

"When are you due?" Frankie asked.

"Eight weeks," Trish said.

So she would have been just a few weeks pregnant when Uncle Frank had had the ranch accident that landed him in a coma in the hospital.

"It's late," Brett said. "And she needs some sleep. I was trying to get her to take my bed and I'll sleep on the couch."

"Why not Uncle Frank's room?" Frankie asked.

It was apparently Trish's turn to suck in a breath. "You want him to take my dad's room?"

"I wouldn't," Brett said, shaking his head as if the very idea of it horrified him.

"I meant Trish," Frankie said. "Why don't you take his room?" Nobody else in the house had wanted to disturb it—leaving it like a shrine to the man they all loved and missed so much.

But Trish was his daughter, and ironically, she was the least close to him of everyone who currently lived in the house, with the exception of Elise and baby Lucy, who had just recently moved in with them.

Trish was shaking her head, too. "I… I'm fine with the couch."

"I can take the couch," Frankie offered. "And you can have your bed back. But it's just a full-size."

Trish patted her belly again. "You're saying I'm too big for it?"

Remembering how sensitive Trish had once been about her weight thanks to her mom constantly monitoring it, Frankie shook her head. "No, of course not."

"I know, but you're right," she said. "I don't know about taking my dad's room, though." She glanced around then. "Where's Buster?"

Tears stung Frankie's eyes at the mention of her uncle's old hound dog. "Buster passed away when Uncle Frank was in the hospital. He missed him too much."

Brett cleared his throat, as if struggling with his emotions, too. "I… I…uh, I should get to bed then. If you're sure you won't take mine?"

Trish's eyes widened for a moment as if she wondered if Brett was offering to share it with her instead of giving it up to her. Trish had no idea how much Brett disliked her for how she'd abandoned her dad.

"I would be fine on the couch," he said, as if to clarify what he'd meant.

"Don't worry about it, Brett," Frankie said. "I'll make sure Trish gets settled in for the night." But she really hoped her cousin wasn't staying longer than that.

Brett handed the bag he held over to Frankie, and then he lowered his voice and said, "This is her overnight one. But there is a truck and a trailer full of the rest of her stuff."

So Trish wasn't here just for a quick visit to finally settle her father's estate. She was moving in, and from the gruffness of Brett's voice, he wasn't happy about it.

Frankie didn't blame him. He'd worked too hard for too many years at the ranch to turn it over to someone who'd never appreciated what she'd had here.

Earlier that day, when Trish had sent that text to Maci, Frankie had hoped that everything was going to work out, but that hope evaporated now. They were a long way from settling anything. In fact, things were probably just going to get even messier than they'd already been. As Brett walked away, Frankie fought the urge to call him back. She didn't want to be alone with her cousin.

"You can go back to bed," Trish told her. Maybe she didn't want to be alone with Frankie either. She reached for her bag. "I've got this."

"And apparently everything else you own, too?"

Trish's face flushed slightly, and she nodded. "Yes."

"Why?"

"I didn't come home just to settle the estate," Trish said. "I'm going to live here."

Yup, life was definitely going to get even messier...

CHAPTER TWO

ONCE HE'D GONE to bed, Brett hadn't been able to sleep very deeply or for very long. Having Trish in the house made him uneasy for so many reasons.

He didn't trust her. Her text to Maci in which she'd promised to explain everything when she arrived didn't mean that she was going to back down from contesting her father's will, just that she was going to explain why she was doing it.

After meeting her and seeing how pregnant she was, Brett could figure out why she was doing it. She wanted the ranch for herself and for her children.

And part of him understood and respected that. He'd even been concerned when she'd looked like she was about to pass out from exhaustion. So he hadn't pushed her to talk. Instead, he'd wanted her to get some rest.

If only he'd been able to get some sleep himself, he might be able to think clearer. But he woke up at the crack of dawn, before anyone else was awake, and he fed the animals in the barn, including the calf that had lost its mother earlier that month. Frankie had been mothering it, feeding it with a bottle. She usually slept in the stall with it, too. But last night she'd been in her bed.

A couple of the barn kittens kept Cocoa company. The two black kittens snuggled up against the little brown calf. Brett sighed as he petted them. He wanted to focus on the cattle; he and his brothers had more than enough work with the beef business. But someone had dropped off a litter of kittens. They'd managed to find homes for three of them, one with Brett's widowed dad and two with Maci. Liam and Elise had adopted an orange one who'd moved into the house, which left these two yet to find homes. No wonder they'd bonded with the orphaned calf.

One of them rubbed against his hand and purred. He scratched under its chin, and it closed its eyes as if in bliss. They were cute.

An image of Trish popped into his head. She was cute, too. Her dark hair just barely reached her shoulders, and with its wild curls, was even more unruly than Frankie's long spirals. Trish had brown eyes like her cousin, but hers were very light brown. Almost the same color as the black kitten's, whose eyes stared at him unblinkingly.

Trish had barely been able to keep her eyes open last night, she'd been so exhausted. She would probably sleep in today. Or so he hoped.

He wasn't ready yet to hear her explanations.

What he'd already learned about her unsettled him. She was recently divorced and very pregnant and had what looked like all her worldly possessions packed into that big truck and trailer. She had plans.

And Brett had a horrible feeling that those plans were going to affect him whether he wanted them to or not. But he wouldn't let himself think about them or about her. Instead, he focused on saddling his horse and then riding out to check the pastures and the cattle.

After he returned to the barn, and had unsaddled and cooled down his horse, he walked around the corner of the barn to where his truck was parked. Fortunately, the keys were in it, so he hopped inside and started it up. As he drove down the long driveway toward the street, he glanced into the rearview mirror and peered at her vehicle through the dust his tires had kicked up. The trailer was there, but the truck that had hauled it to the ranch was gone.

She must have gone somewhere, but it was clear she was coming back. And planning to move in, which left Brett wanting to move out. Despite how big and sprawling the ranch house was, it was already starting to feel crowded. Liam was married with a baby living there, and Frankie hadn't gone back on the road. And Blake…

Now that he was with Maci Bluff, would he move out or would she move in?

Trish and those babies that were due in a couple of months would push the house to capacity. Lucy had just begun to sleep through the night; he couldn't imagine having two newborns crying nonstop.

If Trish moved in, Brett wasn't sure that he could stay, regardless of whether she continued to contest her father's will or not. If he lost the ranch, where else could he go? And what if he didn't lose but had to find some way to work and live with the woman who'd tried to take it away from him?

Mulling over what he might do and because he'd had no idea where he was headed, he was surprised when a little less than an hour later he turned into the long driveway that led to Ranch Haven. He'd just been there the day before, for his grandfather's birthday party and he'd had no intention of returning so soon. It was as if his truck had just driven him here, or maybe his subconscious.

Sadie March Haven, his new stepgrandmother, insisted that all the Lemmons had a home at the ranch. His younger brothers and sister certainly felt that way—they came and went without ringing the doorbell. They even called Sadie Grandma now, which she clearly loved.

But when he stood on the front porch minutes later, Brett couldn't quite bring himself to turn that doorknob without ringing the bell first. And the word *Grandma* stuck in his throat when she opened the door to him.

Maybe he was still slightly in awe of this woman. Sadie was a legend around Willow Creek, Wyoming. She stood over six feet tall in her cowboy boots. Her white hair was tied back in a long, thick braid. And her hands, which were rumored to have fought off wolves, were as big as his, but now her knuckles were swollen with arthritis. She'd worked hard and long her entire life. And she'd endured so many losses. She was probably one of the strongest people he'd ever had the privilege of meeting. That was why he was here: he needed to borrow some of that strength of hers.

"Brett, are you okay?" she asked, her voice husky with concern. She reached out to him, clasping his shoulders. While she pulled him into the house, she didn't pull him into a hug as he'd watched her do with his sister and brothers.

Maybe that was just because she respected that he wasn't a hugger, though. He'd never been particularly affectionate with anyone, which was why he had usually been dumped whenever he'd dated. He had to take his time to get to know a person and for a person to get to know him before he let anyone in. His dad was like that: quiet, thoughtful, independent. Frank Dempsey had been the same way as well. Maybe that was why they'd become friends so quickly.

"Brett?" Sadie repeated his name as a question, and her grasp on his shoulders tightened a bit.

He released a breath and nodded. "Yeah, I'm okay."

"You look exhausted."

"I am," he admitted. "She came back last night."

"Trish?" Sadie asked.

He nodded again.

"Did she explain herself?"

"Not yet," he said. "And I probably should have stuck around to hear her reasons but..." Emotion rushed up on him as he relived the past few months. Losing Frank and then the limbo of the will being contested. It had all been too much.

And now Sadie did what she'd done with his siblings, she pulled Brett into a hug.

He found himself winding his arms around her and holding on tightly, as if he hoped some of her strength would transfer to him. Because as the oldest of his siblings, he'd always felt like he had to be the strong one. The one who'd held it together when they'd been forced to move away from Willow Creek as kids and to the big city that he and his brothers had hated. He'd been the one who'd held it together when their mom died. When their grandma died...

And when Frank Dempsey, Brett's best friend and mentor, died, he'd held it together then, too. For so many years, Brett had forced himself to put his own feelings and fears aside so that he could assuage his siblings' fears and feelings.

Now they all had someone who would do that for them. Liam had Elise, and Blake had Maci, and Livvy had Colton. And Brett was alone. More alone than he'd ever felt in his life despite living in a house full of people. And that was why he'd come here.

So he wouldn't feel so alone.

TRISH WAS A little older than Frankie and Maci, so she'd had her license first and had driven the route between the ranch and Maci's house many times over the summers she'd come home. She knew it well, and her lawyer had verified that Maci still lived there, that she still drove the same vehicle she had since high school, and that she also rented office space in Willow Creek. So, to know all of that, he must have been spying on her, just as Maci had accused him of doing. Trish needed to learn more about those accusations and the will. Fortunately, since she'd woken up so early, she'd caught Maci at home instead of at her office. She would have gone on to it if Maci's little SUV wasn't parked in the driveway and there wasn't a light on inside. Yet she hesitated to ring the bell or knock on the door.

Those summers long ago, she would have just walked right in, but she wasn't the teenage girl she'd once been any more than Maci and Frankie were. Even though Frankie had helped her change the sheets in the main bedroom suite at the ranch, she'd barely spoken to her. Trish had felt strange being in her dad's room now that he was gone, and she would have liked Frankie to stay with her, the way they used to when they were kids. Trish had felt like a little girl again, afraid of whatever monsters might be lurking in the dark.

But Frankie had refused; maybe she believed that Trish was the monster. She hadn't admitted it, though; she'd just said, "You're tired. We'll talk tomorrow. All of us, together."

Frankie had clearly aligned herself with the Lemmons, leaving Trish to feel left out and alone. She didn't want it to be her against them. She didn't want to have to explain herself to all of them at once. She wasn't even sure she wanted to explain herself at all to the Lemmons. What she'd gone through with her divorce and IVF and the usual drama with her mother wasn't something she cared to share with anyone but the women she'd once considered her sisters.

But with Frankie being so cold toward her the night before, Trish worried that she might have permanently damaged her relationship with her cousin. Maci had also defended the Lemmons to her, insisting that they weren't the con artists Nolan Stokes thought they were. And apparently it was possible Maci had fallen for one of them, but Trish figured Maci was more likely to pick whatever side Frankie was on than anyone else's. Those two had always been so close. Trish had lost that closeness with them years ago, long before her dad had died.

She'd started slipping away from them after she got engaged. Her mom, and her expectations for the wedding, had taken over Trish's life. She'd let her mother and then her ex-husband take over way too much of her life. And now some men she'd never met before were taking over the ranch.

It was all too much.

She didn't have to be here alone, though. Her lawyer had offered to handle everything for her just as he'd handled her divorce. But after talking to Frankie and Maci over the phone, she had some concerns about his motivation.

"Why aren't you just walking in?" The question came from behind Trish, and she turned to find Frankie walking up the driveway from where she'd parked her old conversion van along the curb a short distance down the street.

"Did you follow me here?" Trish asked. She'd been so quiet when she'd awakened that morning that she hadn't thought anyone else had noticed her leaving.

"I think your bigshot lawyer has made you paranoid," Frankie said.

She couldn't necessarily argue against that; Nolan Stokes *had* made her a bit paranoid about her ex and about the Lemmons. He'd been right to caution her about her ex, so he could possibly be right about the Lemmons, too. Maybe they had conned her dad into including them in his will, as Nolan suspected, and maybe they'd also conned Maci and Frankie into thinking that was really what her dad had wanted.

"I came to Maci's to talk about you," Frankie brazenly admitted. "About how you showed up last night all knocked up and how you disappeared already this morning. And here you are, so I guess I don't have to talk about you behind your back."

Instead of being offended, warmth filled Trish. She'd missed Frankie so much. She'd missed how open and honest her cousin was. Appreciative of the honesty, she closed her arms around Frankie's shoulders and hugged her. And one of the babies pushed against her belly, kicking with his or her usual vigor. She gasped.

And so did Frankie. "Was that a kick?"

"Yes, they do that a lot," Trish replied. And she thanked God every time that they did, grateful for the assurance they were strong. They were healthy. They were viable after all the failed pregnancies.

"They..." Frankie shook her head. "I can't believe you're having two."

Trish patted her huge belly. "I can. Sometimes it feels like I have a whole chorus line in there."

"A what?"

The question came from behind Trish, and she

turned around to find the door open behind her and Maci standing in the opening. Then Maci saw her belly, and her blue eyes widened in shock.

"Chorus line," Trish replied as she patted her belly. "From the way they kick me."

"They?" Maci asked.

"Just two," Trish said. "That's all I had left of my embryos and the money I'd saved for my IVF treatments."

Maci's forehead creased with deep furrows. "I don't understand any of this…" She turned toward Frankie as if she had the answers.

Frankie shrugged. "I don't know. She showed up late last night, and I thought she would fill us all in this morning. But after I took care of Cocoa, who I think Brett must have already fed, I found her truck gone. Her trailer was still there, though."

"Trailer?" Maci asked.

"Cocoa?" Trish asked. "Who's Cocoa?"

"The calf who thinks Frankie is her mother," Maci answered her question.

"You have a calf?" Trish asked with a rush of happiness. During the days when she'd been confined to complete bedrest so she didn't lose this pregnancy, she'd had so much time to think. She had come up with so many plans for the ranch, plans that might be even easier to implement than she'd thought.

"The Four Corners is a beef ranch," Frankie

said. "Of course we have calves. Lots of them right now. Calving season just ended."

Trish's happiness dimmed with the way that Frankie was talking to her, as if she assumed that Trish didn't know anything about the ranch. Until college, she had spent every summer at the Four Corners. It was part of her and held the happiest memories of her life.

"This particular calf, though, lost its mother at birth," Maci said. "Frankie saved the calf, though. And now they've bonded. We keep teasing her about how she's going to take Cocoa on the road with her when she goes back to traveling with her band."

We. The *we* used to be the three of them: Frankie, Trish and Maci. But Trish knew that the *we* now meant Maci, Frankie and the Lemmon brothers. It stung that she'd been replaced.

"I'll figure out how to bring Cocoa with me," Frankie said. "Right now she's still small enough to fit in the van."

"I'm sure the calf would be happier at the ranch," Trish said. Just like she was sure she would be happier there, too. That was why she'd packed up everything she owned. "I could keep her for the petting zoo I want to start for kids' day camps and summer camps at the ranch."

"What?" Both Maci and Frankie asked the question at the same time.

Excitement bubbled up inside Trish. She had

so many plans for the ranch, to make it the ideal place for her children and for other children to enjoy, just like she had as a child and even as a teenager. She'd lived all year with the anticipation of spending her summers at the Four Corners. And she knew that, like her, other kids from the city would benefit from the fresh air and open space of the ranch. They would love it as much as she had.

Before she could launch into all her plans for the place, Frankie asked, "You're going to stay?"

Trish nodded. "That's the plan." And it was the only one she had. So she had to figure out a way to make this work for her and for her babies.

"THANKS, GRANDMA..." Those words echoed in Sadie's head and her heart long after Brett left Ranch Haven. The last of Lem's grandchildren, their grandchildren now, had called her *Grandma*. Happiness curved her lips into a smile.

"Hey, there, my beautiful bride," Lem said as he and Feisty, their long-haired Chihuahua, joined her on the patio just outside the open French doors of the kitchen.

His white hair and snowy white beard were a bit damp around his flushed face. He was taking his exercise seriously these days, and it showed, because his belly, which he'd never needed to pad to play Santa Claus for Christmas in the Willow Creek town square, was much smaller now.

"Was that a truck from the Four Corners that I saw when Feisty and I were heading back from our walk?" he asked as he dropped into the chair across the table from her.

She nodded.

"I couldn't tell who was driving," he said. "It was going so fast, I couldn't catch a glimpse of the driver. Who was it?"

"Brett," she replied.

"And he put that smile on your face?"

"Yes," she said. "He called me Grandma for the first time."

"Wow," Lem said, and he reached out to squeeze her hand. "That's wonderful."

Her smile slid away. "It would be if he hadn't been so upset," she said.

"Oh, no. More trouble with Trish and her lawyer?"

She nodded. "Trish showed up last night, very pregnant..."

"Pregnant?" Lem asked, his blue eyes widening with surprise. "I thought she just got a divorce."

Sadie nodded. "She hasn't explained anything yet either. And the reason Brett was in such a hurry when he left was because Blake called him. That lawyer of hers showed up at the ranch."

"And you didn't go back with him?" Lem asked, his blue eyes widening with even more surprise.

He knew her so well that she smiled again. "I offered," she admitted.

"Of course."

"And he thanked me for wanting to help," she said. That was when he'd said it, when he'd called her *Grandma* for the first time.

"But he declined," Lem surmised, then he sighed. "Brett is the most like his father. Stubborn. Independent."

Sadie chuckled. "Is he more like his father or his grandfather?"

Lem shrugged. "Perhaps both. But like his father, Brett is also a loner."

Lem had never been a loner. He'd always been there for his family, whether they'd wanted his help or not. He had also been there for the entire town he'd served for years as mayor and now served as deputy mayor. And for her…

Lem had always been there for Sadie despite how much they'd butted heads when they were young, when they weren't as wise as they were now.

"Brett came here," Sadie reminded him.

"Yes, but then he refused your help."

"I don't think he came here for help," Sadie said. "I think he came here to remind himself he has a place to come if he has to leave the Four Corners."

"So she is still contesting the will?" Lem asked, his voice ripe with resentment.

Sadie shrugged. "They didn't talk last night." She updated him on what Brett had told her.

"But in that text she sent Maci yesterday she said that she would explain everything," Lem said.

Sadie nodded. "Maybe she'll do that now. Maybe that's why her lawyer showed up at the ranch."

Lem let out a noise that sounded like one of Feisty's growls when she was tugging on the cuff of someone's jeans. "We should be there, too," he said.

Sadie patted his hand. "He said no. But he promised to fill us in on what happens."

Some tension eased from Lem's stiff body. "Okay. That's good."

"And once we know what's going on, then you and I will figure out what *we* need to do." Step in and help with a lawsuit or with what they'd done for so many other of their grandchildren: matchmaking. Because there had been something curious in Brett's tone when he'd talked about Trish Dempsey…

Something that hadn't sounded like resentment at all.

CHAPTER THREE

BRETT SHOULDN'T HAVE left the Four Corners that morning. Because while both he and Trish were away from the ranch, her lawyer had shown up—or so Blake had told him when he reached him at Ranch Haven.

"Have you told Maci that he's there?" he'd asked his brother.

"Yeah, I called her first."

Of course he had. After all, Maci was not only the executor of Frank Dempsey's estate but also the love of Blake's life.

"Trish is at Maci's house with Frankie," Blake had continued. "She told Maci to ask everybody to meet at the ranch. That's why I'm calling you. You need to get back here as soon as possible."

And so Brett had driven as fast as he safely and legally could back to the Four Corners. When he pulled up to the house, dust billowed in behind him. He didn't see Frankie's van or Trish's truck in the driveway yet, or even Maci's little SUV. But he immediately recognized the flashy black

Hummer as the same vehicle that had left tracks near the Four Corners property not long ago.

This lawyer, Nolan Stokes, had personally spied on the ranch as well as hiring Brett's dad's assistant to spy for him, too. Had he done so for his client? Or for himself?

Brett didn't like that the guy was alone here with his brothers, sister-in-law and baby niece. Again, he mentally kicked himself for leaving that morning. It was his job to protect the ranch, and his family as well. That was why he couldn't get into a relationship: ranching was hard work with long hours. It made it difficult to have a family because the needs of the ranch always came first. That was why Frank's wife had left him and taken their young daughter with her. And it was why Frank hadn't gotten more custody time with Trish.

Liam was already married and Blake would probably be proposing to Maci soon. Brett would make sure their relationships weren't at risk, at least. He would pick up the slack on the ranch—that is, if they managed to keep it. It would destroy them all if they lost it. After being forced to move to the city when they were kids, he and his brothers had dreamed of having a place like this one day.

And for a while that dream had come true for all of them. But it was being threatened now.

Brett hated that the minute he had turned his back, this snake, Nolan Stokes, had slithered out from beneath his rock and onto the Four Seasons property. He parked his truck close to the driver's side of the man's expensive vehicle, so close that Stokes would struggle to open his door wide enough to get inside again. Then Brett hopped out of his truck and rushed up the porch steps. He pushed open the door to the living room, which was oddly quiet despite all of the people occupying the space.

Even baby Lucy wasn't making a sound. Liam held his daughter close to his chest, protectively. And Brett didn't blame him. He found himself edging closer to where Liam sat on the long couch with his wife and their child, so that he stood between them and the stranger.

Despite Nolan Stokes's fearsome reputation as a lawyer, the man was younger than Brett had expected him to be, probably just four or five years older than Brett's thirty-two. He was about the same height, hovering somewhere just under six feet tall. His dark blond hair was slicked back, and he had very pale blue, almost silver eyes. Cold eyes, Brett noted.

Blake stood behind Stokes, and he was staring out the front window. "We're not supposed to talk to him until Maci gets here," Blake told him.

As if Brett had anything to say to the guy. But Stokes wasn't really the problem anyway. Trish was the one who'd hired him, who'd turned him loose not just on Brett and his brothers, but on the two women who'd considered her like a sister to them.

"You don't have to talk," Stokes said. "But I need you to listen. Trish has been through a lot over the past several months—actually, the past few years. She's suffered much more than you all know. And then she lost her father and was blindsided with his will."

A pang of sympathy struck Brett for whatever suffering she'd endured, but he also remembered all too well how Frank had suffered, too, from loneliness and disappointment.

"She didn't lose her father when he died," Brett said. "She lost him years before when she turned her back on him and on the Four Corners."

Blake cleared his throat and shook his head, signaling Brett to shut up.

But fury bubbled up in Brett now, fury that he had tamped down last night when he'd seen how pregnant and exhausted Trish Dempsey had been.

"She should have been blindsided that she was included in the will at all given how she didn't care about her father or the ranch," Brett continued. "I find it really interesting that she only came back to the Four Corners after her divorce. Didn't you get her a good enough settlement for that, Stokes? Losing your Midas touch?"

Stokes snorted and smirked. "Midas touch?"

"I see your Hummer parked out there, the same vehicle that left tracks by the property a couple of weeks ago," Brett said. "I know you hired someone to spy on us, but you did some of your own spying, too. Bunch of good that did for you. All you would have seen was us working our butts off on the ranch. What has Trish done for the Four Corners but cost us contracts and caused stress?"

"Brett!" Blake exclaimed.

He glanced away from Stokes then and saw that Maci, Frankie and Trish Dempsey had walked into the house.

Stokes turned toward the women, too. "This is why you shouldn't have come here on your own," he said to Trish. "It isn't safe for you to be here with *them*."

Like Brett and his brothers were dangerous.

Brett snorted. "Are you still trying to convince her that we hurt her father? Or conned him? We all loved Frank. He was more than a boss to us. More than a friend..." Emotion rushed up on Brett, nearly choking him. Frank had been more like a father to him. While Brett loved his dad, he'd had more in common with Frank Dempsey than Bob Lemmon. Brett had always wanted to be a cowboy, a rancher, which was all Frank had ever been, while Bob was a numbers man, an accountant who spent more time in his office than outside.

Frank had definitely been more than a boss to Brett. And now Brett couldn't help but wonder if Trish was more than a client to Nolan Stokes.

Or maybe he was just thinking like that because everybody else in his life was pairing up with someone else. And not all of those pairings were because of his grandpa and Sadie's meddling.

Trish was beautiful, so he could understand why a man would be interested in her. Surely, Stokes was, or why else would a man as busy and successful as he was rumored to be take the time and go to the trouble to personally spy on them for her?

Why else would he be so concerned about her that he rushed to her rescue this morning?

WHEN TRISH WAS a teenager, her mother had caught her eavesdropping on one of her conversations with her stepfather about her father. It had been about their divorce and custody battle, about how Frank had chosen the ranch over fighting for more custody time with Trish. She'd been devastated then, and her mother hadn't been very sympathetic.

If you're going to eavesdrop, you're going to risk hearing things you don't want to hear...

She'd loved and worshipped her father and had longed to spend more time with him, more time at the ranch. Until that day, she'd always believed that it had been her mother's fault that she hadn't been able to, and then she'd learned the truth. That her dad had agreed to just have her during the summer and on some random holidays in exchange for keeping the ranch and not having to sell it to pay her mother her share of it. Learning that had devastated Trish.

Now she'd inadvertently eavesdropped when she, Frankie and Maci walked into the house during Brett's argument with Nolan Stokes. And what Trish learned was that Brett Lemmon had genuinely loved her father.

And that he didn't have any respect for Trish herself. Wondering if anything her mother had told her was the truth, Trish found she suddenly didn't have a whole lot of respect for herself and how she'd handled things.

Or maybe what bothered her the most was that she hadn't handled things how she should have: on her own.

"Trish, surely you see that coming here was a mistake," Stokes persisted. "Why don't you come back to my place, and we'll hash this out in probate court as we intended."

She shook her head. That had been his intention, not hers. She'd always intended to talk to Maci and Frankie. But she hadn't been in the greatest physical shape until recently. And she hadn't wanted to risk losing these babies as she had the others by putting too much stress on herself.

"You're still contesting the will?" Maci asked the question.

"Let them try, Maci. You've got this," one of

the Lemmon men remarked. Trish had only met Brett, so she didn't know which one was Blake. The one who looked like Brett and had spoken, or the younger man with the baby? Then she remembered that Liam had the wife and baby, so that was Blake who'd championed Maci, who clearly loved Maci. He stared at her with a look of such awe and pride and affection.

Trish couldn't remember anyone ever looking at her that way except one man—her father. He had loved her. And she had loved him, even though she hadn't seen him as much as she should have, as she'd wanted to.

Tears stung her eyes over all her regrets. She blinked furiously in an attempt to keep them at bay, but at least two of the men had seen them because both Stokes and Brett took a step closer to her.

"Let's get you out of here," Stokes said.

"I'm sorry," Brett said, his deep voice gruff with regret. "I didn't see you there…"

"So you're sorry that I heard, not that you said it," she concluded.

He sighed, then nodded.

Appreciative of his honesty, she smiled. Then she turned toward Stokes, uncertain of his honesty. He'd helped her with her divorce, but she wasn't sure if he was acting in her best interest regarding the will. Maybe he thought she deserved to inherit the entire ranch, but, like Brett Lemmon, she wasn't sure that she really deserved any of it, let alone all of it.

But she didn't want any of it for herself. She wanted it for her children. She wanted to give them the childhood she wished she'd had. And that idyllic childhood was here, at the ranch. She patted her belly, drew in a breath and told Stokes, "You can leave. I don't need you here."

She was going to make sure that she didn't need anyone ever again. She was going to take care of herself and her babies.

"Trish, this is a mistake," Nolan persisted. "You can't trust these people."

"She can't trust you!" Frankie exclaimed. "You're a sleaze, spying on us, threatening us—"

"I have never threatened anyone," Stokes interjected, his voice sharp with defensiveness and outrage.

Trish smiled at how offended he was and probably rightfully so. He was well-known and respected for being a champion for the weak and the poor. That was why he'd stepped in to help her all those months ago, or so he'd told her. But Trish didn't want to be weak. And thanks to the divorce settlement Stokes had helped her get, she wasn't poor either. She wasn't rich, but she would have enough to support herself and her babies.

If she could live here at the ranch, if she could make it what she wanted it to be for her kids, she might even have enough to buy out the Lemmons, if they would let her.

"You're not denying the spying," Frankie pointed out, her face close to Nolan's as she argued with him. "Go ahead and try to take us to court. Maci will be sure to expose you as the sleazeball fraud that you are."

"I am not a fraud," Stokes said. "You're the one who has been conned, and you're not astute enough to realize it."

"Are you calling me stupid?" Frankie asked, her face flushed with anger.

Stokes didn't deny it. He added, "And disloyal. You're betraying your cousin for strangers."

"You're the only stranger here," Frankie said.

"And your client told you to leave," Brett said. "But then you don't care about respecting other people's wishes..."

Stokes glared at Brett. "You don't know anything about me."

Brett shook his head. "No, I don't. And I don't want to, and I don't need to. Trish, your client, asked you to leave."

"But you're the one who really wants me to go," Stokes said, "so you can take advantage of her like you took advantage of her dad."

Exclamations of outrage came out of the mouths of everyone in the room. Even the baby began to cry. And Trish's head started to pound with the pressure and stress of the confrontation. She hated conflict; it was why she'd always caved to her mother's and even Harold's wishes. It had been easier than fighting them or even worse yet, disappointing her mother.

But, like the baby, she'd had enough.

"Stop!" she shouted, flinching at the volume of her own voice.

For a second, even that beautiful little girl stopped crying.

"All of you need to stop arguing," she said. She turned back to her lawyer. "And you need to leave—"

"But they're going to—"

"No!" she interjected. "Nobody's going to take advantage of me or coerce me into anything I don't want to do." *Ever again.* She'd promised herself that when she'd started her divorce proceedings. It wasn't just her marriage that had made her feel powerless; she'd felt that way her entire life because of her mother.

But after taking back her name, her life and her dreams, she was empowered and stronger now than she had ever been.

"You heard her," Brett said to Stokes, and he glanced at her.

She wondered if that was a glimmer of respect she saw in his dark eyes. But then she remembered what she'd heard when she'd walked into the house, how he'd been talking about her. He obviously didn't respect how she'd handled her relationship with her father. If she had the opportunity to make different decisions, to talk to him again, she would take it in a heartbeat. But it was too late to undo what had been done.

And tears stung her eyes again.

"Walk me out," Stokes implored her.

"What? Aren't you *astute* enough to find that obnoxiously big vehicle of yours on your own?" Frankie said, her husky voice even huskier with sarcasm.

A smile tugged at Trish's lips as she noticed the annoyance on Nolan's face. He was used to being revered for his intelligence and his appearance. The man was very good-looking, so he probably wasn't used to anyone, especially a young woman, talking to him like Frankie was, with so much disdain.

Then Trish remembered that Nolan had gone through a horrible divorce of his own before helping her with hers. So there had been another woman in his life who'd treated him badly, who'd actually walked out and abandoned not just him, but their children as well. Guilt jabbed her.

"I'll walk you out," she said, relenting. She had to get him away from Frankie before her cousin was even meaner to him than she'd already been. But maybe it was easier for Frankie to blame him for the holdup with the estate than it was for her to blame Trish.

Desperate to get him out of there, Trish headed

to the door and held it open. Nolan waited another long moment before he finally walked out onto the porch with her. When she pulled the door closed behind them, she caught the speculative look that Brett was giving them, as if he wondered if there was more than just a client-attorney relationship between them.

And maybe there was.

They had bonded over their mutual disillusionment with marriage and their commitment to stay single from now on; they had become friends and allies. They both felt that being a single parent would be much safer and healthier for their children.

Maybe Brett suspected there was something romantic between them, but romance was the last thing that either she or Nolan Stokes was interested in. The only thing they shared was their determination to give their children the best life possible…on their own, without having to depend on anyone else. Period.

NOLAN STOKES DRAGGED his feet across the front porch of the Four Corners ranch house. "Trish, you really shouldn't be here on your own. It's not safe."

She chuckled and shook her head. "Nobody is going to hurt me."

After everything she'd been through, it was amazing that she could still be so trusting. That wasn't a mistake that Nolan would ever make again. To trust…

It wasn't worth the risk. It was much better to be safe than sorry.

And he was worried that if she stayed here, she would wind up being sorry that she had.

"We should just handle this in court," he persisted.

She shook her head and smiled. "Frankie is my cousin. She won't hurt me."

"She might be the worst of them," he said, his pride stung from all the insults the young woman had hurled at him. Nobody had spoken to him like that in…maybe ever. Not even his ex-wife. She hadn't said anything at all; she'd just left him and their children in the middle of the night. She'd written a note, but even in that, she'd said very little.

Trish's smile slid away. "She's family. Like my sister, just like Maci is," she said. "They won't hurt me."

"The Lemmons have fooled them—"

"Stop," she said, like she had in the house moments ago. "I don't think the Lemmons have done anything wrong."

"I don't trust them," he insisted.

"Why not?" she asked. "Do you have proof of any of your suspicions?"

He nearly growled with the frustration overwhelming him. "No."

"Then I'm fine," she said. "You can leave."

"Promise me you won't agree to anything until you speak to me again," he implored her. He was genuinely worried about her. He also didn't want to leave the Four Corners. And it wasn't just because he felt like he was about to abandon his client. It was because he was close…to finding out the truth. Not just about the Lemmon brothers and how they had come to be included in Frank Dempsey's will. But also about himself.

About who he really was…

CHAPTER FOUR

ONCE TRISH PULLED the front door closed behind herself and her lawyer, the room fell as eerily silent as it had been when Brett first walked in a short while ago. Even Lucy had stayed quiet after Trish shouted at everyone to stop.

"So that went well..." Maci remarked. "I'll be surprised if you don't get sued for slander, Frankie."

Her voice sharp with defensiveness, Frankie said, "He can't sue me for speaking the truth."

Brett wondered what the truth was. He glanced out the window to where Trish stood with Stokes in the narrow space between Brett's truck and the Hummer. Were they more than client and attorney? If they had a personal relationship, it would explain why Stokes seemed so protective of her and so invested in what happened with the ranch that he'd personally spied on them.

Or maybe Brett just thought that because of the constant coupling up and matchmaking happening all around him. It was possible that Stokes was actually the good guy his reputation claimed he was, and he just felt sorry for Trish and all the suffering she'd endured.

He wondered what exactly Trish Dempsey had been through besides what sounded like a nasty divorce. But, more importantly, why did he even care? Was it just because he'd been close with the man who'd loved her most, her father?

"You still need to be careful," Maci told Frankie. "He seems to have a lot of influence over Trish, and we don't want him to turn her against us any more than he already has."

"Why?" Brett wondered aloud now. "Why would he do that? I don't understand what he stands to gain." Unless he had a personal interest in Trish or maybe in the Four Corners.

"A bigger fee," Frankie said. "More money in his already deep pockets."

Brett shook his head as he studied them through the window. "This seems personal to him for some reason." But as he studied them, he didn't pick up on anything romantic between them. He had definitely just let Lem and Sadie's matchmaking make him suspicious of a romance. The man didn't touch Trish, and she didn't touch him. They really didn't even look at each other; instead, they kept glancing at the house. They probably saw him standing there, watching them, but he didn't care. He wanted Stokes to know that he was keeping an eye on him. He definitely didn't trust the man. There was something about him, something that crept under Brett's skin, needling him.

Did he remind him of someone?

Brett's sister had once been engaged to a narcissist, but that neurosurgeon hadn't looked or acted anything like Stokes. He had been very controlling of Livvy, though. Was Stokes trying to control Trish?

She'd made it clear that wasn't going to happen, that whatever she was doing would be her decision. But what was that decision?

Was she going to keep fighting the will? Or would she find a way to work together with the other heirs?

Finally, Stokes hopped into his Hummer—or, rather, *squeezed* in between his vehicle and Brett's truck. Then he backed slowly down the driveway.

Trish seemed to take a deep breath, then square her shoulders before she headed toward the house, as if she needed to brace herself to deal with them.

Brett thought back to how she had looked when he'd finally glanced up and realized she'd overheard everything he'd said about her, and he could understand why Stokes would feel the need to protect her. She seemed so vulnerable, and all alone.

He'd apologized once. But she was right. He was only sorry that she'd heard him. It was how he felt—that she hadn't treated her father well, that she didn't really deserve any part of the ranch. But she was Frank's family, like Frankie, and Frank had included her in the will just like he had Brett and his brothers.

The hinges creaked as the door opened, and she stepped back inside the house.

Elise broke the silence now, jumping up from the couch to greet her. "Trish, I'm sorry we didn't have a chance to introduce ourselves yet. I'm Elise, Liam's wife." She gestured for Liam to stand and join them near the door. She pointed at him. "This is Liam and our daughter, Lucy."

Trish smiled at the baby, and something about the look on her face, the wistfulness of it, struck a chord inside Brett. "She's beautiful," she said. "I'm happy to meet you, Elise. And Liam."

"This is Blake," Maci said, as she grabbed his hand and pulled him forward. "Stokes probably already told you about us. That we're seeing each other, but that just happened recently."

Trish shook her head. "I didn't know for certain. But the way he looks at you..." That wistfulness was in her voice now. "That's great."

"You don't care?" Maci asked with surprise.

Brett nearly chuckled.

"Why would I?" Trish asked. "I'm not a fan of marriage anymore, myself, but that's my personal choice."

She sounded so much like her father now. And like Brett. After seeing how Frank Dempsey's divorce had nearly destroyed him, Brett wasn't a fan of marriage either. He didn't want to risk getting hurt like his friend had. His dad hadn't divorced, but losing Brett's mom to cancer had nearly destroyed him. No, he was definitely not a fan.

While he chuckled, Maci and Blake heaved huge sighs of relief.

"What?" she asked looking from him to the couple. "I don't understand..."

"These two were worried that you or Stokes would use their relationship against the rest of us," Brett explained. "Blake was even willing to sign away his rights to his inheritance to avoid any backlash against Maci or the other heirs."

"Backlash?" Trish shook her head. "I don't understand how that could be used against anyone."

"You were contesting the will I wrote," Maci said. "I did everything right. The only way to legally contest it would be to prove a fraud of some kind had been perpetuated. Like I wrote the will that way because I would benefit from it somehow."

Trish shook her head. "I would never think that of you, Maci."

Maci let out another huge sigh. Then she blinked as tears rushed to her eyes.

Blake put his arm around her, drawing her close to him. "See, I told you."

"I did wonder about the rest of you, though," Trish said. But Brett was the only one she looked at as she continued, "I wondered how ranch hands were suddenly included in his will. It didn't make sense to me."

Brett sucked in a breath. "Ranch hands?"

Frankie laughed. "You really have no idea what was going on with the ranch," she said. "Uncle Frank nearly lost it because he had to refinance to buy your mom out in the divorce. The mortgage payments were so high that he struggled to make them."

Trish shook her head. "That's not true. He didn't do that. He chose to have less custody of me, so that he could keep the ranch."

"Let me guess? Your mother told you that," Frankie said, stepping closer and staring intently at her. "That wasn't true."

"It wasn't like she told me that outright," Trish said. "I accidentally overheard her saying it."

"When?"

"When I got home after that last summer, before I left for college."

"The last time you were here," Frankie said. "I wish you had talked to me about that. I wish you had talked to me before you hired Stokes. Why did you shut us all out, Trish?"

Brett cleared his throat. "Uh, maybe you, Maci and Trish should have this conversation in private," he said to Frankie. He didn't think it was fair for Trish to have to share everything with strangers. He looked at his brothers and Elise. "We can head out to the barn for a bit." He started toward the door, confident that the others would follow his lead. But when he reached for the handle, a hand closed over his. A small female hand.

It wasn't Elise's.

He knew that from the jolt of awareness that shot through him. Elise was like a sister to him. So were Frankie and Maci. But Trish was not.

For some reason, he found this irritating, independent, very pregnant woman attractive. And now knowing that she hadn't stayed away from her father because she hadn't cared, but because she'd been hurt, changed a lot for Brett. He didn't resent her anymore; he understood that she hadn't thought she'd mattered that much to her own father. And his will must have reinforced that false notion she'd had, hurting her even more.

But understanding her was more dangerous than resenting her because now he didn't want to fight with her anymore.

He wanted to fight *for her.*

TRISH HAD REACHED out to stop Brett from leaving, but once her hand touched his, she lost all reason for a moment. She actually felt a little lightheaded as sensations rushed through her, making her nerves tingle.

What was this?

She hadn't reacted giddily to a touch like this in…ever, maybe? This was even headier than when she, Frankie and Maci had had a crush on a very attractive ranch hand years ago. But Brett wasn't a ranch hand; he'd seemed to take offense when she'd said that.

What was he?

More sensitive than she would have thought, because he'd been willing to leave her alone to have this conversation with just Frankie and Maci. That was what she'd wanted when she'd driven to Maci's house that morning.

But now…

She knew that it didn't matter. Her father's will had entwined her life with the Lemmons'. Hers and Maci's and Frankie's.

"Stay," she said. "I promised that I would explain what was going on to everyone."

"Why you're contesting the will," Maci said. "We all deserve to know the reason."

Maybe Maci most of all, because she'd written it. And as Frankie had told Trish in a voicemail, Maci had been incredibly stressed out over it. So much so that she'd even passed out once or twice.

Realizing that she was still touching Brett's hand, Trish jerked hers away and turned back toward her friend. "I'm sorry," she said. "I wasn't so much as contesting it as just stalling so it wouldn't be settled before my divorce was. I wanted to make sure that the man my father disapproved of me marrying wouldn't get any part of it. Dad was right about Harold. He wasn't in love with me. He was in love with my stepfather's money and with moving up the company ladder. And because of his obsession with money, I didn't want him or my mother to find out about the inheritance. She took his side in the divorce." After her mother's betrayal, Trish had been reluctant to trust anyone, but Nolan Stokes had genuinely wanted to help her. And he'd advised her to trust no one but him, not even the women she loved like sisters. He'd been concerned that they would betray her for the Lemmon brothers, just as her mother had betrayed her for her ex.

"You should have told us that," Frankie said. "We could have been there for you through your divorce."

Not wanting Frankie to hate Stokes any more than she already did, Trish didn't blame him. "Harold and my mother were watching my every move once I filed for divorce. I think they might have had cameras planted in the house, too. I couldn't talk on the phone because I didn't want to risk him finding out that my dad had died. I didn't want my mother to know either. She definitely would have used it in some way to get me to drop the divorce proceedings. I wouldn't have put it past her to come after the ranch then, too."

Brett cleared his throat. "So you're saying you contested the will in order to protect the ranch?"

She sighed. "And to protect myself, too," she admitted. "I couldn't handle much more at the time..." She touched her belly. "I—I hadn't had much luck with IVF before this pregnancy." Tears rushed to her eyes. "I had several miscarriages…" A tear trickled out.

Suddenly Frankie and Maci were there, one on either side of her, their arms wound tightly around her. "Aw, Trish, you should have told us," Frankie said. "I would have been there for you all the way. I would have beat up your ex and your mom. I would have taken care of you."

Trish wrapped an arm around Frankie and held on tightly. Then she wrapped her other arm around Maci. She'd missed them so much, but that had been her fault. "Even before the divorce, I pushed you both away, just like I did my dad."

"Why did you do that?" Frankie asked, her voice cracking with emotion.

Trish groaned. "My stupid pride. I didn't want you all to know that my dad had been right about Harold, and that I'd been a fool again. And after I pushed you all away, I didn't know if you would come. If you would care…"

"We love you," Maci said. "You're our sister."

"I'm sorry," Trish said. She was so very sorry for all the stress she'd caused, not just the two of them but herself as well.

And the others…

She still didn't know what to do about the Lemmons. She pulled away from Frankie and Maci then. They both had tears streaking down their faces. Blake wrapped an arm around Maci, as if to comfort her.

But Brett didn't step forward to comfort Frankie. Elise did. She wrapped her arm around her shoulders. And for a moment Trish wondered if Brett might comfort her. But he stayed near the door, and it was clear from the look on his face that he wished she hadn't stopped him. This was obviously way too much emotion for him, and that reminded her of her father, when he'd struggled to deal with the drama she and Frankie and Maci had sometimes found, like the summer that ranch hand had tried to simultaneously date the three of them.

"I'm sorry," she said to all of them. "I know I handled everything so badly. Probably the worst way that I could have."

"You had help," Frankie said, her voice sharp with irritation again. "That sleazeball lawyer—"

"Nolan is really a good guy," Trish insisted. "He fought very hard for me in the divorce. Since that's over, we'll be able to settle the estate." She'd had to promise Nolan that she wouldn't sign anything and make any final decisions without consulting him, though. Or he wouldn't have left her alone just now.

"How?" Brett asked the question. "How do you want to settle this, Trish?"

The thought of wrapping this up suddenly filled her with dread. Maybe because she hadn't seen her father in the hospital or attended his funeral, she'd been able to hold on to him by not dealing with the estate. But now, in order to do this, she would have to let him go.

She drew in a breath to steady herself as tears rushed in again. She blinked them back and focused on Brett, on his dark eyes. "I want to know what my father really wanted. What his wishes actually were for the Four Corners."

And then she would have to respect them. But she wasn't sure that she would be able to live with them if that meant living with the Lemmon brothers.

Or maybe just this Lemmon brother.

"DIDN'T YOUR LAWYER show you the will?" Maci asked Trish as she set a copy of it on the coffee table in Frank Dempsey's den. She'd brought Trish in here to show her, and it was just the two of them now.

The others had stayed in the living room. Or maybe they'd gone out to work the ranch. This was the legal stuff, and they trusted Maci with that. She hoped she deserved their trust and was able to get through to her old friend that the settlement laid out in her father's will was really what he'd wanted.

Trish leaned forward from where she sat on the leather couch and stared down at the document. But she didn't read it. "Stokes told me what was in it, and he thought it was strange that my father would leave the same amount to a ranch hand as he would to his daughter."

Maci grimaced. "You really have to stop calling them ranch hands," she said. "They were so much more than that to your dad. They were more like your father's sons."

Trish flinched then. "Sons? How? He didn't know them that long."

"Brett's worked here for five years," Maci said. "After his first year working at the Four Corners, he convinced Blake to leave another ranch and come here to help him save your father's ranch. Without them…" She trailed off as emotions overwhelmed her. Then she cleared her throat and continued, "Without them, it wouldn't be here. The bank would have foreclosed and sold it already."

Trish flinched again. "It was really that bad?"

Maci nodded. "I didn't know either until I wrote the will. Your dad paid for my law school—"

"And for some of my wedding," Trish said. "Even though he didn't approve and wouldn't come."

"That was what? Four years ago?"

Trish nodded.

"It was bad then. Brett would have already been working here for about a year. I don't know how he kept the place going. He certainly wasn't getting paid for quite a while."

"But he still worked here anyway?" Trish

asked, her light brown eyes wide with surprise. There were probably few people in her world like the Lemmons, so she didn't understand that kind of selflessness.

Maci nodded. "They're really good guys, Trish. All of them."

"You love Blake."

That love warmed Maci, making her smile. "With all my heart. But that's not why I wrote the will this way. I wrote it because it was what your father wanted. He wanted the Lemmons, you and Frankie to each have an equal share. He wanted you all to work together to run it, too."

"Why?"

A little annoyed, she replied, "I just told you that they literally saved the ranch—"

"No, why does he want us all to work together to run it?" she asked. "Frankie doesn't want to do that, right? Isn't she still touring with her band, doing shows?"

Maci shrugged. "She says she is, but she doesn't seem in any hurry to get back at it."

"Oh…" Trish shook her head again, tossing her curls around her face. This was the prettiest she'd ever looked. She was actually glowing, like people always said pregnant women did. "But did he really think *I* would come back to run it with some strangers?"

"Frank didn't consider the Lemmons strangers," Maci said. "They were all so close."

Trish looked her in the eye. "What about me, though? I more or less became a stranger to him."

"You weren't a stranger either," Maci said. "He loved you, and he knew you loved the ranch once."

Trish sighed, and it was such a wistful sound. "I still do," she said. "And it would be such a great place to raise the babies."

"Yes, it would," Maci conceded.

"Will they let me buy them out?" she asked eagerly. "I have some money from my divorce settlement."

Maci shook her head. "The Lemmons love this place, too. It's not just where they work now. It's their home, and their life, especially for Brett. It's really all he has."

Trish sighed again, but this one sounded as if it was full of disappointment. "So I won't be able to buy them out."

Maci shook her head again. "They won't want to sell. To you. Or to anyone. They have so many plans for the place."

"So do I."

"Try to work *with* them," Maci urged. "It's what your dad wanted." But clearly it wasn't what Trish wanted. She'd said she would honor his wishes, but would she when they weren't the same as hers?

Tears shimmered in Trish's eyes. "I know that's what you're saying…"

"But you don't believe it's really what he wanted?"

"I don't know..."

"What are you going to do, Trish?" Maci asked, her heart heavy again with dread. She'd hoped this would all be settled soon, and she could keep the promise she'd made to Frank to make sure his will was carried out the way he'd wanted.

"I promised Nolan I wouldn't make a final decision without talking to him first," Trish said.

"You know he'll tell you to keep fighting," Maci said. "Is that what you want?"

"I don't want to fight anymore. That's why I would just rather buy them out."

"Well, that's not happening," Maci said. "You're going to have to accept this is what your father wanted or..."

Go to court. But she couldn't even bring herself to say those words. She'd been so hopeful that this would all be over once Trish showed up at the Four Corners. But it was clearly not going to be that easy.

CHAPTER FIVE

BRETT BACKED AWAY from the door to the den hoping that neither of the women inside it had seen him. But he didn't head back toward the living room where the others were still gathered. Instead, he slipped out the back door off the kitchen and started across the yard toward the barn.

Now Brett knew how Trish had felt when she'd heard him talking about her, because he'd just overheard what Maci had said about him. *It's really all he has.*

She wasn't wrong. The ranch was all he had. But for some reason it sounded sad when she'd said it. And Trish had looked sad when she'd heard it.

No. She'd looked disappointed. She didn't want to work with him. She wanted to buy him out. Him and the others. She wanted the ranch all to herself and her babies, which he couldn't even blame her for. If this had been his family ranch, he would have felt possessive of it. Heck, he felt possessive now.

And Frank hadn't really been family at all, except in Brett's heart. That was how he'd felt about the older man—like Frank could have been another father to him. Kind of like Sadie Haven March was now another grandmother to him.

He'd had two. Lem's first wife, Mary, who'd been an incredibly sweet woman even when she'd suffered from dementia. And then there was his maternal grandmother, whom he hadn't even been able to call Grandma. She'd preferred Mimi or Gigi or anything that didn't make her sound too old. Not that they'd seen that much of her, even after his dad had moved them from Willow Creek to Chicago to be closer to them or maybe farther away from Grandpa Lem and his meddling.

Brett had hated living in the city and had counted the days until he graduated high school and could head back west again. He'd worked a few other ranches before accepting the foreman position from Frank Dempsey. And he'd known the moment he'd seen it that the Four Corners was home.

No. It was more than that for him. For him, it was his life, like Maci had said.

Did that mean that losing it would kill him? He hoped he wouldn't have to find out, but even though Trish had explained her reason for holding off on settling the estate, it was also clear that she didn't want to share it with them.

She wanted to buy them out.

But there was nothing that Brett needed that money for if he didn't have the Four Corners. So if he refused the buyout, would she continue to contest the will? Her lawyer was obviously eager to fight for her to get everything he thought she deserved. And he thought that Trish, as Frank Dempsey's next of kin, deserved it all.

TRISH WAS ALONE in the den. At least physically, since Maci had left her. But she didn't feel alone. She could feel and still smell her father's presence in the sweet scent of cigars and leather and horses.

Maci had left the will with her. And for the first time, Trish read through it and noted the thick scrawl of his signature and his bold initials on every clause. This was what he wanted. Not for his family, she and Frankie, to split the estate, but for the two of them to share it equally with each of the three Lemmon brothers.

These were definitely his final wishes. She had no doubt about that now.

Maci had told her, and now he was telling her in the way that he'd signed the papers. It wasn't a faint scrawl, but a thick one, purposeful and definitive. Her father had never asked for much from her; he'd known how hard it was for her to deal with her mother and the fallout she would face had she asked to live with him instead.

But she regretted now that she hadn't done that. That she hadn't been stronger, for herself and for him. She patted her belly, and one of the babies kicked in reaction. She would be stronger now for herself and for them.

And for her dad, too.

She would honor his final wishes no matter how hard it might be for her to run the ranch with strangers who probably had their own vision for it. Maci had mentioned that they had plans.

Nolan had implored her not to make any final decisions until she talked to him. She wasn't prepared to have a discussion with him until she had all the information she needed to make that final decision.

She needed to know what the Lemmons had planned for the Four Corners. And so she tried to lever herself up from the couch to go find them. But the couch was low to the ground and the leather was slippery, and she struggled to get enough momentum to lift herself and her belly up.

"Need a hand?"

The voice sounded similar to Brett's, but it wasn't as husky as his. And she didn't get that little shiver in reaction like she did when he spoke to her.

Blake walked around the couch to the front and held out a hand to her. "I'll help you."

Trish understood right away why Maci had fallen for him. In addition to being good-looking, he also seemed kind. She hesitated for just a moment before putting her hand in his. Then he hoisted her up.

"Thank you," she said.

"Do you need anything else?" he asked.

And she nodded. "Yes, I'd like to know more about the ranch."

Brett might have judged her for asking, might have given her that look of disapproval he had last night when he'd told her how lonely her dad had been. But Blake just nodded.

"Sure, I can show you the books," he offered. "I'm the one who usually does the invoicing and pays the expenses."

"Not Brett?" she asked with surprise. For some reason he had struck her as the leader of the group.

"He was doing it before I came to work here," Blake said. "But I have more of our dad's head for numbers than Brett does. Our dad is an accountant. He has an office in Willow Creek. Maci rents office space from him."

So Nolan hadn't lied when he'd told her that Maci was enmeshed with all the Lemmons, not just the ones at the ranch. He had sounded disapproving of that. But now Trish wondered why.

If they were men as good as Maci and Frankie thought they were, why shouldn't Maci associate with them?

Maybe Nolan was just bitter and cynical from his divorce. Trish was, too, but not to the extent that she considered all men selfish and controlling just because her ex-husband had been. Her father hadn't been. Nolan didn't seem to be, so why would he naturally assume that the Lemmons were?

Blake picked up a laptop from the desk, and then he asked, "Do you want to sit back on the couch or at your dad's desk?" He glanced at the chair, almost as if he could still see her father sitting there.

She could envision him there, too, with Buster at his feet, as he puffed a cigar and signed his name on checks. Or on that will he'd had Maci write up for him. Almost as if he'd known that he was going to have that accident…

That he wasn't going to be able to run the ranch himself much longer.

Tears stung her eyes, and she blinked to clear them away.

"Yeah, we can't sit there yet either," Blake said, as he carried the laptop back to the couch and sat down. Then he held up his hand for her to use to lower herself back onto the cushions.

"Not even Brett?" she asked as she settled onto the leather again.

"Brett least of all," Blake said. "It's been tough on all of us losing your dad, living here without him, but Brett seems to be struggling the most."

"How so?" she asked.

Blake shrugged. "I don't know. He's just not happy."

A twinge of sympathy struck her heart. She had been unhappy for so long, wanting something that the people in her life just hadn't been capable of giving her. Unconditional love. And her babies. She touched her belly again, and a little foot or fist moved against her palm. She'd wasted years waiting for happiness to come to her, for other people to make her happy, before she'd figured out that she was the only one who could do that.

Blake sighed. "Maybe Brett's so unhappy because he's all alone. I'm lucky. I have Maci." He grinned so brightly. "And Liam has Elise and Lucy."

"What about Frankie?" Trish asked. "Brett doesn't have her?"

Blake laughed. "She and Brett are like brother and sister. That's never going to happen no matter how much meddling my grandpa and grandma try to do."

"Your grandpa and grandma would meddle like that?" she asked, her heart beating a bit faster as she thought of all the times her mother had meddled in her life. Like with her ex-husband. He worked for her stepfather; her mother had picked out Harold for her and coached him on all the things Trish liked and wanted. Like the children Harold had said he wanted when he'd really had no intention of ever having them, had even had a vasectomy. Trish shuddered at the memory of how she'd been manipulated and how Harold had just acted the part of the husband she'd wanted. But he had never really been that man. The man she'd wanted—a loving, supportive family man—had never existed. He and her mother had duped her.

But Blake didn't sound upset with his grandparents. He actually laughed over their antics. "They're infamous matchmakers."

That didn't slow the pounding of Trish's heart. "Did they set you and Maci up?"

"I'm sure they would have had we not already started falling for each other ourselves."

She released a shaky breath of relief that her friend hadn't been tricked or coerced like she'd been. "So you already fell for each other before they got involved?"

He nodded. "The first time I saw her. Your dad always talked about how smart she was and how sweet. He hadn't told me how beautiful. And the first time I saw her, I was done. I was in love."

"So you've been together awhile then?" she asked.

He tensed for a moment. "Is that what Stokes told you?"

She shook her head. "No. You just said you fell for her at first sight."

"Yeah, but I didn't think I was good enough for her," Blake said. "She's smart and successful and so driven. I'm just a cowboy."

A very sweet, humble cowboy. And Trish definitely saw why her friend had fallen for him.

"She's so smart that she realized what a good man you are," she told him.

And Blake blinked. "That's really nice. We were so worried that you wouldn't approve, that you would think I was trying to manipulate her or the will or something."

She shook her head again. "I know how smart Maci is." Far smarter than Trish was. "I know she wouldn't fall for that, and if, for some reason, she had, Frankie would have shaken some sense into her." Like Frankie had tried shaking some sense into Trish before her wedding. But she hadn't listened to her cousin any more than she had her dad. And because Frankie and her dad hadn't approved of her marriage, she'd pulled away from them. Even when the relationship got bad, she hadn't reached out to her family because she'd been so embarrassed that they'd been right and she had been so very wrong.

Blake chuckled. "Yeah, Frankie would have taken me out for sure if she thought I would ever hurt Maci."

"She's given me a couple of earfuls over stressing Maci out about the will," Trish admitted. "Deservedly so. I was so caught up in my own mess that I didn't realize the turmoil I'd caused back here. I'm really sorry."

"Wow," Blake murmured.

"What?"

"You're not at all like I expected you to be," he said.

She patted her belly. "Pregnant?"

"Yeah, I definitely didn't expect that," he said with a grin. "But you're nice, too."

She chuckled. "And you didn't expect me to be?"

He shook his head. "That was just because of the lawsuit, though."

"I never actually sued anyone," she pointed out. "Nolan just filed for the extensions because we didn't want the estate to get settled before my divorce was. That had gone on too long, and I didn't want to give my ex another excuse to put it off. But now I realize I was putting you all through what he was putting me through. And I am genuinely sorry."

Blake smiled at her. "We're good."

"You and I," she said. "But the others?"

"Maci is, too. She told me that when she suggested I check on you," he said. "And Liam and Elise will be. They're so happy, in love with each other and Lucy, that nothing bothers them as much as it does…"

"Brett or Frankie?" she asked when he trailed off.

"Both of them," he admitted. "They've been the most upset about all of this. And they'll struggle the most to let it go."

Trish sighed. "That's going to make it tough for

me to work with them," she said. Especially since, with the way her father had set up his will, she would need a majority vote to make the changes she wanted for herself and her babies.

"Once the estate settles, Frankie will probably be off with her band again," Blake said as if trying to make her feel better.

"But that's not going to mend our relationship," she pointed out. And she'd already been apart from her cousin for too long.

"Doesn't distance make the heart fonder or something?" he asked.

"That did not work with my parents," she said. No. She would have to fix things with Frankie before her cousin took off, if she took off. While Blake seemed to think she would, Maci, who'd known her longer and better, wasn't as certain.

And as for Brett…

Trish wasn't sure what it would take for him to forgive her for not seeing her dad as much as she should have, and for not coming to the funeral. She wasn't sure she could ask him to forgive her for the things she wouldn't be able to forgive herself.

But she did want to figure out a way for them to be able to work amicably together. Given the way he made her tingle with awareness, though, maybe it would be better if she kept her distance from him. But how would she manage that when they would both be living at the ranch?

FRANKIE COULD NOT remember the last time she'd been this angry. When she'd found Uncle Frank after he'd fallen off his horse, she'd been upset. Scared. When Trish hadn't come to visit him in the hospital or even shown up for his funeral, Frankie had been disappointed. And maybe a little angry—but not like this.

Then, when Trish and her lawyer had contested the will, Frankie had gotten a little angrier. But she still hadn't been furious.

Today, however, seeing that lawyer in her uncle's house, trying to manipulate her cousin into contesting her father's last wishes, had infuriated Frankie. Even after he left, she couldn't stop shaking with fury. How dare he pit her family against each other?

And that was what the Lemmons were to her—they were her brothers. And Trish had always been more like a sister to her than a cousin. Even as mad as she'd made Frankie, Frankie would never stop loving her. Now that she'd learned about the divorce and the miscarriages and pregnancy that Trish had gone through all alone, Frankie wasn't just upset with her cousin. She was upset for her. And she wished she'd been there for her.

But after Maci took Trish into the den to show her the will, Frankie had headed out to the barn. She needed to calm down before she talked to Trish again. She wanted to be there for her cousin now.

Being on the ranch had always calmed Frankie

down. It had been where she'd come after her parents died. And it had been her safe place after that devastation. Any time she was going through something tough, a breakup with a band, a canceled tour, she'd come home. And usually she hung out in the barn with the horses or out in the pastures with the cows.

But one of those cows was in the barn now. The baby she'd personally pulled from her mama's womb. She'd saved Cocoa, and she was counting on Cocoa to save her right now. To calm her down.

And once she was calm maybe she could figure out how to convince Trish to look at the Lemmons as family, too.

CHAPTER SIX

BRETT STEPPED INTO the dim light of the barn and breathed in deeply of hay and horses. The smells cleared his head a bit and reminded him what mattered most: the livestock, the ranch and Frank Dempsey's last wishes.

Would Trish accept them? Hopefully, Maci would be able to get through to her.

But Brett wasn't naive enough to think that would end their problems. It would just create a whole new set of them because Trish was here.

And someone else was in the barn.

Brett tensed as he heard someone murmur as they shifted within a stall. Then a husky voice began to sing, and he relaxed again.

Frankie really had a beautiful voice. Too bad it was being wasted here on the ranch where more animals than people got to hear it. He walked over to the stall where she'd moved Cocoa, next to the horse that Frank had given to Maci. He opened the stall door and leaned against the opening.

Cocoa was cuddled up against Frankie, who sat

with her back against some hay bales. The calf stared adoringly up at her mama.

"You're spoiling her," Brett said.

Frankie jumped and glanced up at him. "I didn't hear you come up."

He nodded. "I know."

"And let's talk about spoiling her," she said. "You must have fed her this morning before I got in here because she wasn't interested in her bottle."

He nodded again. "Yeah, she was hungry so I grabbed the milk replacement for her."

"You didn't have to do that," she said. "I promised I would take care of her."

Their veterinarian, who was also one of Brett's new stepcousins, had offered to bring the orphaned calf to his practice. But Frankie hadn't been willing to let her go.

"You got up and took care of Trish last night," he reminded her. "I owed you."

"She's my cousin," Frankie said and uttered a heavy sigh.

"That doesn't make you responsible for her," Brett said.

She snorted. "Like you don't take responsibility for every member of your family?" she asked.

Heat climbed into his face over sounding like a martyr. That really wasn't what he was; he just wanted to make sure that they were happy and felt secure at the ranch. "I don't know what you mean.

Liam and Blake and Livvy all take care of themselves." His sister, a doctor in the emergency department at Willow Creek Memorial Hospital, had never seemed to need him that much. But maybe if he'd been there for her more, Livvy wouldn't have gotten engaged to that narcissist.

Frankie snorted again. "And you don't worry about them? You don't wish you could help them, protect them?"

She knew him too well, so he groaned and admitted, "Okay…"

"I wasn't there for Trish," Frankie said.

"She didn't let you be there for her," Brett reminded her again.

"But still…" She sighed. "I don't know. The whole situation is just so frustrating. We spent all these months thinking she was just being vindictive or greedy…"

"And all along she may have just been protecting the ranch, and us," Brett finished for her. Another emotion moved through him, and he wasn't sure that it was just respect for Trish.

"May have been?" Frankie asked. "You don't believe her?"

"I don't know what to believe," Brett said. "I don't know her. What about you? Do you believe her?"

Frankie sighed yet again, and this was a very ragged sigh. "Her mother really is awful," Frankie said. "But I think part of the reason she and Uncle

Frank got divorced was because of me. Even before my parents died, they left me here a lot when they were on the road with their band. Aunt Belinda made it clear that she didn't want to raise anyone else's kid. She didn't seem to like her own very much. She constantly criticized poor Trish."

Sympathy shot through Brett. "That must have been tough for her."

Frankie nodded. "I wish Uncle Frank had had full custody of her, but despite fighting for it, he couldn't convince the judge that a young girl would be happier with her father than her mother. So he lost, meaning Trish spent so much time with that woman."

"You once accused her of being like her," Brett remembered.

Frankie grunted. "I know. That was a low blow."

"But you wondered if she was," he said. "Did you have some other reason to think that? Like all the time she spent with her?"

Frankie shrugged. "I don't know. Trish and I haven't seen each other for years, and we've haven't even spoken on the phone that often in all that time either. I really don't know her anymore."

"So you don't know what she'll decide? If she really will honor her father's wishes?"

Frankie shrugged. "No idea. I would hope that she would, but that lawyer seems to have as much influence over her as her mother used to."

"And for some reason he really doesn't seem to like us Lemmons." Brett couldn't help but wonder why. Why did he mistrust them so much?

"He's an idiot," Frankie said.

Brett laughed. "You're not a fan of Stokes? I couldn't tell."

Frankie laughed, too. Then her smile slid back into a frown. "I just hope she doesn't let him manipulate her."

"Man, I really do need to stop eavesdropping," a female voice remarked.

Now Brett was the one who was startled. He glanced over his shoulder to see that Trish had walked into the barn.

"My mother was right," she said. "You don't hear anything good about yourself when you do."

"I was trashing Stokes, not you," Frankie assured her. She climbed to her feet, then rubbed her lower back. The calf headbutted the side of her leg. "I have to go get a bottle made for this one. Now she's hungry. I'll be right back." She brushed past Brett and then Trish and hurried out of the barn.

Brett was tempted to yell after her to come back. Or to call her a traitor for deserting him like this. He did not want to be alone with Trish Dempsey. But he wasn't just alone in the barn with her.

Because she moved closer to the stall, stepping into the small opening with him, to stare at the calf. Her body was so close to him that he could smell the strawberry shampoo she must have used to wash her hair that morning. He heard her sigh when she saw the calf. He was much too aware of Trish Dempsey, but she barely seemed to notice him at all as she went over to the small animal.

In that moment, he knew that he was in trouble no matter what she decided about her father's will. Maybe in even more trouble if she decided to honor his wishes and stay on the ranch.

TRISH'S PRIDE WAS stung from what she'd overheard in the barn just minutes ago, how her cousin thought she was so easy to manipulate. Not that Frankie was wrong.

Maybe that was what bothered Trish most of all: how weak she'd once been. But she wasn't that person any longer. She patted her burgeoning belly, which reminded her of that. She'd fought to have her babies. And then she'd fought for her freedom from her bad marriage and from her mother.

She wasn't weak anymore. Except when she stepped too close to Brett Lemmon—then her knees felt funny, a little shaky. Maybe she just needed to lie down; she really didn't get much sleep last night. That was why she'd begged off before Blake could explain the ranch bookkeeping to her.

Once he'd mentioned how hard it would be to

change Brett's and Frankie's minds about her, she'd had to find them. And of course everyone had figured they were in the barn. Or somewhere on the ranch, riding around, checking on things. She'd headed to the barn first and found them talking to each other about her. Not that she could blame them for that. She'd caused all this upheaval in their lives.

Or had her father's death caused that?

She had questions about that, too, but she wasn't ready yet to hear all the details. She wasn't weak anymore, but she might not be strong enough for that, not until she got more rest. So she focused on the calf instead, pushing herself past Brett to settle onto a hay bale next to the chocolate brown baby. "She's adorable," she said.

The calf nuzzled against her, as if looking for that bottle that Frankie had gone off to get for her. "She *is* hungry."

"She's growing fast," Brett remarked.

"Hopefully not too fast," Trish said. "She would be perfect for the petting zoo I want to start on the ranch."

"What?" he asked, and he pushed his hat back farther on his head as if he needed to see her more clearly to understand her. "What petting zoo?"

"I want to start a day camp and summer camp for kids on the ranch," she said, her heart beating fast with the excitement she felt over her idea.

"Where? How?" Brett asked. He sounded appalled. “This is a working cattle ranch. It would be too dangerous for kids to be running around here.”

She patted her belly. “There will be kids running around here someday soon. And they’ll be running around here with your niece, Lucy.”

Now his mouth fell slightly open as his eyes widened. But maybe he was genuinely worried about the safety of the children.

“We could have a separate area for the camp,” she said. “Away from the bigger animals.”

“We?” He repeated the word, and then he arched one dark auburn eyebrow. “You’ve made your decision?”

“About the petting zoo and kids’ camps, yes,” she said. She’d made that decision long ago. Once she’d believed she wouldn’t miscarry this time, she’d allowed herself to start dreaming about where and how she would raise her children. She wanted them to live the life she wished she’d been able to live here, with fresh air and animals, and not just for the summer but 24/7. Then she’d considered how lonely they might be without other kids to spend their time with, and so she’d dreamed up the day camps and summer camps for other kids who’d been like her, forced to spend too much of their lives in the city.

“And about the ranch?” he asked. “Are you going to respect what your dad wanted, his final wishes?”

His question reminded her of why she'd sought him and Frankie out in the first place. Then the calf had distracted her and she'd let Frankie slip away. But she was coming back. While Trish waited, she sat on the hay bale petting the calf, and she noticed another movement in the stall. Some loose straw moved, and then a little furry black head popped out of it. Two topaz eyes blinked up at her. Then, from the back of the hay bale where she sat, another little black furball launched itself at the other one. And the two kittens tumbled across the floor.

"Ah, kittens, too." Tears stung her eyes at how perfect it was. She could already imagine her children playing here with the calf and kittens. But she wanted more animals. And more children. She wanted her kids to have friends like she'd had in Maci and Frankie. When she'd gone back to the city after her idyllic summers on the ranch, she'd been so lonely without them, but she'd lived on the memories of everything they'd done together at the Four Corners. Riding horses. Feeding the cattle. Camping out under the stars. She'd been so safe and happy here.

"Somebody dumped a litter off here a few weeks ago," Brett said. "We've managed to get rid of all but those two."

She gasped. "Get rid of?"

He grimaced and looked appalled again. "We didn't hurt them. Blake delivered one to my dad and two to Maci. And there's a little orange one living in the house."

"Why are these two still out in the barn?" she asked. "Are you leaving them out here to take care of rodents?"

They hissed and spit at each as they rolled around the stall floor in their tight embrace. Then one broke free and bounced around on all fours, her back arched high and her hair raised.

"They're a little young to hunt mice. But they certainly have a lot of energy and that's why they're out here," he said. "The orange one is calm. We couldn't have these wild ones in the house waking up Lucy. She's just finally starting to sleep through the night."

"Oh…"

"I answered your question," he said. "So when are you going to answer mine? What have you decided about the will?"

"You asked me if I can respect my father's wishes," she reminded him. "And I want to know if you and Frankie can respect mine. I came out here to talk to the two of you."

Frankie had escaped as fast as she could. Even though she'd claimed to need a bottle for the calf, she wasn't back yet. Trish couldn't imagine it would have taken her that long to fix it.

Brett pushed his hat back farther yet, and his forehead had deep furrows in it as he stared at her with narrowed eyes. "What do you mean by respecting your wishes? It seemed like, with this lawsuit, that you wished to get rid of me and my brothers and even your cousin. That you wanted the whole place to yourself. I can't respect that when I know it's not what your father wanted."

Heat rushed to her face. "I don't mean that. And I never really intended to sue—"

"Then your lawyer wasn't respecting your wishes," Brett said.

She did need to speak with Nolan again to make sure that he knew her decision was hers alone and nobody influenced it. But she wasn't sure she could make that decision just yet.

"I didn't really mean my wishes," she said, and her head was beginning to pound with the weariness that suddenly overwhelmed her. "I meant me. Can you and Frankie respect and work with me?"

"Why are you just worried about me and Frankie?" he asked, his dark eyes narrowing even more.

More heat rushed to her face that she'd slipped up and revealed more than she'd intended to. "I… uh…" She didn't know what to say without risking him getting upset with Blake and Maci.

"Because the ranch is all I have?" he asked. "Because it's my life?"

"So I'm not the only one who's overheard things today," she surmised.

He nodded. “Yeah, your mother might have been right to warn you about eavesdropping.”

“That was the only thing she was right about,” Trish said.

“Difficult relationship?”

“Difficult woman,” she said. “I’m sure my father must have told you about her.” If they were as close as everyone seemed to think they’d been.

His face flushed a bit now. “Yeah, he told me to never get married. That women can’t be trusted not to break your heart and take everything away that matters most to you.”

Tears stung her eyes as sadness rushed over her. “He never got over the divorce.”

“He never got over losing you,” Brett said.

She pressed a hand against her heart that ached with loss and regret. Tears slid down her face.

“I’m sorry,” Brett said, and then he was there, on his knees next to the calf. “I didn’t mean to upset you.”

She peered at him through her tears. “Really?”

He groaned. “I don’t know. I just…” He shook his head. “It’s hard…”

She nodded in agreement. “Much harder than I thought it would be.” To deal with all the guilt that overwhelmed her. She could have done more, should have tried harder. Like Frankie had said, she should have asked her or her dad when she’d overheard her mom saying that her father had given her up for the ranch.

Brett reached out then and lightly touched her cheek. Her skin tingled, and her breath caught at the sensation of his fingertips against her face. He jerked his hand back. "I…you look exhausted. Why don't you go back to the house and rest for a while?"

Despite the little zip in her pulse from his touch, she was wiped. Beyond exhausted. And it wasn't just from the long drive and the little sleep she'd had; it was the emotional toll of being here at the ranch again.

And dealing with the fallout from her recent actions. She wanted to talk to Frankie, too, but she wasn't sure she was up for more recrimination. She already felt so horribly guilty.

She nodded. "I think you might be right."

His lips curved into a faint smile. "You'll find that I often am."

She smiled back at him. "We'll see about that."

He nodded. "Yes, we will." Then he helped her up from the hay bale like his brother had from the couch, by taking her hand.

Once more, she felt that zip of awareness and attraction rush through her that she only felt with Brett. She quickly dropped his hand and hurried toward the open door of the horse stall. It was only after she was halfway back to the house that she realized he hadn't answered her question about whether or not he could respect her.

They wouldn't be able to work together, let alone live together, if he couldn't. She'd been in relationships before where she hadn't been respected, and she wouldn't be in another one like that.

Not that this relationship with Brett Lemmon would ever be anything but professional. That was the only kind of relationship she would allow herself beyond the ones with her family. And no matter how her dad had felt about them, the Lemmons were not family to her.

NERVES JUMPED AROUND in Blake's stomach. "I think I blew it," he admitted to Maci in a whisper once they were alone on the front porch of the house.

She wound her arm through his and leaned against his shoulder. "Why would you think that? You offered to show her the books. It wasn't your fault she didn't want to look at them right now."

He groaned. "It might have been."

"Why? What did you do?" She sounded more curious than alarmed. Thankfully, she trusted him.

"We were talking about everyone being able to get along," Blake said.

"She and I talked about that, too," Maci admitted.

"And I might have mentioned that she'd only have to worry about Frankie and Brett…"

Maci groaned now.

"So you think I screwed up?"

"I told her the same thing," Maci said. "That they're not as likely to forgive her."

Blake nodded. "That's why she didn't look at the books. She went outside to find them."

"And I saw Frankie head back here right after Trish left," Maci said.

"I know. So Frankie didn't give her a chance to talk about it." Not that Blake was particularly surprised by that. Frankie had lit into that lawyer. He couldn't blame her for that, though. He'd been tempted to do the same after all the stress Nolan Stokes had caused Maci.

"And Brett?" Maci asked.

Blake pointed to where Trish was walking slowly back from the barn. Alone. Her shoulders were slumped, and her steps were small as if she barely had the energy to put one foot in front of the other. "She doesn't look like that conversation went well, either."

"Then we weren't wrong to warn her," Maci said. "But, hopefully we're wrong now, and everything went well."

When Trish looked up and noticed them standing on the porch, her posture stiffened. Then she grasped the railing beside the steps, using it to pull herself up to join them. "I'm really tired right now," she said. That much was apparent from the dark circles beneath her eyes and the paleness of her skin. "I don't want to talk anymore today about the will or the ranch or…" Her throat moved as if she was struggling to swallow. "Or my father…"

"Go, get some rest," Blake urged her.

"You must not have eaten much either," Maci said. "I can make you something and bring it in."

Trish shook her head. "No. I just need to sleep right now."

Blake pulled open the door for her and held it. Then he murmured, "I'm sorry…"

Trish stopped and stared up at him. "Why?" she asked. "You've been very kind."

"I'm not apologizing for myself," he admitted. He was apologizing for whatever his big brother and Frankie had done that had exhausted her so much.

She smiled and shook her head. "That's not necessary." She walked through the open door and through the one to the main bedroom without telling him why his apology was unnecessary.

"What do you think she meant by that?" Blake asked Maci as he closed the door behind her old friend.

Maci shrugged. "I don't know. Maybe she didn't talk to either of them, and we've just been jumping to conclusions. Or maybe she did talk to them, and it didn't go as badly as we think. Or…"

"Or?" Blake prodded when she trailed off.

"Or she knows you're not responsible for whatever Brett or Frankie might have said to her, so she doesn't think it's necessary for you to apologize," Maci said.

Blake sighed. "That's what worries me. Whatever Brett or Frankie said…" He groaned again. "She was so close to agreeing to accept the terms of the will."

Maci tilted her head. "I'm not so sure. She promised her lawyer she wouldn't agree to anything until she talked to him—"

"And he's going to do everything he can to make sure she doesn't settle," Blake finished.

Maci groaned now. "I know from experience how good he is at stating his case." Despite how hard Blake knew that Maci had worked, Stokes had kept getting extensions from the probate judge to put off settling the estate.

"I thought this was all going to be over once she got here," Blake said. That was why those nerves kept jumping around in his gut, because he had a feeling that nothing was going to be settled.

He glanced back toward the barn just as Brett rode off on the back of his black horse. The hooves kicked up dust from how hard and fast Brett was riding away from the house. Away from Trish Dempsey…

Was that because he was angry with her? Or for another reason? Like maybe he couldn't stay as angry with her as he wanted to be. Brett had adopted Frank Dempsey's attitude about relationships—that they weren't worth the risk. While Blake had always admired and idolized his older brother, he knew how wrong Brett was about that.

Love was worth every risk.

CHAPTER SEVEN

BRETT HAD SPENT another restless night tossing and turning in his bed. He awoke early the next morning with his head pounding from stress, sleeplessness and all the thoughts that had kept him awake the night before.

Trish.

All his thoughts had revolved around her and what she was going to do. She hadn't told anyone yet. When he'd suggested Trish get some sleep the day before, he'd figured she would just take a nap. Maybe sleep for an hour or two. But he hadn't seen her again after she'd left the barn.

Not that he'd been around that much. He'd spent the entire afternoon riding around the pastures, checking on the cattle, making sure the other calves were doing well. He should probably call the veterinarian to check on them again. The vet he'd been using the past five years was now his stepcousin. Dr. Cash had become more than just his vet, though; they were good friends. Cash had let his fees slide for a while when the ranch was struggling. Brett was glad that he could pay him back for that.

What if Trish wanted to use a different vet? What if she wanted to change everything about the ranch? Maybe not even focus on the cattle that Brett and his brothers had worked so hard to turn into a healthier, organic beef business?

The only thing Brett knew for certain was that Trish intended to start some kind of daycare at the ranch. Or just a summer camp? He understood the appeal of such a place. As a kid stuck in the city against his will, he would have loved spending his summers at a ranch out west. But adding a camp to the ranch would increase the workload and liability. Hopefully, she would understand that while it sounded fun, camps and petting zoos wouldn't be practical.

But in order for her to understand, someone would need to talk to her about it. No one else at the house had seen her again yesterday. She'd stayed in her room. Maybe sleeping. Or maybe she'd just been avoiding them.

Brett wanted to avoid her now, too. Maybe he couldn't sleep because of her presence, her closeness to the room where he'd tossed and turned. Clearly she didn't think that he and his brothers, as *ranch hands*, should even be in the house. And if she decided not to respect her father's wishes, she might want them to move out.

Brett would fight her over the ranch, but he

didn't really care where he slept. So after tending to the livestock that morning, he walked from the barn to the two-story bunkhouse with its weathered clapboard siding. The long building was on the other side of the barn from the house. When he pushed open the door, something scurried across the room, tiny claws scraping across the bare hardwood floor.

A startled scream escaped the lips of the woman who was already standing in the bunkhouse. Trish jumped at the sight of the mouse that raced across the floor in front of her, and her scream echoed off the high ceiling.

"Not going to have mice in your petting zoo?" Brett couldn't resist the urge to tease her.

She shuddered. "No. Absolutely not."

"Maybe we should put the kittens in here," he remarked. "Have them handle the mice."

She shuddered again. "No. This place needs a lot of work before it'll be safe for anyone."

Brett wanted to ask who anyone was. Him?

But he focused instead on the building. The big open space was all wood, floor, walls and open raftered ceiling. Cobwebs hung from the ceiling beams, illuminated by the sunlight streaking through the dirty windows. There was a long table near the small kitchenette and then a couple of couches with stuffing sticking out of some holes in the worn fabric.

Trish was looking around, too. "Looks like this hasn't been used for a long time."

"It hasn't," Brett confirmed. "The last ranch hands we had didn't live on site. They commuted from their homes to the Four Corners because they lived close."

"You don't have them anymore?" she asked.

He shook his head. "My brothers and I can usually handle everything. We just hired extra help during calving season or when one of us was going to be gone. Not that the young guys we hired were much help." If they had been, Frank Dempsey might not have lost his life. He'd been out checking pastures alone when he'd fallen off his horse.

"What?" Trish asked as she studied his face. "Was there a problem with them?"

He sighed. "One of them is the reason that baby Lucy was abandoned in the barn."

"Oh my gosh," she said, her hand going to her heart like it had yesterday when they'd talked about her father. "Someone abandoned her?"

He nodded. "The mother didn't realize that the ranch hand had lied to her about his name. She thought he was really Liam Lemmon, and that's what she put on the baby's birth certificate. The child protective services investigator believed he was the father even though a rodeo accident made it impossible for Liam to ever have biological children."

She gasped again. "That's sad."

Brett shook his head. "No. He has Lucy, and I'm sure he and Elise will adopt more children. Elise is the CPS investigator who helped make sure that Lucy stayed where she belongs, here on the ranch."

Trish's lips curved into a slight smile. "Are you worried that I'm going to throw Lucy out of the house?"

"Yes," he admitted. "We've all worried about that during the limbo we feel like we've been living in while the estate stays unsettled."

She sighed. "I understand the frustration of that. I've been living in limbo for a while myself."

"So?" he asked. "What have you decided?"

"Is that why you followed me out here?" she asked. "To find out my decision?"

"I didn't follow you out here," he said. "I was checking out the bunkhouse for myself. Clearly you're not comfortable with strangers in your father's house."

"So you're considering moving in here?" she asked. She glanced around and shuddered again.

"What about you?" he asked. "Why are you out here? Are you considering moving into the bunkhouse?"

She shook her head. "I was just checking it out." She headed toward the stairwell on the inside wall of the long room. As she started up the steps, she reached for the railing. It wobbled, then creaked as it gave way, falling off the stairs onto the floor below.

Trish wobbled on the steps, as if she was about to fall, too. Then she let out another little scream like she had over the mouse.

Brett raced toward her, desperate to catch her before she tumbled down the stairs and hurt herself or the babies she carried.

THE SECOND THE railing gave way beneath her hand, Trish struggled for balance. Her arms flailed as she searched for something to grab on to, for something to stop her fall, but then her feet slipped and she floundered in open air, bracing herself for the crash to the ground.

Thankfully, strong arms wrapped around her, catching her. Holding her. “I’ve got you,” Brett said. “You’re not going to fall.”

But she already had. She just hadn’t hit the ground because of him. Because he’d rescued her.

Her breath shuddered out in a ragged sigh of relief. She found his shoulders with her hands, holding on to him as she regained her footing on the floor. “Thank you.”

He hadn’t only rescued her; he’d rescued her babies, too. They kicked now and moved around in her belly, and she couldn’t imagine what might have happened had she fallen to the ground. She wouldn’t let herself imagine. But still a tear trickled out as her fears overwhelmed her.

Brett tightened his grasp on her for a moment. "You're fine," he said. "You didn't get hurt."

"Scared," she admitted in a shaky voice. "That scared me." And she was even more frightened of the feelings coursing through her as he held her. She forced herself to push back from his shoulders until his arms loosened around her and she slipped free of his embrace.

"You need to be more careful," he said. "This place is in bad shape. Why in the world are you checking it out?"

"For the camps," she explained. "It's a great open space for kids to play and has a kitchen and a couple of bathrooms."

"They're in bad shape," he said.

"It can be fixed up," she said. She wasn't thinking about anyone living there full-time. Clearly her father had wanted the Lemmon brothers to live in the house. So she imagined instead all the possibilities for the bunkhouse. She could envision the space as it had once looked, years ago. It could be that fun open area again that had once housed a pool table and ping-pong table. She and Frankie and Maci had had so much fun here, and the kids who would come for the camps would, too.

"It would take a lot of money just to get the electrical and plumbing up to code," he said. "Let alone fix the structural things."

"Does the ranch have that money?" she wondered aloud. Or would she need to use her divorce settlement?

"Didn't Blake show you the books?" he asked.

"He offered," she said. "But then I went out to find you and Frankie."

"To find out if we can respect you," he said.

"And you never told me if you could," she said.

"I don't know you, Trish," he said.

"And I don't know you," she pointed out. Yet, when he'd held her, his arms had almost felt familiar to her. Or maybe they'd just felt safe, like she was home.

But Brett Lemmon wasn't home. The Four Corners was.

"So you still haven't made a decision about the will," he said.

She had made her decision, but she intended to keep the promise she'd made to Nolan Stokes. "I want to talk to my lawyer again before I make any rash decisions."

"Like packing up everything you own in a truck and trailer and driving for hours to move into a house with strangers?" he asked, his mouth curving into a slight grin.

She laughed. "Yeah, like that."

"Why did you do that, Trish?" Brett asked her, his head tilted as he studied her face.

She patted her burgeoning belly. "For them. I want to raise them here where I was happiest."

He sucked in a breath. "I wish your dad knew

that." He blinked as if he was fighting the same tears that were rushing up on her. "That this is where you were happiest."

"I hope he knows," she said. "I loved it here. I loved him." And Frankie and Maci.

"Then why did you stay away so long?" he asked.

She shook her head. "I don't know. Pride. Stupidity. Stubbornness." She had so many regrets. But she would be careful to make sure she didn't do anything else she would wind up regretting.

He didn't say anything then, just stared at her as if trying to figure her out.

"I can't undo the past," she said. No matter how much she wished she could. "All I can do is focus on the future."

He nodded in agreement. "And what do you see in that future, Trish? And who?"

She patted her belly again. "Them." Her children were most important to her now, and doing whatever she had to in order to secure their happiness. "They're all I really need."

"Not Frankie or Maci?"

"I would like them back in my life," she admitted. "But I know I pushed them away." And maybe she'd done irreversible damage with Frankie at least if not Maci as well.

"So your plan is to raise your babies alone?" he asked.

She nodded.

"Babies are a lot of work," he said. "Lucy showed me that." He shuddered now like she had when she'd seen the mouse.

"You don't like babies?"

"I love my niece," he said. "But she just reinforced my belief that I'm not cut out to be a father."

A twinge of disappointment struck her. "You're not? Why not?"

He shrugged. "Ranching and raising kids are both a lot of work. Too much work to do both well from what I can tell. One or the other will suffer."

She sucked in a breath. "You think the ranch was failing because of me?"

He shook his head. "Not you. But the divorce took a toll on your dad and the ranch. He had to take out a mortgage on it and still pay child support to your mom. You can tell from the books that it was hard for your dad to take care of you and the ranch."

Fury bubbled up inside her that her mother had lied to her about so much. But she shouldn't have been surprised that she had. If only she'd known the truth sooner…

"Also," Brett continued, "ranching is hard. It takes long hours and there are always emergencies that unexpectedly pop up. That puts stress on a relationship and on a family."

"So what about Liam and Elise?" she asked. "Are you worried about their relationship? And

Blake and Maci? Will ranching destroy those relationships?"

He shook his head. "I'll do my best to make sure that doesn't happen. That all the hard stuff and the long hours fall on me, not them."

"So you're sacrificing yourself to make sure your brothers are happy?" she asked. Could anyone really be that selfless? She couldn't remember ever meeting anyone else that was.

He shook his head again. "It's not a sacrifice. Ranching is all I've ever wanted to do."

"Despite how hard it is?" she asked.

He grinned. "Maybe because it's hard, it's even more rewarding when it prospers. But it is hard, so before you talk to your lawyer, you need to think about that, about if this life is really what you want. You might have enjoyed your summers here, but ranching day in and day out can be grueling work. And then to try to raise two babies while doing it..."

"It's not like I intend to be out on horseback cutting cattle from the herd or anything," she murmured. Her dad had taught her and Frankie how to do it, but it had been so long ago. And who would watch the babies while she helped out? If she'd been able to buy out the Lemmon brothers, she would have had to hire ranch hands to help with that part of the work.

"What do you intend to do, Trish?"

"The kids' camps..."

"Summer and day camps," he said and sighed. "I still think that isn't a good idea. They'll just add more work for everyone else when there's already so much work to do around here, especially in the summer."

For the first time, doubts about her plan crept into her mind. The camps obviously wouldn't support the ranch on its own. The beef business would have to continue, which she knew was hard work with long hours.

Had she romanticized the ranch? Would it not be the best place to raise her kids like she'd believed it would be?

LIAM HATED LIVING in limbo like this. They'd spent entirely too many months doing it. If he hadn't had Lucy and Elise, he probably would have lost his mind by now. But because of Lucy and Elise, he wanted to know that their future was secure, that they could continue living on the ranch while he worked it with his brothers and Frankie and maybe Trish.

"Do you think she's really staying?" he asked Blake as they walked from the barn to the house. Brett had beat them back some time ago from the pastures. His horse had already been tended, its black coat shiny and clean from Brett brushing him out. As a former rodeo rider, Liam appreciated animals and especially appreciated how well his brothers took care of the ones on the ranch.

Frankie did, too. She was still in the barn tending to her calf.

Where was Brett?

Blake pointed at the trailer as they passed it on their way to the house. "She hasn't unloaded it yet, but it sure seems like she brought everything she owns with her."

Liam nodded. "But like you said, she hasn't unpacked it yet."

"That might be a little hard for her to do in her condition," Blake said.

"We should help her," Liam said.

"We need to know if she's really staying," Blake said. "I think she wants to see if she'll be able to get along with Brett and Frankie before she makes any decisions."

"Brett and Frankie definitely aren't happy with her," Liam said.

"And you?" Blake asked.

"I hate living in limbo, but I understand now that she has her reasons." The babies she carried. Since becoming Lucy's father, Liam knew that children had to come first. They had to be protected because they couldn't protect themselves.

"Hopefully Frankie and Brett can accept that, too," Blake said.

Liam wasn't all that hopeful that would happen. Even though Frankie and Brett loved Lucy, they were determined to never become parents themselves. They didn't understand how parents thought.

He followed Blake up the steps to the front door. Then he followed him inside the house. As he turned to pull the door closed behind them, he noticed someone else walking toward the house now.

It wasn't Frankie. She was probably still inside the barn with Cocoa.

But the woman walking next to his brother Brett looked a lot like Frankie. If her hair was a little longer, her eyes a little darker and she wasn't pregnant, Trish would have looked like Frankie's twin. Despite how much they looked alike, their personalities seemed very different, though.

Frankie was decisive and strong and an open book with her thoughts and feelings. Trish was harder to read.

But as they drew closer, Liam noticed the glances she kept shooting at his brother. Maybe he'd been spending too much time around his grandparents because he found himself wondering where they'd been and what had happened between them and if there was any chance of more than a working relationship between the two of them.

CHAPTER EIGHT

She was gone. Brett knew it even before he glanced out the front window and saw that her truck was no longer parked in the driveway.

In the time it had taken him to shower off his work day plus their expedition into the rundown bunkhouse, she must have slipped out of the house. He wondered where she was going.

To her lawyer's?

If not for her trailer still being in the driveway, he might have figured that she'd taken off for good. That he'd scared her away from ranching. It wasn't as easy and fun as she seemed to think it was.

Didn't she realize how hard her dad had struggled?

She should have gone over the books with Blake. Instead, she'd taken off.

Maybe she'd gone to see Maci. But then Maci's little SUV appeared in the driveway, heading toward the house. She would have passed Trish on the road if Trish had been going to see her.

He waited for her at the front door.

"Hey, Brett," she greeted him. "What's going on?"

He shrugged. "I really have no idea. Did you pass Trish on the road, by any chance?"

She shook her head. "No. Was she coming to see me or heading to town?"

"If she'd been doing either of those, you would have passed her," he pointed out. "So she must be going to see *him*." He thought as highly of Stokes as Frankie did, which wasn't very high at all despite his sterling reputation as a champion of the underdog.

He hadn't considered Trish an underdog. But now, knowing the struggles she'd had with her mother and her ex-husband, Brett realized that she might have been in those circumstances. That wasn't the case with the ranch. At the moment, it definitely felt as if she had the upper hand.

"Hey, beautiful," Blake said as he walked out of the kitchen to greet his girlfriend at the door. He passed Brett and pulled Maci into a hug.

A jab of envy hit Brett like an elbow. He'd felt that before when he'd seen how happy Blake was with Maci and Liam with Elise and Lucy. At the time he hadn't realized it was envy, though. He'd just figured he was concerned about his brothers, worried that they might wind up getting hurt like Frank Dempsey had been. And their dad, when their mom died.

Was love worth that kind of pain?

Hopefully, his brothers and his sister, who was engaged, would never know that pain, only the love and happiness they were experiencing now.

Was he jealous of that love and happiness?

He shook his head at the thought. Absolutely not. If they wanted to put themselves at risk like that, that was their choice. It wasn't one he was ever going to make for himself. And that was good, because one of them had to put the ranch first.

"You okay?" Blake asked when he noticed that Brett was still standing there.

He nodded.

"He's worried about Trish," Maci said.

"What about Trish?" Frankie asked, as she walked in the door Maci had left open. "Where is she?"

"Brett thinks she went to see her lawyer," Maci said.

Frankie sucked in a breath. "Well, better that she goes to him than that he comes here again." She shuddered. "I don't want to see him ever again."

"I don't think that's going to be an option," Brett said.

"Why?" Blake asked. "What happened between the two of you today? Liam and I saw you walking back to the house together. Where were you?"

"The bunkhouse," he replied.

"You thinking of moving out there?" Liam asked as he carried Lucy out from the kitchen. He must have been cooking because delicious aromas drifted out with him. "I hope Lucy's not chasing you out of the house."

"I don't think it's Lucy he wants to get away from," Frankie said. "It's Trish."

It was Trish. But now that she was gone, he had a strange feeling. Like a hollowness. That was probably just about the ranch, though. He was worried that lawyer still might talk her into going after all of it.

"But she was out there, too," Blake said. "Why?"

"She wants to start a kids' camp at the ranch," Brett said.

"She was serious about that?" Frankie asked.

"She mentioned it to you, too?"

She and Maci nodded. "She seems really excited about it," Maci added.

"It's a stupid idea," he protested. "It will expose us to all kinds of liability."

"And children," Liam said, chuckling. "Isn't that really what you don't want? A bunch of kids running around the ranch?"

"Who's running around the ranch?" Elise asked from the kitchen doorway. "Come and eat. It's all ready."

"Children," Liam said and shared with his wife Trish's desire to start the camps.

"I love that," Elise said.

"Brett doesn't," Liam said.

He shook his head. "That's not the case. I would have loved it when we were kids."

Blake and Liam nodded.

"It would have been great to spend our summers on a ranch," Brett acknowledged. "It might have made up for our parents moving us to the city. But now, with all the work we already do around here, why would I want to add more work? Because that's all this will be, more work and more trouble."

"And more kids," Liam said with a mocking grin.

"I love Lucy," he said. "And I love being her uncle. But this camp idea… I'm just not sure that it's feasible."

When no one else said anything, he sighed and added, "But I'm not going to worry about the camps and her petting zoo idea until I know what she's decided about the will." None of it would matter if he wasn't able to keep his inheritance of the ranch.

"So you think that's why she's meeting with her lawyer," Maci said. "Because she's made a decision?"

He nodded. "I think so."

"And? What do you think she decided?" Liam asked.

He shrugged. "I don't know. When we were in the bunkhouse and she was talking about her plans, I reminded her how much work a cattle ranch is. Maybe she's changed her mind about wanting to be part of it."

Or she just wanted it all for herself now so she could turn it into what she wanted without any resistance from him.

"I MADE MY DECISION," Trish said when Nolan Stokes opened the front door of his new, two-story modern house. With its metal and glass and sharp roof lines, the place looked like it belonged downtown in some big city, not in the middle of fields and pastures. Even the barn matched the house with its sharp angles and black metal.

"Come in," he said as he stepped back for her to enter past the ten-foot-high entrance door to the foyer.

The ceilings soared even higher in the wide-open spaces. He gestured in one direction and said, "The kids are still eating…"

Through a doorway, she caught a glimpse of dark cabinets and a long table where three kids sat staring at plates of vegetables. There were two girls with pale blond hair. One was probably seven or eight, and she sat next to the younger one, who was probably just three. Her hair was wispy with little tendrils curling softly around her face. A boy, who was probably somewhere in the middle of their ages at five or six, had black hair and Nolan's pale blue eyes.

"They're beautiful," she murmured.

"They're stubborn," he said with a sigh. "Nobody wants to eat their vegetables." He raised his voice. "And they know they don't get dessert until they eat at least half of them..."

The boy sighed but picked up his fork and stuck it into a spear of broccoli. The older girl lifted her chin, and the younger one stuck out her bottom lip.

Instead of getting irritated, Nolan laughed. "Who knew my toughest negotiations would be with my own children?"

Babies are a lot of work. That was what Brett had told her just that afternoon. And Lucy was still a baby. The work didn't stop when they got older.

And Trish had decided to do this on her own. But plenty of people did. Nolan Stokes was doing it. She could, too.

She had to.

She didn't have a choice now.

"Here," he said as he slid open a pocket door off the foyer. "Let's step into my office, so that they have time to hide their vegetables without me catching them."

She laughed now. This was a side she never would have suspected him of having. "You're a good dad," she said as she followed him into the room with its high ceiling, tall windows and dark furniture.

He sighed. "I have no idea what I'm doing half

the time, like moving them out of the city to this ranch," he said. "Hopefully they survive to adulthood."

She touched her belly. For her first few pregnancies, she hadn't let herself think much beyond the pregnancy. But these babies were doing well. They would make it, and then she would have to figure out how to get them to adulthood.

"What about you, Trish?" he asked. "Do you know what you're doing?"

"As a mother?" She shook her head. "All my mother taught me was what not to do."

"Sometimes that's the most important stuff to know," Nolan said. "What about the will? What are you going to do about that?"

"I'm not going to fight it."

He groaned. "You've only been there a couple of days, and they already coerced you into giving them what they want. No wonder they were able to get your dad to change his will."

Trish shook her head. "The only person who ever coerced my father was my mother. After her, I seriously doubt he would have let anyone else do that."

"You don't believe that the Lemmons conned him?"

"No," she said. "I believe they worked hard, and my dad always rewarded hard work." That was why he'd paid for Maci's law school.

"But you are his rightful heir," Nolan said. "You shouldn't have to share what's yours with strangers."

She might have only been at the ranch for a couple of days, but the Lemmons didn't feel like strangers anymore. Especially not Brett. He wasn't happy she was there, but he had been kind to her. He'd also been very honest today, and that had scared her. But he was right. Ranching and raising kids were both hard work.

Trish glanced out the big window at the pasture. "Do you manage this ranch, too?"

He snorted. "It's not much of a ranch," he said. "Less than a hundred acres and not much livestock. But one of the reasons I bought the land and built the house was because I like being self-sufficient."

Self-sufficient.

That was what Trish wanted to be. She wanted to take care of herself and her children. And even though it wouldn't be easy, she was determined to do it.

"Are you going to be able to work with the Lemmons?" he asked. "Let alone live with them?"

"I don't know," she admitted. Brett had never really answered her question. She didn't know if he would respect what she wanted. And Frankie…

She and Frankie still had a long way to go to get back to how close they'd once been, if that was even possible after everything that had happened.

"I'm actually more worried about my cousin than I am the Lemmons."

He grunted. "Your cousin is unhinged."

Trish tensed. "Not at all. Frankie is very loyal."

"Just not to you."

"I haven't earned that loyalty," she admitted. "Not with how I handled things."

"You had no choice," Nolan said.

"I could have—I should have—handled everything much better," she said. "Especially with my cousin." Until these babies came into the world, Frankie was the only biological family she had left. Her mother had disowned her over the divorce.

Despite being angry with her, Frankie had hugged her, along with Maci, when Trish had talked about her divorce and her miscarriages, but they hadn't had a one-on-one conversation since that day. Frankie seemed to be avoiding her.

She'd thought Brett might have been, too, with the way he was always the first one out of the house and the last one back at the end of a long day. But he'd shown up at the bunkhouse. Fortunately. Or she might have been seriously hurt when she'd fallen from the staircase. But he'd caught her and held her in those strong arms. And for a moment, she'd been more afraid of how he'd made her feel than she had been of what might have happened had she struck the ground.

Nolan shrugged. "I don't know that there would

be a right way to handle anything with a woman like your cousin."

"She's really a very good person," Trish insisted. "And I think the Lemmons are, too."

"You've only been at the Four Corners for a few days," Nolan said. "I wish you would take more time before making your decision. I got that last extension from the probate judge, so we don't have to settle anything for a couple of weeks yet."

She shook her head. "I had to live in limbo for months because of my ex fighting everything. I can't keep doing that to Frankie, the Lemmons and Maci."

"*You* are a good person, Trish Dempsey," he said. "And I hope the other heirs aren't taking advantage of that."

"Nobody's going to take advantage of me again," she assured him.

"Then let me try to get you a bigger share of the estate," he said.

She shook her head again. "No. I do believe that this is what my father wanted." A pang struck her heart over that, over things having gotten so strained between them that he hadn't told her what he wanted before he died. That she'd had to find out this way.

"That doesn't mean he was right," Nolan said with a faint smile. "The Four Corners was your home, not the Lemmons'."

"After my parents divorced, it was only for the summers," she reminded him. Those amazing summers that she'd longed for all the other months of the year. If she hadn't had those, her life would have been so empty. "And Maci did a good job with that will. I doubt you could fight it."

"I can fight anything," he said.

"But would you win?"

He released a ragged sigh and shrugged. "I don't know."

"It doesn't matter," she said. "I'm tired of fighting."

"Then you should let me do it for you," he said. "Because I think running this ranch with that many other people is going to be another big fight for you. And you're not going to get what you want done around the place."

She'd had that fear, too, that she wouldn't get what she wanted. The day and summer camp for kids. The petting zoo. Brett thought they would be too much liability and too much work for a working cattle ranch.

And maybe he was right.

But that wasn't going to stop her. Just like raising her babies alone would be a lot of work, but she wanted them more than anything else. And she would fight to give them the life she wanted for them. To make sure that they were happy.

NOLAN STOOD AT his office window watching Trish Dempsey's truck drive away. She was going back to the Four Corners, back to *them*.

And he couldn't help but worry about her. Even though she was much stronger than she'd been when they'd first met, she was still vulnerable. And despite how people in her life had treated her, she was still too trusting.

That was something he would never be. Never again.

He'd learned his lesson, and he would make sure that nobody was ever able to hurt him again. But Trish…

She had too big a heart not to let more people into it. That was why she'd wanted children so badly. She wanted to love unconditionally and be loved unconditionally.

"Daddy!" Zoe shouted. "Daddy!"

Nolan ducked out of his office and ran back to the kitchen, to his baby, who'd called for him.

She sat in her booster seat, the plate in front of her piled high with broccoli. Tears pooled in her silvery blue eyes. "Daddy, they gave me all the veg-tub-alls."

Hope's and Xavier's plates were curiously clean.

He sighed. "Not a real great job of hiding them, guys," he said. Then he sighed again and pulled open the freezer. Ice cream was good for a person, had calcium and vitamin D. He wasn't being a bad father by giving in.

He wasn't a bad father anymore. But like Trish he regretted things he'd done or hadn't done. Because of his career, he hadn't always been there for his family like he should have been.

He was changing that now. He was going to be there for *all* of his family, whether they liked it or not.

CHAPTER NINE

SHE WAS BACK. Alone. Once Brett saw her truck pull into the driveway, the tension eased from his body… even before he noticed that no other person was in it with her and no other vehicle followed hers.

"Good, no sign of the snake," Frankie remarked. She stood beside him at the window.

Brett must not have been the only one who'd worried that Stokes might return with her. But maybe he didn't need to because he'd gotten what he wanted—for her to continue fighting the will.

"I hope he didn't talk her out of settling," Frankie said.

Trish didn't jump out of her truck after she parked it. She sat behind the wheel for a while. And that concerned Brett. Was she okay?

She'd nearly fallen that morning. While he'd caught her, maybe something else was going on with her. Like maybe she was dizzy or something, like she'd seemed that first night she'd shown up at the ranch after driving for so long. And then she'd basically slept most of another day.

Maybe she'd just needed to recover from packing up all her stuff and driving. Or being as pregnant as she was, she could be having any number of medical issues. He didn't need to be a doctor like his sister Livvy to know that.

He stepped back from the window, to move around Frankie and start toward the door, to make sure that Trish was all right, but then she stepped out of the truck. The wind tousled her curls, tumbling them around her face, which she lifted toward the sun. She seemed to take a deep breath and square her shoulders before she began to walk toward the house.

"Uh-oh." Frankie voiced aloud the concern that hit Brett. "She looks like she's bracing herself to tell us whatever she decided."

"Or maybe she's just bracing herself to deal with the two of you," Blake said.

Brett turned to find his brother standing behind him, his arm around Maci's shoulders.

"Or maybe she's just going to put us off some more before telling us what she's going to do," Frankie said. She was as cynical as Brett had become.

Maci shook her head. "No. I don't think that's the case. Trish sent me a text a few minutes ago asking me to meet her here." Clearly, she hadn't known that Maci was already at the house.

The door creaked as it opened, and Brett turned to watch Trish step inside the house. She glanced from Frankie to Maci to Blake. But she didn't look at him.

A sharp jab of disappointment took Brett by surprise. He shouldn't care that she wouldn't look at him, that she didn't like him. He didn't need her to like him. And he didn't need to like her. But…

He was starting to; he actually understood some of the reasons she'd done what she had. It was clear her mother and ex-husband had had more influence on her than she'd wanted, that they had manipulated her.

Had her lawyer just done the same?

"Are Liam and Elise here, too?" she asked.

"Here," Liam said, his voice just a whisper, as he ducked out of his bedroom. Elise followed him out and softly closed the door behind herself.

"We just got Lucy down for a nap," she said.

"Can we talk in the den?" Liam asked.

Trish nodded and whispered back, "Yes, of course."

Everyone waited, letting her lead the way to her father's office. When Brett followed the others, he found her sitting on the couch next to Liam and Elise while Frankie, Maci and Blake stood. He couldn't sit either. The only other seat in the room was Frank's chair. And he still couldn't bring himself to sit there.

Seeing that Liam had the baby monitor in his hand, Brett closed the door behind himself, then leaned against it. He didn't want to wake up Lucy in case voices got raised. But for another long moment nobody said anything.

Finally, Frankie cleared her voice. "So? What did the sleaze convince you to do?"

Trish grimaced. "Nolan really is a good man," she said. Then she smiled. "Which is what I just told him about the Lemmon brothers."

"That we're good men?" Blake asked.

She nodded.

"So he was still trashing us to you," Brett concluded. "What's his deal with us? None of us met the guy until the other day."

Trish shrugged. "I don't know. I think he just struggles to trust anyone."

So Brett had something in common with the lawyer after all.

"And he didn't convince me to do anything," Trish continued, speaking directly to her cousin. "I had already made up my mind."

Brett wasn't surprised. He knew what she wanted for the ranch; she wanted to recreate the childhood she wished she'd had for her children and for other kids as well.

"And?" Maci prodded.

"I want you to do whatever you have to do to settle the estate," Trish replied.

Maci nodded. "That means that Stokes has to withdraw his request to postpone the probate court hearing. In order for everything to be settled, the judge has to rule that the will is valid, review all the documentation we've forwarded regarding the ranch books and inventory, and reissue the deed for the ranch to show all the heirs as the rightful owners."

Trish drew in a breath and then nodded, too. "I'll have him do that, and we can get this settled. But..."

"But what?" Frankie asked.

Trish drew in another deep breath, and her face flushed slightly. "I already asked Brett this question, but I've wanted to ask you, too."

Frankie glanced at him. "What question?"

"After everything that's happened, do you still respect me enough to work with me?" Trish asked. "Or will you not be able to get over it?"

Frankie glanced at Brett again, as if she was waiting for him to share his response before sharing hers. But as Trish had already pointed out to him, he hadn't answered her. She glanced at him now, but then her gaze bounced back to her cousin.

Frankie shrugged. "I understand some of your reasoning," she admitted. "You were going through a lot. I wish you had let us be there for you. I wish we would have known what was going on with you."

Trish blinked, but there was still a sheen of tears in her light brown eyes. She nodded. "I know. I'm sorry."

Frankie released a shaky sigh and nodded. "I

know. And yeah, we can do this…all five of us can run this ranch…although…once the estate is settled I'll probably be on my own way, back to the road." She didn't sound all that excited about returning to her old life, though, not like she once had.

"I still have some concerns about running this ranch together," Trish began, and she sat up a bit straighter on the couch. "I feel like I'm at a real disadvantage."

"I'll show you the books," Blake said. "Bring you up to speed on everything we have going on."

Brett knew he'd already offered, but Trish had been more interested in whether or not she could work with him and Frankie. "I don't think that's what she means," he said, then had to clear the gruffness from his voice. "She has plans for the ranch."

"The petting zoo and kids' camps," Liam said.

"I love that idea," Elise added. "I think it would be great for kids who otherwise wouldn't have the opportunity to get a taste of living on a farm. We can teach them responsibility, too, by having them help take care of the petting zoo animals."

Trish smiled. "And here I was worried that you would all vote against my idea."

"Ah," Blake said. "You thought all the Lemmons would stick together and side against you."

"And Frankie," she added with a glance at her cousin.

"How will this work?" Frankie asked, and she looked at Maci. "If someone wants to do something on the ranch, do we have to put it to a vote?"

Maci shrugged. "Frank didn't put that into the will. I guess he assumed you would all figure it out."

"Maybe he assumed that some people would sell their shares to the others," Brett said with a glance at Trish. "That they wouldn't actually be interested in running the ranch."

Trish cleared her throat. "If that was what he thought, he would have been wrong."

Brett had respected Frank for how much he'd loved the ranch and his family, for how hard he'd worked to try to hang on to them both. "But was it wrong to assume that somebody who hadn't shown any interest in the place for years wouldn't want to be part of the day-to-day running of it?" He shrugged. "That seems logical to me."

Trish sucked in a breath, and the color left her face.

A pang of guilt struck Brett. He hadn't wanted to upset her. But he also had to defend his friend since Frank wasn't here to defend himself. Annoyed with himself more than anyone else, he shook his head. "I can't deal with this right now, with talking about petting zoos and kids' camps that we don't have the money or the manpower to get up and running. We need to focus on the cattle, on what actually makes the money to keep this place going."

He turned and pulled open the door and then walked out. He couldn't stand around while Frank's daughter destroyed the ranch that he had worked so hard to save. But he didn't know how to fight her and her ridiculous ideas when he didn't want to hurt her or her feelings. Clearly, she'd already been through a lot in her life.

If only she would just sell her share and leave… but he had a feeling that she wasn't going anywhere. So would he have to? Because he wasn't sure how he was going to work with Trish Dempsey, let alone live with her and the twin babies she was going to bring into the world soon.

BRETT CLEARLY DIDN'T want to work with her. Or live with her.

And she wasn't sure if he just really didn't like her plans for the petting zoo and camps, or if it was her that he didn't like. That hurt, and the sting of pain stole her breath for a moment.

Elise reached out and patted her hand. "Are you okay?"

She nodded. "I'm fine." She'd known it wouldn't be easy coming back to the ranch. But then, she'd been more concerned about dealing with the loss of her father than with the others who were still living at the ranch. And sitting here in his den, with the scent of leather and sweet cigars on every breath she inhaled, she felt as if her dad was still here in some way.

No matter what Brett Lemmon thought, her dad had to have known how much she'd loved the ranch, too. How much she'd loved him.

"You look really pale," Maci said. "Are you sure you're okay?"

Trish nodded. "Just tired." She patted her stomach, where the babies moved restlessly. Even when she was in bed, she didn't get much sleep. She had to keep getting up, keep moving to find a more comfortable position.

"Don't let my brother upset you," Blake said. "He's just really protective of the ranch. And it's been tough going for years."

"But it's turned around now, right?" Trish asked.

Blake sighed. "It's getting there. I wanted to make the beef business organic, make sure that there were no harmful chemicals in our feed that could be passed on to consumers."

"Blake, Liam and Brett lost their mother to breast cancer," Maci said.

"Brain cancer, actually," Liam said, his voice gruff. "She survived the breast cancer but then it came back in her brain."

Trish gasped over their loss. She wanted to ask questions but didn't want to pry, so she just offered her condolences. "I'm so sorry."

The brothers nodded, and Blake continued,

"Nobody knows how she got it. So, I just thought it would be safer and healthier to go organic."

"Of course," Trish said. "I wholeheartedly agree. And I can't imagine that hurting the ranch."

"It makes things more expensive," Blake said. "And causes more work for us to grow most of our own feed. But…what really hurt was not getting a contract we were counting on from a wholesaler who supplies whole foods stores."

"Tell her why the Four Corners didn't get the contract," Frankie said. But then she didn't wait for Blake to explain before adding, "Someone had told them that the ownership of the ranch was in dispute. And he was worried that the new owner might not honor the deal he was working out with the Lemmons." She narrowed her dark eyes. "Can you guess who might have told them that?"

"Not me," Trish assured them. "I didn't know about any of this."

"Bet your lawyer did," Frankie said.

It was clear that Nolan and Frankie were never going to be friends. Was that going to be the same situation with her and Brett?

Brett probably blamed her for them not getting that contract. And maybe it was her fault. If she hadn't dragged things out like she had…

She couldn't go back and change the past, but maybe she could smooth things out right now, at least with the purchaser. Her plans didn't have to affect the rest of the ranch; she had the settlement money from the divorce to remodel the bunkhouse and buy the animals for the petting zoo. But because she wasn't the sole heir of the ranch, she had to work with the others. And she doubted that there was any way she could get Brett's cooperation. He didn't want anything to do with her plans for the ranch—or probably with her, either.

"NOW I KNOW how Dad felt waiting up late for us to come home," Blake remarked to Liam, who sat on the porch steps next to him.

Liam chuckled. "Brett was always the one who pushed curfew."

"I'm a little old for a curfew." A deep voice spoke from the darkness.

Blake jumped; he hadn't noticed Brett walk up from the barn. But he recovered quickly and said, "That's the exact same thing you used to tell Dad."

"Yeah, when you were sixteen," Liam added.

"Well, thirty-two is definitely too old," he said. "Why are you guys waiting up for me? Are you giving me a heads-up that we're selling off all the cattle and turning the entire ranch into a daycare and a zoo?"

"That would be great," Liam said.

Blake didn't know if his younger brother was just teasing or serious. But from the way that Brett stiffened, he clearly wasn't amused. "It's not happening," Blake said.

"You guys voted down her petting zoo?" Brett asked, his voice lighter with surprise.

"No," Blake admitted. "But it's not going to affect the ranch or the cattle business. In fact, Trish called that purchaser for the whole foods stores. She got us the contract!" He stood up to high-five his older brother, but Brett didn't slap his hand. "Okay, leaving me hanging…"

"You should be happy," Liam said. "What's your deal, Brett?"

Their older brother just grunted and shrugged. "I don't trust her."

"I know a lot has happened, but I blame her lawyer for most of that," Blake said.

"Frankie certainly blames him," Liam said with a chuckle. "He would be smart to not show his face around here again until after she leaves."

"Or ever," Brett added.

He was obviously not a fan either. Neither was Blake. The man had put Maci through a lot of unnecessary stress.

"But he's not really the problem," Brett said.

"You think Trish is the problem?" Blake asked.

"You don't?" Brett sounded surprised again.

Blake shook his head. "She got us that contract. She doesn't want to hurt the ranch. She wants to keep it going, make it prosper. She understands everything we've been doing and respects it. She just wants to be respected in return, Brett." Blake didn't think that was too big an ask.

Apparently, his older brother did because he shook his head as if denying her his respect. "She doesn't know anything about ranching," he said. "I don't think she even knows anything about petting zoos and kids' camps. She just dreamed up this fantasy from her childhood and doesn't realize how much work it will be to make it a reality."

"I think you're underestimating her," Blake said. Or maybe Brett just didn't want her to stick around because she made him uncomfortable. Was he a little more interested in the single mom than he was willing to admit?

CHAPTER TEN

HIS SLEEPLESS NIGHTS and long days working the ranch caught up with Brett a few days after Trish's arrival, and for once he didn't manage to wake up early enough to beat everyone else out of the house. He liked being gone before anyone else was up and about, and he liked getting back after everyone else had gone to bed.

Then he didn't have to talk to anyone. No. He didn't have to talk to *her*. Or see *her*.

Except not talking to her, not seeing her, hadn't stopped him from thinking about her, from wondering what she was up to. But whenever he ran into his brothers out in the pastures or in the barn, or if they waited up for him like they had a couple of nights ago, he didn't let himself ask about her. He didn't want to care, and he certainly didn't want anyone else to think that he did.

He would not let Trish Dempsey get to him. He would focus on what mattered to him: the ranch, the cattle and his family.

He grimaced with guilt that his family came

last. And they had since her arrival. He'd been avoiding them as much as he'd been avoiding her. Maybe he was a little annoyed with Blake and Liam for being so agreeable to working with her and so accepting of her plans for the ranch.

Had she started on them?

Remembering how she'd nearly fallen off the staircase in the bunkhouse, alarm flashed through him. What if she got hurt trying to fix things up the way she wanted?

He shouldn't have been avoiding her. He should have been making sure that nothing happened to her. Despite how little he'd seen of his daughter after she'd become an adult, Frank Dempsey had loved her with his whole heart. Brett had kept the ranch running for Frank, but he needed to also make sure that nothing bad happened to his daughter and to his unborn grandchildren, too. He also needed to thank her for securing the contract that he and Blake hadn't been able to.

Sure, that had been her fault since she was the reason the estate hadn't been settled sooner. But she'd secured that contract now. She hadn't had to do that. But she had. She'd settled the will, too.

And he hadn't thanked her for anything yet.

So when he awoke a couple hours later than he usually did, he searched the house for her. She'd left the door open to her dad's suite, and it barely looked as if she'd touched it or brought anything into it. She wasn't in it or anywhere else in the house. But her truck was in the driveway.

Worried that she might be in the bunkhouse, Brett rushed across the yard toward it. But as he passed the barn, he caught the soft lilt of a singing voice. It could have been Frankie's, but Frankie's van was gone. Nobody else drove that rattletrap, which meant she must have taken it somewhere.

So who was singing?

The voice drew him into the barn, and he understood that old myth about mermaids luring sailors to their death with their singing. He wouldn't have been able to resist finding out who this was even though part of him already knew.

He blinked to adjust his eyes to the dim light in the barn. But he still couldn't see her. She had to be where her cousin usually was, so he walked over to the stall where Cocoa was kept with the kittens. He leaned over the top of the stall door and peered inside the small area.

Trish sat on one of the bales of hay, and the calf leaned across her knees as Trish fed it. One of the kittens was in the crook of her free arm, and the other one was curled up beside her. She finished the lullaby she'd been singing and leaned down to kiss the top of the calf's head.

"You are as good with animals as your cousin is," Brett commented.

He must have startled her because she jumped, disturbing all the animals that had gathered on and around her. "I'm sorry," he said. "I didn't mean to scare you."

She pressed her hand to her heart and breathed in deep. "I'm fine. And I'm actually only good with farm animals, not all animals. I have a scar from my mother's dog to prove it." She held up her hand.

He opened the stall door and stepped inside to get close enough to see whatever she was showing him. The scar was so small that he hadn't noticed the fine white line on the side of her palm. "And you still want to open a petting zoo?"

She sighed wearily. "I just said that I have no problems with farm animals. That's partly why I want to do the petting zoo, because the animals on the farm were always easier to take care of than pets like my mother's aggressive dog."

"What's the other part of why you want the petting zoo?" he asked, as he'd been wondering why she was so set on opening one at the ranch.

"The summers I spent here were so magical," she said. "I loved taking care of the animals and spending so much time outside in the fresh air."

He understood that all too well; he'd missed so much when his family had moved away from Willow Creek.

"I want other kids to experience that magic," she said, and she touched her belly. "Not just me or even my kids. But I shouldn't have said anything because now you're going to use this—" she held up her hand again "—as another reason that I shouldn't proceed with the camps."

"It's not just my decision to make now," he said. "And I thought I was already outvoted on it."

"Is that why you've barely been around the past couple of days?" she asked, and then her face flushed a bright pink. "Not that I noticed or…"

"Cared?" he finished when she trailed off.

Her skin color deepened to rose. "Well, I thought you were probably pouting."

He chuckled, then sighed himself. "I don't know if I was pouting, but it did sting that my brothers couldn't understand my concerns about the petting zoo and kids' camps."

"I expected them to side with their big brother," she said. "That as the oldest, you're the boss."

He chuckled again. "I don't want to boss anyone around," he said. "And I don't need to with my brothers. They know what needs to get done around the ranch, and they don't need supervision. That's why we all work so well together." And that was why he knew they would pick up his slack today. They did that for each other without anyone having to ask or anyone complaining about extra work. But he wanted to make sure that Blake and Liam didn't work so much that it affected their relationships.

"I want to work well with everyone, too," Trish said. "That's why I haven't started on my plans."

"How will you and I work well together when

we don't want the same things for the ranch?" he asked.

The truth was, the ranch wasn't the only thing they had differing opinions on. They obviously didn't want the same things for their lives, either. Brett wanted the peace and quiet of spending his days on horseback, working the ranch; he wanted to focus solely on the Four Corners. Trish wanted the chaos and noise that kids brought.

"We both want the Four Corners to be successful," she pointed out.

He nodded. And then he remembered why he'd sought her out. "I owe you a thank-you," he said.

She arched a dark eyebrow. "For what?"

"For reaching out to that purchaser and getting a contract with them," he said. "Blake and I tried, but we couldn't get him to agree to it."

"Because of the dispute over ownership of the ranch," she said. "That was my fault. I just tried to fix it."

"You did fix it," he said.

She smiled. "Does that bother you? Is that why you've been so scarce?"

He sighed. "It's just a lot for me to process, Trish," he admitted. "You didn't come here just to explain yourself. You're moving in."

"I haven't done that yet," she said.

"Why not?" he asked. "I looked in your room. You haven't touched any of your dad's stuff."

"I know that I need to," she said. "But I haven't

quite been able to bring myself to start packing up his things, probably for the same reason you haven't sat in his chair in the den," she said, her voice cracking.

"It's hard," Brett acknowledged. "But I know that he would have wanted us all to move forward, and to put his things to good use at a shelter or something."

She sniffled and nodded. "I know. There are so many things that could be useful to someone else. And that makes me feel selfish for keeping everything. But I guess getting rid of his stuff makes me feel like I'm losing him all over again, even though I know he's already gone." A tear slipped down her cheek.

Brett found himself moving closer to her. He dropped down to his knees next to the calf and the bale of hay where Trish sat. Then, using the pad of his thumb, he wiped away her tear.

Her pale brown eyes widened, and her lips parted as if his touch surprised her. Or maybe it affected her like it affected him, making his skin tingle and his heart beat faster. And the sudden urge to lean closer, to press his mouth to hers overwhelmed him.

ONE MINUTE BRETT's thumb was on her cheek, wiping away her tear. The next, he was stumbling backward in his frantic haste to get away from her. He tripped over one of the calf's gangly legs and sprawled onto his back on the floor of the horse stall.

The kittens jumped up with their backs arched. One of them dropped down from the hay bale and pranced across the floor toward Brett, who had yet to move.

Had he felt what she had? That sudden rush of attraction? Or had he just noticed that she'd felt it, that for a brief moment she'd been tempted to kiss him? Maybe that was why he'd backed up so fast that he'd fallen—he'd been horrified that a heavily pregnant woman was about to kiss him.

The kitten pounced on him. And then the other one jumped down to join her littermate.

Trish tried to stifle a laugh that bubbled up, but it slipped out between her lips anyways.

"Mmm-hmm, very funny," he muttered, but his lips were curved into a slight grin.

"What happened?" she asked.

He sat up, with the kittens in his lap, and shrugged. "Lost my balance."

"That's been happening to me a lot lately," she admitted. Usually around him. "Thankfully, you caught me in the bunkhouse before I fell." She touched her belly, concerned over what might have happened to her babies. Then her stomach stiffened, the skin stretching taut across it. Were the babies having a growth spurt? She doubted she had much more room to give them. And she had seven weeks left to go in her pregnancy.

She had an appointment soon with her current ob-gyn, but she would rather switch to one in Willow Creek so she didn't have as far to drive. And so that she would be prepared if the twins came early as twins sometimes did.

"I was worried that you might have started working on the bunkhouse yourself," he said. "I was heading that way when I heard you singing. Being good with animals—I guess that's another family talent you and Frankie share."

She smiled. "Well, I don't have any scars from singing. But I don't come close to Frankie's talent."

"No desire to go on the road with her and her band?"

She touched her belly again. It was still hard. "And the babies? She's going to have enough trouble trying to bring Cocoa with her. I don't think she could handle all of us." Especially when Frankie hadn't really let her back in, not as close as they'd once been.

The Lemmon brothers, at least Blake and Liam, and Liam's wife, Elise, had been more welcoming to her than the two women she'd considered sisters. But because they'd once been so close, she had probably hurt them the most when she'd pulled away from them.

Just like she must have hurt her dad.

A pang struck her, first in her heart and then in her side, as regret overwhelmed her for a moment.

"Yeah, and it would be hard to run your petting zoo and kids' camp from the road," he said.

"You're not going to fight me over those?" she asked.

He sighed. "I don't think it's going to work, but since I'm obviously outnumbered, I don't get a say."

She flinched now with another little jab of pain. "That doesn't seem fair," she remarked. She knew how hard he'd worked. She'd recently sat down and had Blake show her the books for the ranch, and she'd seen the years that Brett had deferred his salary in order to keep it going.

"How else are we going to run the place?" he asked. "Having one person in charge doesn't seem fair either."

"Are you worried that I want to be that person?" she asked.

"You are a Dempsey, Frank's daughter," he said. "You thought once that you should have been the only heir—"

She gasped at another sharp jab. "I never thought that. Frankie was like another daughter to him. Maci was, too."

"But me and my brothers were strangers," he said. "Just ranch hands."

Heat rushed to her face. "I'm sorry. I made some assumptions that I shouldn't have."

He sighed. "I think I did, too."

"That I was greedy and selfish and uncaring?" she asked, curious what he thought of her.

He grimaced. "Maybe."

"And now?"

He blew out a breath. "I don't know, Trish. I still don't know you."

"Maybe that's because you've been avoiding me," she said with a slight chuckle.

"What?" he asked, as if the thought hadn't occurred to him. "I've just been working…"

"From before dawn to after dark?" she asked. "You always work that hard?"

"During calving season."

She patted Cocoa's head. "This is the last calf birthed. I think you're avoiding me."

He sighed again. "I'm avoiding the situation. I don't know how this is going to work with so many cooks in the kitchen."

She gave an exaggerated shudder. "You won't catch me in the kitchen. I'm not much of a cook. I'm kind of surprised by how much cooking you and your brothers do."

"Dad taught us when we were younger," he said. "It was probably when Mom had cancer the first time, but we didn't know it. They didn't tell us until it came back. We were all out of the house then."

"I'm sorry about your mom," she said.

He nodded. "Thanks. It's been a couple of years

now, but we still miss her. Dad the most. He's been struggling I think."

"I can't imagine how hard losing his wife must be for your dad. Due to my stupid pride and stubbornness, I didn't even see my dad that much the past seven years, and I'm missing him so much. I can't imagine losing someone who was a part of your everyday life like that."

"You weren't a part of your husband's?" he asked.

She snorted. "He's not dead. But he wasn't really around much either. We had our separate lives. He had work and golf. And I..." She rubbed her stomach. She had the dream of being a mother.

"What did you have?" he asked when she didn't continue. "What are you, Trish? Singer? Animal lover?"

She patted her hard belly. "Mother. That's all I've ever wanted to be."

"Why?"

"Because I love kids. I was going to college to become a teacher when I met my ex-husband during my summer internship at my stepfather's company."

"And you quit college?"

"Eventually," she said. "After we got married. I only had a year left. It was another reason my father disapproved of my marriage. He thought my husband should have encouraged me to finish instead of pressuring me to quit."

"He was right," Brett said.

"He definitely was," she wholeheartedly agreed. "He really wanted all his girls to be self-sufficient."

"That's why he paid for Maci's law school."

"That and he loved her." Just like he'd loved the Lemmons, too. That was why he'd included them in his will; Trish had no doubts about that any longer. And she could see that that love was mutual. The Lemmons were grieving her father, too.

"He loved you," Brett said. "So much…"

Guilt and regret coursed through her now, and maybe that was the cause of the pain she suddenly felt. She nodded. "I know." She hadn't always believed it, though. She'd let her mother plant doubts in her mind, and maybe she felt the guiltiest about that, for not being as loyal as she should have been.

"Because he loved me, he wanted me to be self-sufficient," she said. And she wished so much that she'd listened to him then, that she'd never lost touch with him. "I can keep the petting zoo and the camps self-sufficient from the ranch. As an intern and after I left school, I worked at my stepfather's business in marketing and events. I can handle the camps on my own. You don't have to invest any money or time in them. I'll take care of it myself, both financially with my divorce settlement, and laborwise."

Brett shook his head. "No, Trish."

Frustration bubbled up inside her. "No?" She shook her head. "That's not for you to decide. All the months that I was on bedrest for fear of losing my babies, I could think of nothing else but my dad and the ranch. I know that I'm not cut out to be a rancher. I couldn't be out riding a horse all day like you and your brothers and Frankie. But I love this place. I loved my summers here with the animals." With her dad. With her sisters. "And I want other kids, not just mine, to have that experience."

He held up a hand and said, "Trish—"

"No!" she yelled again. "I know what I want. And nobody's going to manipulate me into giving up my dreams. Never again!" Then she felt another cramp. And not just in her side but across her entire belly.

What was happening?

Was she going into labor?

It was too soon.

Way too soon.

FRANKIE'S STEPS SLOWED as she approached the barn. She could hear Trish's voice and a low rumble that sounded like Brett's. They were having an intense conversation from what she could overhear, and she didn't want to intrude.

Frankie understood what had driven her cousin to do the things she had. But Brett had worked so hard on the ranch for Uncle Frank. He'd been more than an employee; he'd been a friend, probably the best friend Uncle Frank had ever had. The two men were so much alike. Frankie loved Brett like she loved Trish, like they were family.

And if they were fighting, she wanted no part of it. So she turned to head back to the house.

CHAPTER ELEVEN

ALARM SHOT THROUGH Brett as he watched Trish's face go from red with anger to deathly pale. He surged up from where he'd been sitting on the ground to kneel in front of her again. "Trish, are you okay?"

The last thing he'd wanted to do was upset her.

She just sat there on the hay bale, her hands on her belly. Maybe the babies were kicking again.

"You've misunderstood me," he said. "I'm not trying to stop you from doing the petting zoo and kids' camps. I'm telling you that you don't need to do them alone."

Her long lashes blinked as she stared at him.

"We all work together on this ranch," he said. "No bosses. We'll help you with the camps."

She shook her head.

Maybe she didn't want his help.

"Liam and Elise love the idea, too," he said. "They'll help…if you'd rather I not."

She reached out then and grasped his arm. And

the look on her face chilled him. She looked so afraid.

"Trish, I don't know what's wrong," he said, and he was getting scared now. "I really didn't mean to upset you like this. Honestly, I wasn't trying to talk you out of doing what you want."

Her nails dug into his skin a bit, and her beautiful face contorted with a grimace. Finally, he realized what was wrong. She was in pain.

Physically in pain.

"Oh, no..." he whispered. "It's the babies..."

She bit her lip and nodded, and tears slipped down her face. "It's too soon..."

He touched her face, wanting to brush all her tears away. But he understood her fear now. It coursed through him, too. She could not lose these babies; she'd already suffered too many losses.

She needed help.

He considered calling an ambulance, but they could take too long to get out to the ranch and that was if they could find it. His brother-in-law-to-be was a paramedic, but Colton had never been out to the Four Corners. Even his sister, Livvy, an ER doctor, hadn't made the trip out yet. She was usually too busy at the hospital. He grabbed his cell from his pocket and tried calling her, but the call went straight to voicemail. Hopefully, she was at the hospital.

In order to get Trish there as soon as possible,

he had to drive her. "We'll get you to the ER," he said. "We'll get you help."

But right now she just had him.

More tears slid down her face as she bent over her belly, and a cry slipped out.

He slid his arms around her and lifted her up from the hay bale. She wound one arm around his neck as if to hold on while her other was wrapped around herself, as if to hold on to her babies. To protect them.

He wanted to do that, too, so he carried her out of the barn to his truck. Fortunately, he'd left the keys in it. He held her against him as he pulled open the passenger door. Then he tried to ease her onto the seat, but she clung to him for a moment, her body trembling with fear and perhaps with pain.

He wanted to take that pain away from her. "You're going to be okay," he said.

She settled onto the seat, and he stretched the belt across her and clicked it in to secure it. He was going to drive fast, and he wanted to keep her safe. Her and them. He touched her belly and it felt so hard. "They're going to be okay..."

But he had no way of knowing that for certain. He could only hope.

She covered his hand with hers and squeezed. "Thank you."

She was so scared but still so sweet. She would

be a great mother; she couldn't lose her babies. And he had to do whatever he could to make sure that she didn't.

THE SHARP PAIN receded to a dull ache in her side, but the panic remained, pressing down on Trish's lungs, making it difficult for her to draw deep breaths. She might have hyperventilated if not for Brett taking one of his hands off the steering wheel to hold her hand. Something about the strength and the warmth of his grasp lent her strength, so that she was able to breathe evenly, deeply, again.

And the pressure eased on her chest and on her stomach.

She knew he had no way of keeping his promise, of making sure that she and the babies were okay. But somehow she believed that he would, maybe from how fast he drove the distance between the Four Corners and Willow Creek Memorial Hospital.

When he pulled up to the lobby doors, she didn't want to let go of his hand. She didn't want to let go of him. He was the only thing keeping her from all-out panic.

"We're here," he said. "Help is here."

But he had been the help.

She was feeling better now.

"Let's get you into the ER," he said, and he

pulled his hand free. Then he was out of the truck, rushing around the front of it and pulling open her door. He leaned in and unbuckled her seat belt. And then he moved his arms around her, lifting her out of the truck.

She could have walked, but her legs felt weak and she was afraid of the pain returning. So she wound her arm around his shoulders instead and held on.

Leaving the passenger door open, with the keys in the ignition, he rushed toward the glass doors of the lobby. "Help! We need help!" he called out.

"Brett!" a beautiful young woman exclaimed. She wore scrubs with a stethoscope dangling around her neck. Her strawberry blond hair was pulled up in a clip, and her green eyes were wide with surprise as she hurried over to the two of them. A medical ID dangled from the pocket of her scrubs. *Dr. Livvy Lemmon.*

And for some reason Trish felt a rush of relief. She wasn't sure if it was just because this woman was a doctor or if because this woman, who knew Brett, was his sister and not someone he might have dated had he ever left the ranch. But his brothers had already told her how he rarely left the ranch.

The Four Corners was his life.

"What's going on?" Livvy asked.

"I think she's in labor," Brett answered for her. "She doubled over in pain back at the ranch."

"You're having contractions?" Livvy asked.

"I… I…thought so…"

"How far along are you?" she asked.

"Thirty-three weeks," Trish replied. She saw how the doctor looked at her stomach. "With twins."

Livvy nodded. "Okay. Sometimes twins want out early. They don't like sharing that space. Let's check you out." She gestured behind her, and an older woman rushed forward pushing a gurney. "This is Nurse Sue," she said. "We're going to take care of you. And you are?"

"Trish," she replied. "Trish Dempsey."

Livvy sucked in a breath, and her green eyes widened even more. "Oh."

So Livvy knew about her. Knew about the lawsuit over the will, no doubt.

"They'll take care of you," Brett said, as if he felt her fear. He helped to settle her onto the gurney.

But Trish grabbed the hand she'd held in the truck. "Don't go," she implored him.

"I'm not leaving," he said. "I'll just get the truck out of the way. I'm staying."

She believed him, just as she'd believed back in the barn that he would help her. So she released him.

"How long ago did the pain start?" Livvy asked as she and the nurse steered the gurney to the ER.

"A…less than an hour…"

"Wow, Brett must have broken every speed limit there is to get you here," Livvy said, and her lips curved into a smile.

"He drove safely." Trish defended him.

"He was probably afraid to jostle you for fear the babies would fall out," Livvy said. She had her hand on Trish's belly. "How long has it been since your last contraction?"

"I—I...don't know if they were contractions," she admitted. "My belly got so tight, and then I have this pain in my side."

The nurse and doctor exchanged a glance over her gurney.

"What?"

"Hopefully just Braxton Hicks contractions," Livvy replied.

"False labor," the nurse said, and she smiled down at her. "Though it probably didn't feel that way to you."

The woman's hair was such a silvery blond that it was almost white. And her eyes were nearly silver, as well, and vaguely familiar.

"We're going to check you out and check out these babies, too," Livvy said. "We'll make sure everyone is doing well. Do you have an ob-gyn in Willow Creek?"

Trish shook her head. "I was supposed to get a referral from my doctor in Sheridan, but..." She hadn't been entirely convinced that she should stay at the ranch—that she could stay if the Lemmons and Frankie didn't want her there. And while she'd agreed to settle the will, she still wasn't sure that they wanted her there.

"We can get you a referral if you want," Nurse Sue offered as she jerked aside a heavy vinyl curtain.

"Are you staying?" Livvy asked as she steered the gurney between the curtain and a concrete wall. "In Willow Creek?"

Trish nodded. "Yeah, your brothers didn't tell you?"

Livvy's face flushed. "I don't talk to my brothers as much as I should."

"You're busy," Sue said, defending her.

And they were both busy, hooking machines up to her. Checking her blood pressure, pulling over an ultrasound machine. But they talked as they moved around her.

"My brothers are busy, too," Livvy said. "We're getting better at communicating than we used to be."

"I've not even been back a week," Trish said. "Maybe they don't think I'm going to stay." She wouldn't blame them since she hadn't been entirely convinced herself. Then she sighed. "Or they don't want me to stay."

"Well..." Livvy looked uncomfortable. "I know it's been a tough time for everyone after your dad died."

Tears sprang to Trish's eyes. And she nodded.

Sue pressed a tissue into her hand. "Let's get you into a gown," she said. She helped Trish change out of her maternity bib overalls and T-shirt into the gown. Then she lifted the gown and put a dab of gel on Trish's belly.

"We're going to check on these babies," Livvy said. "Make sure they're okay." She pulled the ultrasound machine closer and moved the wand over the gel on Trish's stomach. "There's your little girl."

Trish stared at the screen and the perfect little profile of her daughter. Then the wand moved, and another little face appeared, a thumb inserted in the mouth.

"Ah," Livvy said. "And this sweetheart is your son. They both look healthy, Trish. And I don't see any signs of active labor."

She released a ragged sigh of relief and eased back against the gurney. "That's good. Just Braxton Hicks." She'd heard about them, but she hadn't thought it would feel like that.

"Your blood pressure is high, though," Livvy said. "Have you been under a lot of stress?"

Trish laughed, and some of the tears that had rushed to her eyes earlier leaked out. She could only nod.

Livvy squeezed her shoulder. "I know you have a lot going on right now. But you need to take care of yourself and these babies. You have to get a handle on the stress."

Trish laughed again, just one short chuckle this time.

"I know, I know, easier said than done," Livvy

said. "And you need to make sure that you're getting enough rest and nutrition, too."

"I was being so careful," Trish said. "I didn't want to lose these babies, too."

"You've had miscarriages?"

Trish nodded as she pressed a hand to her heart, which had a hollow ache from the loss of those babies. "I've been doing IVF, trying to get pregnant for some time." She stared at the ultrasound monitor, at her babies. "I can't lose them."

Livvy squeezed her shoulder again. "Everything looks good, Trish. Their heartbeats are strong. Their lungs are mostly developed. I think, even if you were in labor, they would survive. They might have to spend some time in the neonatal unit, but they would make it. You can stop worrying about that."

More tension eased from Trish. She hadn't realized how concerned she'd been about that until now. "I… I knew I was getting close. That's the only reason I waited this long to make the trip to Willow Creek. Because I knew they were getting to that stage…" Where they would survive if something happened. "But I was still worried it could be too soon. That, as twins, they might not be as developed as a single baby."

"They look strong," Livvy said. "Both of them. Now we have to make sure that their mama is strong, too."

Trish had been working on that for a while.

And she did feel stronger than she ever had. She nodded. "I'm going to be okay." Just like Brett had promised.

Sue patted her hand. "And I'll get you that referral for an ob-gyn."

"Thank you," Trish said. Then it dawned on her who those silvery blue eyes reminded her of. Even his kids had them. "Weird question, but are you related to Nolan Stokes by any chance?"

The nurse gasped, and then all the color drained from her face. She didn't answer the question, just pulled the curtain aside and rushed away.

"I'm sorry," Trish said to Livvy. "I didn't mean to upset her."

Livvy stared after her coworker. "I don't understand how you did. Who is this Nolan Stokes person?"

"My lawyer."

"Oh…him…" Livvy murmured.

"What have you heard about him?" Trish wondered.

"Depends on who's talking," Livvy said. "Some people think he's a saint. But your cousin…" She shook her head and chuckled softly.

"Yes, Frankie is not his biggest fan," Trish said. Then she sighed. "She's not mine either right now. I made a mess of things."

"That's life," Livvy said. "We make messes of

it sometimes. But we can usually clean them up with time."

Tears stung Trish's eyes again. "Unless it's already too late..." Like it was with her father. She'd lost him before she'd had a chance to clean up the mess she'd made of their relationship. She didn't want that to be the case with anyone else. And she should have been thinking of Frankie and Maci then. But the person who sprang to her mind was Brett, and then he was stepping inside the curtain with her.

"I hope it's okay for me to be in here," he said to Trish. "Nurse Sue showed me back." He glanced at the ultrasound monitor, then at her face and then at the ultrasound machine again. "That's them?" His dark eyes widened with awe. "They're moving? They're okay?"

"Yes," Trish said, and the last of the fear that had been pressing on her chest eased. "You were right."

Brett looked at his sister. "Really? They're good?"

Livvy nodded. "Yeah, they're strong, like their mama. She just needs to take it easy. No more stress."

Trish wished that was possible, but she was too realistic to believe that. She'd turned her life upside down with her pregnancy and her divorce and the move. So of course she was stressed.

And she was also unsteady, often feeling as if

she couldn't quite get her balance, as if she was about to fall. But she had a feeling that wasn't because of stress.

That was because of Brett Lemmon and the things he made her feel: things she hadn't wanted to feel again. She'd wanted to focus only on her babies and her plans for the ranch. She didn't want to fall, but she was worried that, if she wasn't careful, she would fall…for Brett.

LIVVY COULDN'T GET over the way Brett had carried the pregnant woman into the ER just moments ago. Or the way he was looking at her now, and at the ultrasound monitor. He looked stunned and maybe a little scared, too. That surprised her so much that she had to duck out of the ER bay. "I'll be right back with that ob-gyn referral. Maybe we can find one in the hospital today who might be able to see you."

Livvy would feel better for Trish if she made contact with her doctor now, because she had a feeling these twins weren't going to wait around for another seven weeks before coming into the world. She also needed to see if Sue was all right. She found the older woman at the nurses' station. "Are you getting that referral?"

Sue's silvery eyes widened. "Yes. Was it okay that I showed your brother back?"

Livvy nodded and glanced toward where she'd left them alone together.

"This seems to be a habit with your brothers, coming into the ER with women," Sue said.

"Women? Liam brought Lucy here after finding her in the barn."

"He wasn't alone," Sue reminded her. "Elise Shaw was with him, and now they're married. And your other brother..."

"Blake," she said.

"He came in with the woman who'd passed out in the brewery."

"Yeah, he did." And he would probably propose to Maci Bluff soon.

"And now this brother..."

"Brett," she said. "He's the oldest."

Sue made a strange noise, then cleared her throat. "And he carried in this pregnant woman..."

A slight shiver passed through Livvy as she remembered how Brett had looked. "I'm not used to my oldest brother showing any emotion," she admitted. "He's always acted so tough, so stoic. When we moved away from Willow Creek and Blake and Liam were crying, Brett never showed that he was upset, too. And when Mom died..." She blew out a breath and shook her head. "Sorry, Sue, I know you hate this personal stuff."

Sue shrugged, but her shoulders moved stiffly. "It's fine. Your family seems to come in and out of this ER quite a bit. I guess I'll have to get used to it, especially now with things about to change..."

Before Livvy could ask her what she meant by that, Sue picked up the phone from the desk and made a call to Obstetrics, asking them to send a doctor to the ER. Livvy heard Brett's deep rumble and turned around to find him on his cell in the wide corridor outside the bay where Trish Dempsey was. He was calling the Four Corners Ranch, letting them know where he and Trish were. He also gave them some instructions.

Livvy smiled at him after he disconnected the call. "That was smart. She really has to take it easy and avoid stress."

Brett nodded. "I'll make sure that she does."

That shiver of uneasiness passed through Livvy again. Brett always took on so much responsibility that his shoulders seemed to bow from the weight of everything he carried. He also had dark circles beneath his dark eyes as if he hadn't been sleeping much. He worked so hard at the Four Corners, had gone through so much with losing his boss and best friend, and then Trish Dempsey had fought the will. While they'd all been at Grandpa's birthday party, Trish had sent Maci a text that she was coming back to the Four Corners to work things out, and the last time she'd talked to Liam, he'd seemed positive that everything would be fine.

But Brett didn't look like everything was fine. He looked exhausted. She reached out and touched his shoulder. “You need to take care of yourself, too, Brett.”

He nodded. “I’m fine, Dr. Lemmon.”

But she knew that he would say that even if he wasn’t. He didn’t want to worry anyone else. But Livvy was worried.

CHAPTER TWELVE

STRESS. BRETT UNDERSTOOD it well since he so often felt it himself. But that was something that Trish couldn't have in her life anymore. The obstetrician had confirmed what his sister had told them. Her blood pressure had to get down and stay down for her health and the health of her unborn babies.

He glanced across the console at her in the passenger seat. Her hands rested on her stomach, maybe for comfort, maybe for reassurance that the babies were still moving.

She had been so scared. Brett had been, too. And instead of feeling comforted when he'd seen the babies on the ultrasound machine, more concern had coursed through him. The babies were real to him now with little personalities showing in the way the girl had moved around and kicked. And the way the boy had sucked his thumb, the same way that Liam had as a baby and toddler.

"Are you all right?" he asked. She'd been so quiet since they'd left the hospital that Brett wondered if he should bring her back. The obstetrician and Livvy had kept her for a while to make sure that her blood pressure came down. But he worried now, as they drove back to the Four Corners, that it might go up again, especially with what he'd told Frankie that she and the others needed to do.

"Yes," she said. "I'm sorry that you had to make the long drive to the hospital for nothing."

"Nothing?" he asked.

"I wasn't in labor," she said. "It was just those Braxton Hicks contractions, false labor."

"You were in pain," he said. "And you have a pulled ligament and high blood pressure."

She touched her side. "The babies are taking up a lot of room."

"And you're taking on too much stress," he said.

She groaned. "I don't want to argue," she said.

"That's the last thing I want to do," he agreed. "I don't want to upset you. And I didn't mean to do that earlier. I wasn't telling you not to do the kids' camps and petting zoo. I was just saying that you shouldn't do them alone."

"So who would help me?" she asked. "You don't want to do them."

"That doesn't mean I won't help you," he said. "And everyone else will, too, Trish. You don't have to do this alone. And you don't have to use your personal money for it. We'll figure out a way for the ranch to finance it but still keep the camps separate from the cattle business." He glanced across to see her smiling. "What?"

"I thought you weren't the boss," she said. "How can you make that decision without talking to the others?"

"You know my brothers and Elise, especially, support your plans," he said.

"Then what about Frankie?"

He shrugged. "I don't even know how much longer she's staying. Since the estate will be settled once it goes through probate, she'll be able to go back out on the road like she wants."

She sighed. "I hope she does what she wants and that it's what she *really* wants to do."

He chuckled. "I can't imagine anyone stopping Frankie from doing what she wants."

"If she's really been waiting to leave until the estate was settled, then I must have stopped her," Trish said, her voice soft with regret.

"I think she's forgiven you." Frankie had sounded so worried when Brett called her from the hospital. "Now, your lawyer…" He chuckled. "She's never going to forgive his part in all of this."

"Never say never," she murmured.

"Why not?" he wondered aloud.

"Look at you, offering to help me with kids' camps and a petting zoo," she said. "I bet that was something you never thought you would do."

He chuckled again. "You've got me there."

She reached across the console and touched his hand on the steering wheel. "Thank you. Thank you for getting me to the hospital. Thank you for keeping your promise."

"Promise?"

"You said that I would be okay and that the babies would be, too," she reminded him.

He grunted. "Yeah, that was a stupid promise to make. Totally out of my control…"

"But you still made me feel better," she said.

"Good," he said. "I don't want to add to your stress." She'd already lost so much; he didn't want to be the reason she lost anything else.

"I've added to yours," she said. "Over the will and now this…" She yawned.

"Don't worry about me," he said. "And feel free to close your eyes and get some rest. We'll be there soon enough." But hopefully not too soon for his family and hers to have done what he'd asked.

Her hand slipped away from his and she moved the passenger seat back until it reclined. Then she turned so that she faced him and closed her eyes.

As he drove, he kept glancing over at her, watching her sleep. The panic he'd felt when he'd seen how much pain she'd been in rushed over him again. But he wasn't afraid for her this time.

He was afraid for himself.

He had decided long ago that he wasn't going to fall for anyone. Ever. He had to focus on the ranch, on keeping it going and making sure that it took care of everyone who relied on it for support. Like his brothers and his niece. Frankie. And now Trish and her babies.

And the camps…

He swallowed the groan that threatened to escape his throat. He didn't want to do them, but he knew that Trish would stress herself out even more if she tried starting them on her own. Frank had been his best friend. Out of respect and loyalty to him, Brett had to make sure that nothing happened to the man's daughter or grandchildren.

And Brett had to trust that nothing would happen to himself. That he wouldn't fall for her. Frank and his dad had proven to him that love wasn't worth the loss that inevitably followed. And there was no way that she was going to fall for him; she was recently divorced and as determined to stay single as he was.

TRISH HADN'T EXPECTED to fall asleep, not after the scare she'd had. But she must have drifted off because the next thing she knew, the passenger door was opening and Brett was reaching to lift her out like he had at the hospital. Instinctively she wrapped her arms around his neck. But the seat belt held her tight to the seat.

She laughed and then awoke fully to realize how close his face was to hers. How dark his eyes were, how strong his jaw…how strong he was.

He'd carried her a couple of times that day. From the barn to his truck and then from his truck into the hospital. Nurse Sue had delivered her back to his truck via a wheelchair, per hospital policy. "You don't have to carry me again," she said, but she didn't release his neck. "You probably hurt your back doing that earlier."

He shook his head. "No." His voice was gruff. And he stared at her so oddly, like his focus was on her mouth.

And then she looked at his. She arched up from her reclining position and brushed her lips across his mouth. "Thank you…"

He tensed. But his lips moved back across hers once. Then again.

The sensation shot through her, making her tingle everywhere. Then one of the babies kicked, and with the way he was leaning across her, he must have felt it because he jerked back, hitting his head on the roof of the truck.

"I'm sorry," she said. "Sorry… I just…wanted to…" Kiss him. And it had been so long since she'd had the urge to kiss anyone, and never as strong a one as that, too strong to resist. "To thank you…" She cleared her throat. "Uh, thanks…"

His lips, which had felt so good against hers, curved into a slight grin. "You're very welcome, Trish." He touched the back of his head.

And she remembered he'd hit it. "Are you okay?"

His grin slipped away. "Yeah, probably needed some sense knocked into me. This…this…is a bad idea…if we want to keep living together and working together."

"Oh, I know," she said, her face heating up with embarrassment. "I shouldn't have… I just…" She touched her head, too, like she'd hit it. And she must have had a concussion or some other momentary lapse of sense since she'd acted on impulse like that.

"You're half asleep," he said. "You can excuse it as a dream, that it never really happened."

She wasn't sure she would be able to do that, but she nodded in agreement. Would he be able to do the same? Would he be able to forget about the kiss?

Of course he would. There was no way in the world a confirmed bachelor like Brett Lemmon would be interested in a recently divorced, expectant single mother. And she shouldn't be interested in him either.

As he said, they lived together. They worked together. They couldn't risk making that relationship any more awkward than it had already been. No wonder he'd been avoiding her the past couple of days; he would probably continue to do that now.

But he didn't rush away from her. He even helped her unbuckle her seat belt since she just fumbled with it, her hands shaking. He caught her hands and held on to them even after he helped her down from the truck. He slowly swiped his thumbs across the backs of her hands.

Goose bumps of awareness rose on her skin, as her pulse quickened. She was supposed to forget the kiss, not want to do it again. And she really wanted to kiss him again.

"Are you okay?" he asked.

No. She was nearly as scared and upset as she'd been when she'd thought she was going into labor too soon. The last thing she'd expected when she'd decided to move to the Four Corners was to find herself attracted to anyone, let alone one of the Lemmon brothers her lawyer had warned her about.

She drew in a deep breath, which meant breathing in the essence of him, of leather and horses and hay, and for a moment she felt lightheaded again. But then one of the babies kicked, reminding her of what mattered. *They* mattered. Her children.

They were most important. And she had to take care of them. And in order to do that, she had to take care of herself. She couldn't rely on anyone else. Not like she just had leaned on Brett. She couldn't count on him taking care of her and keeping his promises.

She'd chosen to have her kids alone, so that she was the only one responsible for them, for taking care of them. So that no matter what, she would never lose them, even for the summers. They would be with her always.

"I'm fine," she assured him and herself. She was strong now. And the doctors had assured her that the babies were strong, too. She could do this…*alone*.

BRETT'S CALL FROM the hospital had rattled Frankie, and guilt had overwhelmed her because of how distant she'd been with Trish. Like Brett, Frankie had been avoiding her cousin as much as possible since she'd moved into the Four Corners. Or as Brett had pointed out on his call, Trish hadn't fully moved in. She'd left all her stuff packed in her trailer. She hadn't touched a thing in her father's room, hadn't done anything to make the space her own. And despite her plans for the petting zoo and the kids' camps, she hadn't pushed to start work on them.

And she shouldn't have had to push. The ranch was as much hers as it was the other heirs. They had all inherited equal shares of it.

But it was clear that Trish didn't feel equal to them. She felt like an outsider. Had that added to the stress that Brett said was the reason for her visit to the hospital? The stress he'd said that his sister warned them Trish couldn't have. While she hadn't been in labor today like she'd feared, her blood pressure had been too high.

And that scared Frankie as much as it must

have scared Brett. He hadn't sounded at all like himself on the phone. And he didn't look like himself, standing with Trish next to the passenger side of his truck. He actually held her hands in his, like he was afraid she might topple over without his support.

"Are you okay?" Frankie asked as she hurried over to them.

Brett jumped and stepped back, and once he was out of her way, Frankie closed her arms around her cousin.

"I was so worried about you," she said.

"I was pretty worried, too," Trish said, and her body trembled. Or maybe that was the babies kicking again.

Her little cousins. Or, since Trish was more like a sister to her, her little niece and nephew. "And the niblings? They're okay?"

Trish nodded and released a shuddery breath that stirred Frankie's hair. "Yes, they're good. We're all okay."

"Thank goodness," Frankie said with relief. "And we're going to make sure that you all stay that way." She leaned back and studied her cousin's face. With the circles beneath her eyes as dark as they were, she looked bruised and so very exhausted. "Let's get you settled back into your room."

Trish's forehead furrowed beneath the errant

curls that had fallen across it. "What do you mean?"

Frankie slid her arm around Trish's waist and began to guide her toward the house, past her trailer. The back doors stood open now, and the only things inside the trailer weren't Trish's—they were Uncle Frank's.

"It's your room now," Frankie said. "Blake, Liam, Elise and I packed up Uncle Frank's things. We put them in your trailer, so you can go through them when you're ready. When Brett called, he said that you wanted to donate them, but we wanted to make sure that we didn't give anything away that you want to keep."

Tears filled Trish's eyes.

Frankie panicked for a minute. "I hope that was okay. We didn't want to upset you."

Trish shook her head. "You didn't. I know it had to be done. I was just overwhelmed with the thought."

"Well, we got the room ready for you now. And we didn't want you to have to worry about packing and unpacking..." Guilt jabbed her. "Well, Brett was worried. He was the one who thought of it and told me about his idea when he called from the hospital."

"You guys got all this done since then?" Brett asked as he stopped at the rear of the trailer and peered inside.

"Yes, it's amazing what we can do when we all

work together," Frankie said. "You don't have to do anything on your own anymore, Trish. We're here for you."

A sob slipped out of Trish's lips and then her shoulders started shaking. Alarm shot through Frankie. "Oh, no. I'm sorry. Was this a bad idea?"

"I'm sorry," Brett added. "I didn't want you to be stressed and—"

Trish grabbed his arm and Frankie's, too. "No. I just..." Another sob cracked her voice. "I just really appreciate this."

"Come see it," Frankie said. "Your furniture looks so nice in the room. We unpacked the baby stuff and put it in the sitting area of the suite. That way they'll be close when they come—" she patted her cousin's belly "—when they're supposed to." One of the babies shifted beneath her palm, then kicked, and Frankie laughed. "Guess they don't like being told what to do..."

"They take after their aunt Frankie then," Trish said with a watery smile. She hugged Frankie and whispered, "Thank you."

"It was Brett's idea," she reminded Trish, not wanting to take the credit from him.

"But you guys did the heavy lifting," he said.

Trish turned her watery smile toward him. "I don't know...you did some pretty heavy lifting when you carried me out of the barn and then into the hospital."

Brett's face flushed as if he was embarrassed.

He shrugged. "You were in so much pain..." And then the color receded from his face as if just the memory had made him feel sick.

Frankie felt sick herself. There had been more than enough pain and loss at the Four Corners. They needed happiness and love now. And something about the way that Trish and Brett were looking at each other made her wonder...

Could these two find love and happiness together?

Wow. She must have been spending too much time around Sadie and Lem. She was starting to think like them. But there was no couple more unlikely than Brett and Trish except maybe for Frankie herself and that sleazy lawyer. Now that would be an unlikely match.

Brett and Trish didn't seem to have much more in common, though. Brett was a cowboy through and through, focused on the ranch, and Trish wanted a family. Something Brett claimed he never wanted.

No. Frankie doubted that even Lem and Sadie would be able to make this match happen.

CHAPTER THIRTEEN

BRETT'S BROTHERS, SISTER-IN-LAW and Frankie had done more than just unpack Trish's trailer. Using non-toxic latex paint, they'd brightened the dark walls in the sitting area of the suite with a soft shade of yellow, making the space lighter and happier-looking for Trish and the twins.

Over the next couple of weeks, he and the others worked on getting a small barn built and created a pasture area for the petting zoo. The work required for the bunkhouse was more extensive, so they'd had to call in professionals for the electrical and plumbing. But that didn't stop Brett and the others from working in the bunkhouse. They made sure the railing to the second story was secure, and they worked on cleaning up the space. Since Trish had landed that contract with the whole foods chain, they had plenty of money for the camps and the ranch.

They did the heavy lifting for Trish—or they tried to—but there were many times that Brett had caught her trying to move something on her own.

So one morning he stopped her on the way to the bunkhouse, took her hand in his and led her to his truck. Her hand felt so small and soft in his, but he detected some calluses, too. Despite them trying to get her to take it easy, she was doing more work than she should.

"What's going on?" she asked.

"We're going for a drive," he said. Riding in the truck would keep her off her feet.

"Why?" she asked, her forehead furrowing with confusion.

"We have an appointment," he said.

"With whom?" She tensed. "Not your grandparents. I know they've called wanting to meet me..."

And he'd kept putting them off. He wasn't sure if that had been for her sake or for his, though. They were such notorious matchmakers. "No, I'm not taking you to Ranch Haven," he assured her.

"Then where? I already went to my doctor this week."

She was going once a week now. Usually Frankie or Maci drove her. Brett was just glad that she was going and that everything seemed fine.

Well, everything but him. He wasn't sleeping well. No matter how much he tried to pretend that kiss had never happened, he couldn't stop thinking about it or about her. And those babies...

"I'm taking you to the vet," he said.

She laughed. "You think the vet can treat me

better than a doctor can? What kind of animal does that make me? Or maybe I shouldn't ask."

"I'm taking you there for the animals," he said as he drove toward the Willow Creek Veterinarian Practice. "They have a rescue there, too."

"Oh..." Her long lashes fluttered.

"The barn and pasture are ready," he said. "We can pick out some critters for your petting zoo."

She reached across the console and grasped his arm. "Thank you...for everything you're doing."

"It's not just me," he said. "Everybody's been working hard to get things done for you."

"But I know this isn't what you wanted," she said.

"What?"

"The petting zoo, the kids' camps..." She chuckled. "Me." Then her face flushed, and she jerked her hand off his arm. "Not that you have me. That's not what I meant. It's just that you're forced to put up with me."

And that was what it should have felt like to him—more work, an inconvenience, a burden...

But when she was as happy as she was now, her face literally glowing, making her happy like this felt like a gift. One that he was receiving as much as he was giving.

"It's fine," he said. But he wasn't sure that he was. Not anymore. He wasn't even sure who he was anymore. Before she'd moved into the Four

Corners, he'd always known that he was a true cowboy, one focused only on ranching. But now…

He seemed more focused on her and what she wanted. But that was just because he didn't want to add to her stress. It wasn't for any other reason. At least not one that he would let himself entertain.

Because Trish was too vulnerable. And he was too set in his bachelor ways. But she was his best friend's daughter. And maybe that made them friends as well.

Just friends.

TRISH DIDN'T BELIEVE BRETT. Not that he was fine. She knew she'd turned his world upside down with her arrival. Probably even before that with how he'd had to live in limbo until the will was settled.

She wasn't sure that it was legally settled yet. She hadn't talked to Nolan since she'd dropped by his house that day. But in her mind, it was settled. The Lemmons were her partners in the ranch as much as Frankie was. And Maci oversaw them all as the executor of the estate. Her dad had made the right decision in his will.

After looking at the books, she knew there wouldn't have even been a ranch left for anyone to inherit if not for Brett and the others helping her father. And now they were helping her. There was no way that Trish could have handled the ranch entirely on her own. She needed the Lemmons. But she knew they didn't need her, especially Brett. He just wanted to work the ranch. And he did. But he also spent so much time helping her with the petting zoo and the bunkhouse. And now this trip to the Willow Creek Veterinarian Practice, which was actually a big barn on the outskirts of Willow Creek.

Excited to see the rescue animals, she clamored down from the truck the minute he parked it next to the barn. It was then that she first noticed he had hooked a small animal trailer to the back of the vehicle. "We'll be able to bring them home with us?" she asked, even more excited than she'd already been.

He nodded. "Yes, we need to get them used to their new surroundings before we open up."

We.

Despite thinking her dream was a bad idea, he was still all in with her. He hadn't tried to talk her out of doing something he hadn't wanted her to do. Instead, he'd put aside his discomfort and helped her. She didn't know if she'd ever met anyone quite like him before. Brett was supporting her even more than her father had. Her dad had refused to come to her wedding because he hadn't approved. She suspected that Brett, had they been friends, would have come.

And were they friends now?

He and the vet obviously were because once

they stepped into the big barn, a blond-haired man stepped forward and heartily shook his hand with one of his while slapping Brett's back with the other.

Brett pulled back and introduced them, "Trish Dempsey, this is Cash Cassidy, or Dr. Cash, as everyone has always called him. He's also my stepcousin."

She shook the hand Cash extended to her. "Nice to meet you."

"Have you met many of us yet?" Cash asked. "There are a bunch of us. Since my grandma married his grandpa Lem, I think we're both related to pretty much everyone in Willow Creek now."

Brett chuckled and nodded. "That does seem to be the case."

"And speaking of relatives," Cash said as a sandy-haired, older woman walked up. "This is my aunt Darlene, mother of my Haven cousins."

"Nice to meet you," Trish said. "There really are a lot of Havens, Cassidys and Lemmons."

Cash chuckled. "Seems like we keep multiplying. Kind of like our animals. We really need to find homes for some of them so we'll have space for more in need of rescuing."

Darlene sighed. "Yes, but it'll be hard to let some of them go."

"Hard for you or for Mikey and Faith?" Cash asked. "Faith is my daughter. Mikey's my nephew.

They pretty much live here when they're not in school."

"They'll be able to visit whatever animals we take," Trish said. "I want them for a petting zoo I intend to open for kids attending day and summer camps at the Four Corners."

"Oh, that's a great idea," Darlene said.

Trish glanced at Brett to see if he would argue. But he didn't say a word. And she felt a pang of regret that he wasn't happy about her idea. Though she appreciated his help, she would have liked to have him be as excited about it as she was.

Darlene led her around the barn, showing animals to her that were healthy again and ready to move into their forever homes. A pair of pygmy goats. A miniature horse and her foal. A trio of bunnies. They even had a skunk who'd lost his ability to spray.

"He can't defend himself anymore," Darlene said. "So it wouldn't be safe to turn him outside again."

"He's cute," Trish said.

"And there's a lamb, too," Darlene said. "Who was orphaned..." Her voice cracked on the last word. "Sorry." She shook her head.

"What is it?" Trish asked as she touched the woman's arm.

Darlene sighed. "I just...my grandsons were orphaned last year when their parents, my son and daughter-in-law, died in a car crash."

"I am so sorry," Trish said, her heart aching with sympathy for the woman. "That's so tragic for everyone."

Darlene tensed. "I—I did a stupid thing years ago. Made some assumptions that were wrong, and I hadn't been in my children's lives for years. I didn't even know that my son had passed..." Her voice cracked. "I just... I have many regrets."

Trish nodded. "I can relate to that," she said. "My dad and I were estranged when he died. I don't know if I can forgive myself for not being around that much...for missing his funeral..." Her voice cracked now. She glanced back at Brett, who stood talking to Cash where they'd walked in. Even though he was helping her, she wondered if he'd really forgiven her. Or if that was even possible...

He'd been so close to her dad, much closer than she had ever been.

"I'm sorry," Darlene said. "I didn't mean to bring up sad things. You're pregnant and starting these camps. You have so many happy things happening in your life right now." She glanced at Brett, too. "Is Sadie's new stepgrandson part of the happy things?"

Trish shook her head. "We're just...we're..." She wasn't even sure that they were friends. "Partners in my father's ranch along with his brothers and my cousin."

Darlene nodded. "I've met them all before at

Ranch Haven and at the wedding, of course." She smiled. "Have you met Sadie yet?"

Trish shook her head. "Not for want of her trying to meet me though."

She must have had a funny look on her face because Darlene cocked her head and smiled. "What? Are you afraid of meeting her? What have you heard about her?"

"I've heard she's pretty strong-willed." After dealing with her mother and Harold, the last thing she wanted in her life was someone who manipulated other people into doing what they wanted them to do.

Darlene shook her head. "Sadie is amazing," she said as if she was in awe. "So strong. She's survived so many losses, but she hasn't let that make her bitter or resentful. She's kept her big heart open for love. And despite everything she's been through, she trusted in love enough to risk it again…with Lem. He's such a sweetheart and so in love with her, too." She smiled. "You really should meet them. They've made me a believer in happily-ever-after again." She glanced toward a man who'd just joined Cash and Brett. He had salt-and-pepper hair and a big grin.

Trish touched her belly. "These two are all I need for my happily-ever-after," she said.

"Two? Twins?"

"Yes."

"My son, a twin himself, and his wife just had twins. A boy and a girl."

"That's what I'm having, too," Trish said.

Darlene beamed. "They're amazing." Then she sighed. "A lot of work, though. I hope you have a good support system."

She did, for the petting zoo and camps, but what about her babies? Would the others help her with them?

She hadn't intended to have them help with anything. She suddenly felt guilty for just adding more work to the already heavy load everyone on the ranch carried. What if all of this was a bad idea? How would she manage two babies on her own and the camps? Maybe she was being as unrealistic as Brett had clearly thought she was. But she didn't want to wait to open the camps. And she had already waited too long to start her family. So she had to figure out how to manage it all.

LIKE SO MANY other things in her life, Darlene wished she could take back what she'd just said to Trish Dempsey. The woman had been so bright and happy when she'd first walked into the barn. Now she was tense and quiet.

Brett Lemmon kept glancing at the young woman with concern in his dark eyes. Darlene was the one who had to point out the animals Trish had liked for her petting zoo.

"Even the skunk?" he asked with a chuckle.

Finally, a slight smile curved Trish's lips again. "His scent is gone and he can't be released into the wild again."

"He's a big baby now," Dr. Forest said as he slid his arm around Darlene. He wasn't her boss anymore; he was her boyfriend.

Boyfriend? That made Darlene think of teenagers, not people pushing their mid-fifties. But Forest made her feel like a teenager again, like Sadie looked when she was with Lem.

Sadie and Lem.

Maybe that was who Trish Dempsey needed. Darlene had obviously scared her that her babies were going to be too much work. Sadie and Lem might be able to convince her that Trish would have all the help she ever needed.

Or maybe Brett Lemmon, who insisted on getting every animal Trish had liked, would be all the help she needed and wanted.

CHAPTER FOURTEEN

BRETT WASN'T SURE what had happened: one moment Trish had been glowing with happiness and the next she was quiet and withdrawn. He'd had to talk her into the animals Darlene had said she'd wanted.

"What happened?" he asked once they were back on the road to the Four Corners.

"What?" she asked as if she hadn't heard him.

"What's wrong?" he asked. "Are you feeling all right?" Maybe she'd overdone it at the vet practice. He'd been trying to get her to spend less time on her feet, and it hadn't worked. She'd walked every inch of that huge barn with Darlene.

Darlene had looked concerned about her, too.

"Do I need to bring you to the doctor?" he asked.

"I feel fine," she said. "Nothing's wrong."

"I don't believe you," he admitted.

She sucked in a breath as if offended. Then she sighed and some of the tension drained from her. "Darlene just mentioned that her son and daughter-in-law have twins."

"Yeah, Dusty Chaps, the former rodeo champ, is her son," Brett said.

"Like Liam? Didn't your brother used to be in the rodeo?"

"Billy the Kid," Brett said with a flash of pride. "Liam got hurt not long into his career. He never made the championships like Dusty did."

"Maybe that's why it's tough on Dusty's wife with the twins," Trish said softly. "She's alone a lot."

Brett shook his head. "Melanie is never alone at Ranch Haven. Her mom lives there, too, and Dusty retired from the rodeo—although he did buy the Cassidy Ranch to start breeding rodeo animals there. But they live at Ranch Haven, where they have all kinds of family helping them with the twins."

Now he realized the reason she'd grown so quiet. She was alone. A single mother about to give birth to not just one baby but two. "You have support, too, Trish," he assured her.

She shook her head. "I didn't want support, though. I wanted to raise my babies alone. I wanted to do the camps and petting zoo on my own. And now I wonder how realistic I'm being. You all had to step in to help me, or I wouldn't have gotten anything done yet."

"You are very pregnant," he reminded her. "You have to take it easy. And we're all happy to help."

She snorted with apparent disbelief. "All of you? Even you?"

"I'm helping," he said. "You don't need to worry about how happy I am." But he *was* worried about her happiness; that—and Trish—were all he thought about lately.

"This isn't fair to you," she said. "Me making all this work for you and for everyone else. I don't know if I made the right decision about anything right now."

"Trish?" He was really worried. The last time she'd been this upset he'd had to take her to the hospital. "Because of your blood pressure, you need to stay calm. You shouldn't be getting worked up about this."

She drew in a deep breath, let it out and then drew in another. "Okay, okay…" she murmured. "I don't know why I'm freaking out."

"I don't know either," he said. "You were so certain that you're doing what you want now for what might be one of the first times in your life. Don't doubt yourself."

She drew in another breath and lifted her chin. "You're right. This is what I want. I just panicked for a moment. As much as I've always wanted kids, I haven't had that much experience with them. I didn't babysit. I didn't have any younger siblings. Just Frankie, and she's always been independent."

He snorted. "She is certainly that."

"That's what I want to be, too," she said. "I don't want to have to depend on anyone else. I want to be capable of taking care of myself and my children."

"You should talk to my dad, Trish," he said. "He was determined to take care of my mom all by himself when she got sick. He pushed everyone away who cared about both of them. Me, my brothers and sister and my grandpa, too. And I know he regrets that now."

She released a shaky breath. "You don't understand, Brett. This isn't about not wanting people to help me. It's about knowing if I can do it without help, if I can handle all this on my own, and I'll never know that if I don't try to do it without help."

"I'm sorry," he said. "I didn't mean to take over. I was just trying to help because Livvy and the other doctor said that you shouldn't be under stress right now, that it could raise your blood pressure too much."

She reached across the console and squeezed his arm. "And I appreciate that so much," she said. "I can't believe, after everything that's happened, that you would help me like you have. I thought you would hate me."

He chuckled and admitted, "I thought I would, too." And maybe it would have been easier if he had. But he liked her too much and that was why he wanted to help her.

"I'm glad you don't," she said, "though I would understand if you did."

He shook his head. "No. You have your reasons for everything that you did, Trish."

"And I have my reasons for wanting to take care of myself and these babies," she said. "I don't want to put them through the childhood I had, split between two parents, missing one, getting manipulated by the other. I want to be the only person they need, so that they don't wind up losing and missing someone so much."

"So you're never going to get married again?" he asked.

She shook her head. "No. I can't."

"Not that I'm proposing," he assured her and tried to laugh it off as a joke. "I swore to myself long ago that I'd stay single."

"Why?" she asked. "What's your reason? Your parents sound like they had a great marriage."

"They did," he said. "And my dad is devastated without her. I wouldn't want to go through that kind of pain and loss. Or what your dad went through. Not wanting to risk that, I decided long ago that it's better to stay single."

She drew in a deep breath and nodded. "Yeah, it is."

"I decided to put all my focus on the ranch, to make sure that the Four Corners prospers and that it takes care of the people who rely on it, like Liam and his family and Blake. I don't want them to risk their relationships because the ranch takes so much of their time," he explained. "Like it did your father."

"My mother hates it still," she murmured.

"Your father loved it," Brett said. "And I love it."

"I do, too," she murmured.

And he believed her. "You have this..." He gestured toward her stomach. "The babies. Parenting. You'll figure it all out on your own. But as for stuff on the ranch, you have four partners in it, five really, since Liam and Elise are partners in his share. So we're all partners in the work, too."

"But you're all doing more work than I am," she said.

He shook his head. "No, Trish. This is all you. You picked out the animals. You designed the bunkhouse remodel. That's all been a lot of work, and I'm sure you'll probably wind up doing the bulk of the work for it once it's up and running."

She sighed.

He was worried that he'd made matters worse instead of better. "Or you can hire someone to help you with the camps and with the babies. You don't need to worry about all of this."

She nodded. "You're right. I will have to hire counselors for the camp. And I have time—more than a month yet—to learn more about kids."

"Trust me, you learn quick when they get here," he said. "None of us knew anything about babies when Lucy showed up in the barn. But we know what we're doing now."

"Yes, you do. She's a very happy baby."

FAMOUS LAST WORDS. A short time later, while Trish walked the floor with a screaming Lucy in her arms, she wondered if she'd jinxed herself. When she and Brett showed up at the ranch, Liam and Elise had rushed out to them in the driveway.

"My mom is having a situation at the foster home she runs," Elise said. "I need to help her—"

"And I don't want her to go alone," Liam interjected. "It's a tricky situation. So we don't want to bring Lucy either."

"We can watch Lucy," Brett offered. "Just let me get these animals put away."

"There's no time," Elise said. "Someone's on their way to help, but nobody's here right now. And I really need to get to my mom."

"Go," Trish said. "I'll take care of Lucy for you while Brett takes care of the animals."

Elise released a breath. "You're sure?"

"Yes, of course." She had to learn, and Brett wouldn't be far away. Besides, someone else was on their way. This was the perfect opportunity for her to get some hands-on experience with a baby.

When Elise and Liam had met them in the driveway, they'd had the baby monitor with them and no sound had emanated from it. "She's down for her nap right now," Elise said.

So Trish shouldn't have had any problem. Except the minute Lucy's parents drove off and Trish stepped inside the house, the baby started crying. Brett was already driving off, too, toward the petting zoo pastures on the other side of the big barn near the bunkhouse.

She didn't want to have to call him for help. Not so quickly. She wanted to figure out herself what was bothering the baby.

But a diaper change didn't calm her down. Or the bottle that Trish fixed per the directions left next to the can of formula in the kitchen. Lucy wouldn't let her put the nipple of the bottle in her mouth, unlike the calf who greedily sucked her bottle down whenever Trish got the chance to feed her.

Lucy wanted nothing to do with her bottle. Or with Trish. She writhed in her arms as she cried. Obviously, she didn't know her and was not comforted by a stranger holding her.

"I'm so sorry, Lucy," she said. "I don't know what to do..." She'd had no business taking on this responsibility when she had no idea. How was she going to raise her babies on her own?

"I want to help you, sweetheart," she cooed. And then she began to sing to her, something soft and soothing, trying to calm her down.

The baby blinked, and the tears cleared from her eyes.

Brett had commented before that Trish sounded

like Frankie, so maybe that was what was making the baby feel better, that Trish wasn't a total stranger. She was a little familiar to her.

She kept singing and finally Lucy closed her lips around the bottle and began to suckle.

Trish breathed a sigh of relief.

And Lucy tensed up again and scrunched up her little face. So Trish started singing.

She didn't dare stop.

SOMETIMES LEM'S NEW hearing aids were as much of a curse as a blessing. They picked up too many background noises and were hard to adjust to the TV volume, and both situations resulted in giving him a headache.

But he could also appreciate things like the sound of his wife's voice. And the beauty of a bird's song or the soft chirp of crickets. Then he was glad that he had upgraded his hearing aids.

He was especially glad when he and Sadie stepped out of his old Cadillac and walked up to the house at the Four Corners Ranch. He would have hated to have missed the singing that he heard so clearly, every note hitting perfectly.

"Wow…" Sadie murmured. "Frankie sure is talented."

"Yes, she is," Lem agreed. He hated to think of her leaving Willow Creek once the estate was settled, but it was clear that she was destined for greater things. He just wished that she'd been destined for Brett.

He hated that his oldest grandson was still single. And not just single but so alone, like his father, Bob. And he wondered if how devastated Bob was over the loss of his wife was why Brett chose to stay single.

Lem and Sadie had a perfect record with their matchmaking, but he suspected Brett might change that. Clearly he and Frankie wouldn't work.

And this Trish…

He and Sadie hadn't even met her yet. Not for lack of trying, though. She obviously didn't want to meet them after what she'd put his family through.

When Liam and Elise called them to babysit, they'd said that nobody else was home. Frankie must have returned sometime after that call, though, because that definitely sounded like her beautiful voice.

He and Sadie climbed the steps of the porch, a little slower than they usually would have due to the long drive from Ranch Haven. Old joints tended to stiffen up on them after sitting for a while, but the exercise was helping Lem. Eighty-one was going to be another great year for him. He was married to the love of his life and nearly all of his family were happy. He and Sadie would make sure that Brett and Bob were soon, as well.

And the singing made him even happier. That, and the fact that soon he would have baby Lucy in his arms. He picked up his pace for the last couple of steps and reached for the screen door. The inside door was open so it was no wonder they'd been able to hear Frankie so clearly.

But the woman on the other side of the screen door turned, and she wasn't Frankie. Not unless Frankie had gotten very pregnant in the past couple of weeks since they'd seen her last. *Very* pregnant.

Her hair was curly like Frankie's, just shorter since it only reached her shoulders. And her face was very similar except her eyes were lighter. They met his through the screen, and she abruptly stopped singing.

And Lucy started crying.

"Let me. Let me help," Lem said, as he pulled open the screen door and hurried inside. "I'll take my great-grandbaby."

Sadie chuckled as she followed him into the house. "Excuse my husband, Miss Dempsey," she said as Lem took the baby from the young woman. "He is a baby hog."

But Trish didn't look upset when he took the child from her arms. Instead, she flashed him a smile of gratitude, and some tension eased from her shoulders, especially when the baby stopped crying and cooed up at him.

Actually, she burped and then she cooed…and

a bubble of formula escaped her perfect little rosebud mouth. "There's my precious," Lem cooed back at her.

Sadie chuckled again. Then she stepped closer to Trish. "I'm Sadie Lemmon and this is my husband, Lem. You are Trish Dempsey, right?"

Trish nodded, then cleared her throat. "Yes, I am."

"Elise said nobody else was home when she asked us to come over and watch Lucy," Sadie said.

"Uh, Brett and I just got back from Willow Creek a little while ago," Trish said.

"You and Brett went into town?" Sadie asked.

Lem caught the significant look that she sent to him. Trish wouldn't have noticed, but he did. He knew his wife so very well.

"Not quite," Trish replied.

Sadie's smile slipped a bit.

"We just went to the Willow Creek Veterinarian Practice on the outskirts of town."

"Oh, to Cash!" Sadie exclaimed. "He's my grandson."

"Yes, Brett told me," she said. "I also met Darlene."

"That dear girl," Sadie said, and she emitted a soft sigh. Just as Sadie had with her son Jessup, she had also lost years with her late son Michael's wife, Darlene, because of misunderstandings and misconceptions.

"She speaks highly of you," Trish said.

Sadie blinked hard. "She's a gem. What were the two of you doing there? All the animals all right?"

Of course that would be his wife's chief concern. She loved animals almost as fiercely as she loved her family.

"Yes, Brett and I picked out some for the petting zoo we're going to have at the ranch."

"Oh, Liam and Elise told us about that," Sadie said. "That's such a wonderful idea. I'm sure all our great-grandchildren will love to visit, too."

Trish cocked her head. "But they all live on ranches, don't they?"

"Mikey and Bailey Ann live in town," Sadie said. "But even the ones who live on ranches would love what you're starting here. I certainly do."

Lem wondered if she was talking about the petting zoo anymore, or what Trish might be starting with Brett. Trish and Brett? Would that be possible?

Brett was the one who'd been the angriest with her for not showing up for her father when he was in the hospital and for his funeral. But Brett was the one who'd taken her to town, so maybe he'd forgiven her. Even if he had, Brett was insistent on staying single, on forever being a bachelor cowboy.

So maybe he would be their first failure with their matchmaking.

CHAPTER FIFTEEN

UNLOADING THE ANIMALS and setting them up in their new homes took Brett longer than he'd thought it would. Hopefully, Trish hadn't had any issues with Lucy. She was already getting nervous about raising twin babies on her own. He could understand that; he was nervous for her doing it alone. And he was nervous for himself, too, that he kept feeling some obligation toward her and those babies.

Was it just because she was Frank's daughter?

Was that why he felt like he had to keep stepping in and helping even when he didn't agree with what she was doing? At least with the petting zoo and kids' camps. He had no intention of helping her with her kids, and despite her nerves she claimed that she didn't want help.

He totally understood why she wanted to raise her kids on her own. He would have hated growing up like she had, shuffled between bickering parents. He hadn't been too happy about the way he'd grown up after his family had moved to the city. So he definitely understood her wanting to have these camps for kids to spend time with animals out in the fresh air.

He would have loved to do that as a kid. And he imagined that all the kids who participated in the camps would love them, too. They'd picked out some perfect animals for the petting zoo. And Trish had mentioned having plans for other activities as well.

After settling in the last of the animals, Brett rushed across the yard toward the house. His stomach dropped when he noticed the vehicle parked in the driveway. The vintage red Cadillac.

His grandparents were here.

Then he noticed what was gone: Trish's truck.

He groaned but continued up the steps to the house. When he pushed open the screen door, Sadie put a finger to her lips and pointed to where Lem rocked Lucy in one of the living room chairs.

"She just got back to sleep," Sadie whispered.

That was probably where Trish should have been after their busy morning. But she'd taken off.

"You two just drop in?" he asked.

Sadie smiled and shook her head. "No. Elise called us to watch her. Nobody was here then."

"Where did Trish go?" he asked, but he tried to make the question sound casual, like he didn't care. He was all too aware how his grandparents loved playing matchmaker, how they loved love.

And each other. They sent each other a sappy-looking smile. But he wasn't sure if that was expressing their love or something else.

Probably some plan that involved him.

"She went into town to follow up with Maci about the will," Sadie said. "She said she wanted to make sure that her father's estate is all settled now."

He narrowed his eyes. "*She* wanted to make sure? Or *you* do, Grandma?"

Sadie's smile widened, and she stood up and kissed his cheek. "*She* does. She brought it up and apologized about holding up the will. She's actually a very sweet young woman."

He groaned.

"What? You don't think so?" she asked.

He swallowed another groan. "I think she's just gone through a very messy divorce, and she has no interest in someone trying to match her up with anyone else, Grandma." He shot a warning glance at Lem. "Grandpa."

Lem arched his bushy white eyebrows, looking all innocent.

Brett knew better.

"What about you?" Sadie asked.

He acted deliberately obtuse. "I have not gone through a messy divorce. That's something I will never do because I will never get married."

Lem sighed and shook his head. "That's a shame for sure. You don't know what joy you're missing."

"And what pain," Brett said.

"Ah..." Sadie sighed. "Pain is part of life, Brett. You know that. You lost your mother and your grandmother. And now Frank Dempsey, your best friend and boss. You can't avoid pain no matter how much you want to try."

His stomach flipped with the realization of how very right she was.

"But in trying to avoid pain," Sadie continued, "you're also avoiding the one thing that makes that pain bearable. Love."

"But if I don't love someone, I don't have to worry about losing them," he said.

"If you don't love someone, you don't have anything worth having," Lem said.

"And you love people," Sadie said. "You love your family. Your friends..."

He had no friends now that weren't family. Frankie and Maci, though not biologically related, were family. And Trish...

He had no idea what Trish was beyond a partner in the ranch. Was she a friend? She definitely wasn't family. But he cared about her, especially after having to rush her to the hospital that day.

He didn't want anything to happen to her. But he certainly wasn't in love with her. He would never let himself fall for anyone, no matter how much his grandparents tried to match him up with someone.

Maybe they'd been doing the same with Trish,

and that was why she'd taken off. She was even more determined to remain single than he was.

TRISH HADN'T INTENDED to drive back to Willow Creek that afternoon. But after trying to care for Lucy and then meeting Brett's grandparents, she'd been so overwhelmed she'd felt as if she was suffocating. She needed air, and so she'd grasped the excuse to talk to Maci.

Not that she didn't want to talk to her friend. She did. She also needed to follow up with her, just as she'd claimed to Sadie and Lem, and make sure that everything with the estate was settled. For all their help with the ranch, it was the least that she could do for her partners in the Four Corners.

So she made the drive back to Willow Creek, this time alone. And for some reason she had a hollow feeling inside her heart, like something was missing. Or she was empty.

But the babies shifted inside her stomach. She wasn't sure if they were kicking her or each other. They seemed eager to get out. But she wasn't ready. Not yet. She wasn't sure, though, if she would ever be ready.

Babysitting Lucy had not been easy. She hadn't known what she was doing with the little girl. Clearly, the baby had had gas since her great-grandfather had gotten a burp and a sweet coo out of her the minute he'd taken her from Trish. For a second, she panicked at the thought of someone taking away her children because she didn't know what she was doing. Someone like Elise, who worked for child protective services.

Would Trish's children need protection from her because she was that incompetent?

No. She would figure out how to be a good mother. While her mother hadn't been the best example, she had Elise in her life now. Even though Trish wanted to raise her kids on her own, she could ask Elise for advice.

She could and would be a good mother. And she also wanted to be a good partner in the ranch like her partners were all being so good to her. Especially Brett.

He'd gone above and beyond to help her get the ball rolling on the kids' camp and petting zoo.

So when Sadie had asked about the estate, Trish had decided she needed to know immediately that it was all settled. She could have called Maci, but she'd just texted her to find out if she was at home or her office. She wanted to talk to her in person.

She had also wanted to get away from Sadie and Lem. While they were very sweet, she hadn't been comfortable with them. After she'd upset their family, she didn't feel as if she deserved their kindness. And something about the way they'd kept looking at each other as they'd asked her questions, especially questions about Brett, had unsettled her.

Were they matchmaking?

But her and *Brett*?

He was the one she'd hurt the most when she'd not immediately agreed to honor her father's wishes. When she'd not been there for her dad like she should have been…

If she could have undone the past, she would have, but that wasn't possible. So she just had to make sure that the present and future were better.

She reached the main street of Willow Creek, surprised to see how busy it was. When she'd driven through at night, she hadn't noticed how much larger the city had grown, how many new businesses there were. And the population had definitely increased with all the improvements. She had to circle the block twice before a spot opened up near the building where Maci rented space from Brett's dad.

Brett had suggested that Trish should meet him, to ask him about his regrets over not accepting help when his wife was sick. There was no way she would ever pose such a personal question to the man, though. She wasn't sure that she even wanted to meet him. Meeting Brett's grandparents had already been a lot for one day.

She should have asked Maci in her text if she was alone in the office. Hoping that she was, she drew in a breath, stepped out of the truck and walked the short distance to the building that she remembered as being a cigar shop the last time she was in Willow Creek. When she pushed open the door, the faint scent of cigars hung in the air. And tears stung her eyes as it reminded her of her father.

This was where he'd bought the cigars he'd smoked in his den. Oh, how she missed him...

How she wished he had had the chance to meet his grandchildren.

She had no doubt that he would have loved them like Lem and Sadie loved theirs. And he would have been happy that she intended to raise them on the ranch.

Maybe doing that and honoring his last wishes for the Four Corners would make up for not being there for him like she should have been, like she wished she could have been. A bell had dinged when she opened the door, but there was no one around when she stepped inside and closed the door behind her. Nobody sat at the desk in the front of the building, and nobody called out from the back.

Then a little gray kitten scampered down a wide center hallway, its back arched slightly. It stopped at her feet and began to purr.

Despite her burgeoning belly she managed to crouch down and pet it. "Oh, you're a sweetie." It rubbed against her hand and purred even louder.

"Smokey is our new receptionist," a male voice commented. "She's great at greeting visitors but her typing skills need some work."

Trish chuckled and looked up at the man standing near her. He wasn't as tall as his sons, but his facial features were very similar to Brett and Blake's. He had that square jaw and dark eyes, and his hair was thick like theirs, just more brown than auburn except for some silver strands.

"So Smokey is actually trying to type when she walks across my keyboard?" a familiar female voice remarked. Maci appeared behind the man from whom she rented office space. But clearly Bob Lemmon was much more than a landlord to her. Maci was in love with his son.

"Of course," Bob replied.

Trish moved to straighten up, but a cramp gripped her side again and she grimaced. Bob reached out, closing his hands over her elbows to help her up from the crouch she'd been ill-advised to try.

"Are you okay?" he asked with concern.

He was as nice as his father had been to her at the Four Corners. Tears stung her eyes for a moment over the difference between Brett's family and hers.

At least her maternal one.

The older man studied her face, his concern in his dark eyes now. "Do you need anything?"

"This is Trish, Bob," Maci said. She moved up next to him. "Are you okay, Trish?"

She nodded. "Yes, I just forget sometimes that I have a couple of extra passengers on board."

"Twins?" Bob asked. "That's wonderful."

"It is," Trish said. This was what she'd wanted for so long, to have these babies, to be a mother. She was going to focus on the gratitude instead of the anxiety from now on.

"Congratulations," he said.

"Thank you."

"Can I get you anything?" he asked. "We have water, coffee and tea in the back. Or I can get you something from one of the shops around here, too."

"That's very kind," Trish said. "But I'm fine."

"That's a bit of a drive from the Four Corners to here," he said. "So if you need anything let me know."

"Thanks," Trish repeated.

"You didn't need to make the drive all the way here," Maci said. "I would have been happy to come out to the ranch later today."

Trish nodded. "I know but…uh…"

"You wanted to talk in private?" Maci asked, and she tensed a bit.

"No, it's not that," Trish said. "I was taking care of Lucy alone when Mr. and Mrs. Lemmon showed up—"

"Mr. and Mrs. Lemmon?" Maci repeated, her forehead furrowing. "That sounds so formal."

"Sadie and Lem," Trish said, remembering what they insisted she call them. Or Grandma and Grandpa since mostly everyone called them that now. She never would, though. While they were very sweet, they weren't family to her.

Bob chuckled. "Ah, scared you off, huh? Were they matchmaking?"

She shuddered a bit at the thought. "I doubt they would try to match me up with anyone." But they had kept asking her about Brett.

"I don't think anyone is safe with those two," Bob said. "Even me." He shuddered, too. Then he bent down and scooped up Smokey. "This is the only companion I want in my life." And he carried the kitten down the long hallway.

"So you're just using me as an excuse to get away from the ranch?" Maci asked, but she was smiling as if she wasn't offended.

Trish hoped she wasn't, that she hadn't done too much damage to their friendship. "I also wanted to make sure that Nolan did everything you needed him to in order to get the estate settled."

"And you're asking me instead of him?" Maci asked. "Don't you trust him?"

Trish sighed. "I don't know if he trusts that I'm doing what's in my best interests."

"I don't think he's worried about just your interests," Maci said.

"I'm sorry that you've had such a difficult time with him," Trish said. "Until you told me, I had no idea that he was having anyone spy on you."

Maci pointed to the empty receptionist desk.

"That's why nobody is sitting in that chair anymore. Robert admitted to spying for Stokes."

Trish shook her head. "I'm sorry you had to fire him."

"He quit," Maci said. "And he feels bad about what he did. Does Stokes?"

Trish shrugged. "I don't know what he thinks," she admitted.

"So the two of you aren't close?" Maci asked.

"He's been kind to me," Trish admitted.

"Is he interested in you?" Maci asked.

Trish laughed and patted her belly. "I don't think anyone is interested in me right now."

"You're beautiful," Maci said.

Trish laughed again.

"I'm serious," Maci said. "And I hate that your mother undermined your self-confidence. You were always beautiful, but you're even more so now."

Tears stung Trish's eyes again. She would have blamed the hormones, but she knew her friend's sweet compliment would have affected her no matter what. "I've missed you," she said. Stepping forward, she closed her arms around Maci and hugged her as tightly as her big belly allowed.

"I was always here," Maci said. "And I will always be here for you."

"Thank you," Trish said.

Maci hugged her back. When she pulled away, she wiped a tear from her cheek. "I'm so glad you're home. And yes, Nolan Stokes withdrew his petition to probate court. Everything is settled."

Trish sighed. "That's good." She waited for the relief to wash over her. But she had a strange feeling—or maybe it was just the nerves from earlier that were still hanging on—that she couldn't relax yet.

Maybe it was just the concern that she'd taken on more than she could handle on her own that was making her feel so unsettled despite Maci's claim. But as Brett had pointed out earlier, she didn't have to do everything on her own. She just wanted to.

TRISH DEMPSEY WAS not at all how Bob had pictured her. He hadn't expected her to be the sweet, beautiful young woman that she was. But she had been best friends with Maci and Frankie, so maybe he should have expected her to be more like them than the lawyer she'd hired.

Not that he'd met her lawyer. But he probably needed to do that to find out why the guy had hired Bob's former assistant to spy on him.

"Excuse me..."

He glanced up from his desk to find Trish standing in the open doorway to his office. "Yes? What can I help you with?" he asked.

She smiled at him. "I just wanted to say again that I'm sorry about what my lawyer did. I had no idea that he'd hired anyone to spy for me."

Bob shook his head. "I don't think that it was just for you," he said. "He had my assistant spying on me even before your father died."

Trish's forehead furrowed beneath the stray curls that lay across it. "I don't know why he would do that. It doesn't make sense."

"No, it doesn't," Bob agreed. "I'm about the most boring man there is. I spend most of my time here in the office or upstairs in my apartment above the office." He flinched over how pathetic that sounded. But that was his fault for pushing his children and his dad away for all the years that he had. He was trying to reach out more, trying to be more social now.

"I know you're always welcome at the Four Corners," Trish said.

Warmth filled Bob's heart. "That's kind."

"I'm starting these camps for kids to spend the day and eventually the summer at the ranch," she said. "We're going to have a petting zoo and other activities for them."

Bob chuckled. "I'm not a kid anymore."

"No, but maybe you'd like to bring some kids."

"Only grandchild I have already lives there," Bob said. "But I would love to see more of her and my sons and daughter-in-law. I'll make a point of coming to visit more often."

She smiled. "That's good. And..."

"What?" he asked when she trailed off.

"Nolan Stokes's new ranch isn't far from the

Four Corners," she said. "Maybe you should stop by and ask him why he's so interested in you."

Bob's stomach flipped. He was not good at confrontation; he was much better at avoidance. He shrugged. "I'm sure he would have reached out to talk to me if it was something that mattered."

Trish shrugged. "Maybe. But talking to him might give you peace of mind."

Or disrupt the little peace he had even more. And somehow Bob suspected the latter was what would happen.

CHAPTER SIXTEEN

SHE CAME HOME. Last night. Brett hadn't been able to fall asleep until he heard her truck pull into the driveway. But even after he'd heard her footsteps in the hallway and her bedroom door close, sleep had still eluded him. He'd wondered what—or who—had kept her out so late.

Stokes?

Not that it was all that late. But with as many long days as Brett worked and with as little sleep as he'd been getting, he had headed to bed early. And despite his restless night, he still woke up early the following morning. He wasn't the first one up, though, because he walked out to the kitchen to find Trish already dressed and awake. Like him, she had dark circles beneath her eyes, so she hadn't gotten much more sleep than he had.

"Good morning?" He asked it as a question rather than a greeting.

She nodded. "Yeah…"

"I wondered if you were coming back last night," he admitted. "Or if my grandparents had scared you away from the ranch." Or more likely away from him. He was their last single grandson, so he had to be the one on whom they were setting their matchmaking hopes.

"They are very sweet," Trish said with a smile. "Your dad, too."

"You met him when you went to see Maci?"

She nodded.

"I wasn't sure that you were really doing that or just using it as an excuse to get away from them," he said with a chuckle. "They can be a lot."

"They were very kind, especially given what they must have thought of me over how I've handled everything."

"They wouldn't hold anything against you, Trish," he assured her. "They were once mortal enemies themselves, and now they're madly in love."

She chuckled and shook her head. "I don't believe it. Mortal enemies?"

"Since grade school," he said. "They were constant rivals over grades and even arm wrestling as the stories go. And when he was mayor, she was constantly complaining to him."

"Wow, I wouldn't have believed that," she said. "Not with how sweet they were with each other."

"She didn't call him an old fool?" he asked. "Because that's what she used to call him. And she was the first to call him Old Man Lemmon, too. Now most everyone calls him that."

"What changed between them?" she asked.

He shrugged, then sighed. "I'm sure they would say love. They think it's the most important thing there is."

"But you're not convinced," she surmised.

"Are you?" he asked curiously.

She shrugged then. "Between a man and a woman? I don't know if that love can be trusted." She cleared her throat. "Or, more specifically, I know that I wouldn't be able to trust it."

"Me neither," he agreed. He should have been happy that they were on the same page about this, but there was an odd hollow feeling inside his chest.

"I know I love my children," she said as she patted her belly that stretched the bib overalls she wore. "But I guess kids can hurt us, too. Like I hurt my dad."

"Trish, you have to stop beating yourself up about that," he said.

"I just wish I could talk to him," she said. "Explain everything. Apologize..." Tears glistened in her eyes.

"So do it," he said. "I go to his grave and tell him about what's happening around the ranch." Sometimes it made him feel less alone since his brothers and sister had significant others now, and he was the odd man out. But sometimes it made him feel even lonelier that all he had of his old friend was a tombstone.

She nodded. "Maybe I will do that."

"I can drive you over there this morning if you like," he offered.

She shook her head, and her curls tumbled around her face. "I have a meeting with the contractor to go over the final things that need to get done for the bunkhouse."

"I can join you for that, too," he offered.

But she shook her head again. "No. I've got it. I know you have things to do on the ranch."

"Yeah, but I'm happy to help out," he reminded her. "We're all partners."

"Yes, we are," she said. "And Maci verified that everything's been settled, by the way."

"That's good," he said, and he waited for the wave of relief he'd expected when that was confirmed. "Frank would be happy." Brett should have been, too, and he was. But he was also concerned. Even though he'd been talking about being Trish's partner, it felt somehow bigger now that it was official. Like they were partners in more than the ranch. That wasn't what either of them wanted, though.

Her lips curved into a slight smile. "I do hope he's happy," she murmured.

"So did you stay out with Maci to celebrate?" he asked, curious about why she'd gotten home so late.

Her smile widened. "Maci and Frankie and I

had a sleepover at Maci's house. We used to alternate houses when we were kids."

"But you came home," he said.

"You were waiting up for me?" she asked.

Heat rushed to his face. "Just couldn't sleep." But he hadn't even noticed that Frankie hadn't been home. He'd just been waiting up for Trish.

"I came home instead of spending the night because I have this meeting." She glanced at her watch. "I better get to it," she said, as she rushed out the side door of the kitchen.

Maybe she was just in a hurry to meet with the contractor, but Brett couldn't help feeling that she might have been in a hurry to get away from him. Hopefully, she didn't think that he would succumb to his grandparents' matchmaking and start falling for her.

That wasn't why he wanted to help her with things. He just didn't want her to get too stressed, not when she was so very pregnant.

But she had made it clear that she wanted to be independent. That she wanted to take care of herself and her children without anyone's help.

And he, the oldest of his family who'd always felt responsible for everyone else, should have been relieved that he didn't have to help her. But that wasn't the way he felt at all. He wouldn't even admit to himself what he was feeling—although, if he could bring himself to admit it, he would say that it felt a lot like disappointment.

A PANG OF regret struck Trish over how she'd rushed away from Brett. He was so sweet to keep offering to help her. But she felt as if she'd already taken enough of his time and caused him enough trouble, and most of that had happened even before they'd met.

At least the estate was settled now. So he didn't have to worry about that. And she would make sure that he didn't have to worry about the camps either since he didn't even think they were a good idea.

And she didn't think it was a good idea for her to lean on him as much as she already had. He'd helped so much already. And when he'd offered to take her to the cemetery…

That wasn't just physical support he was offering but moral and emotional support, too. And that was too dangerous.

She couldn't let her emotions get away from her with Brett. She'd already kissed him once. If she hadn't rushed out of the kitchen when she had, she might have kissed him again.

He probably would have been horrified. He'd made his plans clear to her that he had no intention of ever getting married. He didn't want to divide his attention between a relationship and the ranch. He wanted to focus on the ranch, so that it would prosper without affecting his brothers' relationships. And that was good. She shared that intention. So why was she still so nervous around him?

So aware of him?

She glanced back toward the house then, almost as if she'd instinctively known that he was walking out at that time. That was how aware of him she was. But he walked toward the barn, not her.

And she walked past it, only stopping when she reached the new smaller barn and fenced-in area for the petting zoo. She stopped at the enclosed pens and greeted each of the new animals. They were all so perfect for a petting zoo. The kids would love them. She touched her belly and was certain that her own kids would probably love them most of all.

But she needed more than the petting zoo to keep the kids busy during the day and summer camps. So after feeding her new critters, she headed toward the bunkhouse. She laid out the plans she'd drawn up for the building just as the contractor arrived. She half expected to see Brett with him, especially when the man asked if he would be joining them. When she shook her head, he looked disappointed. He was older, though, and maybe he preferred dealing with men.

She made it clear that she was the one making the decisions when it came to the camps, and the man's disappointment turned to what looked—at least to Trish—like begrudging respect.

She didn't care that it might have been begrudging. At least it was respect. And Trish felt a new surge of confidence. She could do this. Even though she had partners, she was still capable on her own. But she did miss Brett's involvement, like when she'd picked out the animals.

Or maybe she just missed Brett.

ELISE FOUND TRISH out in the old bunkhouse. Dust danced in the air as power equipment rumbled in the building. "Should you be out here?" she asked, raising her voice as she waved her hand around.

Trish tensed, and her skin paled slightly, leaving the circles beneath her eyes as the only color in her face. "Oh, I..." She coughed.

Elise linked their arms, drawing the other woman outside. She handed her the water bottle she'd brought out with her. "Are you okay?" she asked.

"Yes," Trish said after she took a big swig from the bottle. "I just got caught up in the renovation. I should have thought about the dust." She patted her belly with her free hand.

"I'm sure the dust won't affect them," Elise assured her. "I just came to find you to thank you for watching Lucy yesterday for me."

"I didn't watch her very long before her great-grandparents showed up," Trish said.

"They must have made it here in record time," Elise said with a smile. "They're amazing."

"Yes, they are, so I figured Lucy was safe with

them," Trish said. "Probably safer than with me. I don't have much experience with babies."

"You'll be a great mother," Elise assured her.

"How is everything at your mom's foster home?" Trish asked. "Is everyone okay?"

Elise nodded. "Yes, a couple of the teenagers got into a physical altercation."

"Oh, no."

"They're both fine now," Elise said. "We did have to take them to the ER, though, to get X-rays to make sure that nobody broke or sprained anything. They knocked each other halfway down the stairs."

Trish gasped. "But they're okay?"

Elise nodded. "Nurse Sue and Livvy checked them out for us."

Trish smiled. "Like they checked me out when I thought I was in labor." Her forehead creased. "Nurse Sue reminds me of someone…"

"Who?" Elise asked.

"Nolan Stokes," she said. "They both have those very pale blue, almost silver eyes."

Elise's eyes widened as she remembered the man. And she also remembered what Sue had once confided in her. Was it possible…?

She shook her head, unwilling to let herself speculate or gossip about the woman who'd trusted her with such a personal secret. She focused on her mother again. "My mom might need to find a placement for one of those foster girls."

She glanced at the bunkhouse and the barn. "Or maybe a summer job. Working here would be great for some of those kids, give them a real purpose."

Trish smiled. "A real purpose. That's what it feels like to me, too."

"I see how much it means to you," Elise said. "And I think it will be great."

"I have more planned than the petting zoo," Trish said. "I want to have hayrides and scavenger hunts and horseback riding lessons for the kids. I'll need help for all that."

"You have it," Elise said. "I'll do what I can, and I know the others will, too. Even Brett and Frankie."

"I think Frankie will leave soon," Trish said.

"Back to the road," Elise murmured, but she wasn't so sure that Frankie would be able to tear herself away from the ranch. It was her last connection with the man she'd loved like a father, her uncle Frank. "But Brett isn't going anywhere."

Trish didn't look relieved over that comment, though. She looked concerned. Was she worried about Brett taking over when it was so clear that the kids' camps were her babies?

Or was she worried about falling for the determined-to-stay-single bachelor cowboy?

CHAPTER SEVENTEEN

AFTER THAT AWKWARD morning when Trish had realized Brett had waited up for her, he'd been careful to keep his distance from her. He only went near the bunkhouse and the petting zoo barn when she was in the house or off somewhere with Frankie or Maci or Elise. He didn't want her to worry that he was getting too involved with her or attached or interested.

But he was beginning to worry that he was, because even though he hadn't seen her that often over the past couple of weeks, he thought about her all the time. Keeping his distance wasn't working for him at all.

Maybe if he just checked in and had a real conversation with her, he would be able to stop worrying about her and about himself. So once he returned from the pastures, he took care of his horse and was just about to leave the barn when he noticed the wagon with hay bales on it.

Except it didn't just have hay bales on it. A certain curly-haired woman sat on the back among the bales with one black kitten on her lap and the other on the hay bale behind her.

Had that wagon just come back from the fields? The tractor was still hooked to the front of it. And then it began to move. As it jerked forward, Trish slid off one bale and onto another, and she scrambled to hold on to the kittens, as if worried they might fall off.

Brett was more worried about her. And those babies.

His heart pounding madly, he ran to catch up to the wagon, then grabbed on to the edge to hoist himself up and onto it. He fell across the straw that had come loose from the bales. Then he scrambled up to wrap his arms around Trish, holding on to her as she held on to the kittens. "Are you all right?" he asked with concern. He tried to peer over the hay to see who was driving the tractor. "What's going on? Don't they know you're on here?"

He couldn't imagine anyone would have driven off with her sitting on the back like this. She could fall off so easily.

"Of course they know," she replied. "This is a test run for the hayrides we want to have."

He shuddered. "Not we. This isn't a good idea, Trish." He wasn't sure if he was talking about the hayrides or the way he'd wrapped his arms around her, holding her so close that she had to feel the pounding of his heart.

"What do you have against hayrides?" she asked.

"Liability," he said. "Kids could fall off."

"We're going very slowly," she pointed out.

And it was true that the tractor was putzing along. But still…

He shook his head. "Someone could still fall off and then the wagon or the tractor could run them over."

"It's not going to back up," she said. "We'll make sure we have a route mapped out, and we'll have plenty of adults onboard to watch the kids."

She was determined. He could hear it in her voice. So, knowing he was going to lose, he sighed. His breath stirred her hair, and she shivered despite the warmth of the day.

Or maybe he was just hot from running after the wagon. Or from holding her.

"Let's look into maybe getting higher sides on the wagon, so that nobody can fall off, and a gate on the back," he suggested.

"Okay," she said. "That makes sense."

At least he was talking sense because he sure didn't feel like he was thinking it right now. Because all he could think about was her and how close he held her and how much he wanted to kiss her.

And that would not be sensible at all.

TRISH WANTED TO be annoyed that Brett kept jumping in to rescue her. She wanted to be independent. She wanted to be able to handle everything on her own. But he'd looked so worried about her when he'd run after the wagon. And the way he'd vaulted onto it and then wrapped his arms around her had her melting into a gooey mess.

Nobody had ever acted this way with her. Not even Nolan Stokes. He'd sought her out to warn her about the Lemmons for some reason as if he'd been concerned they were conning her dad. He hadn't even known her dad.

After Frank Dempsey had felt her mother had conned him, there was no way he ever would have let anyone else do that. And while her dad had certainly loved Trish, he hadn't rushed to her rescue like this. Maybe if he had actually come to her wedding she wouldn't have married the man he hadn't approved of. He had been right that Harold Trent had love-bombed her in the beginning to win her over. He hadn't really wanted any of the same things in life that she had. He'd just lied and told her that he had.

Whereas Brett was doing the opposite. He said he didn't want the same things, like the petting zoo and the camps and now the hayrides, but he kept helping her anyway. The only thing they really agreed on was that getting married was too risky and not worth the pain.

Her heart was beating fast like his as he held her. And she felt more like she was falling now than when the wagon had first lurched into motion. But she wasn't falling off the wagon.

Brett's strong arms wrapped around her were making sure of that. She couldn't remember anyone ever holding her like this, so close but yet so carefully, too. Like he didn't want to hurt her.

If only she could trust that…

If only she could trust anyone…

Most of all herself.

But she was trusting herself. She had so many hopes and dreams and plans. And she had no intention of letting anyone derail them again.

Not even Brett Lemmon.

Though he hadn't really tried to stop her from doing anything. He just wanted her to be safer when she did it. She let herself relax against him and enjoy the ride. And when the tractor finally lurched to a stop, she turned her head and skimmed her lips across his square jaw. The stubble on it tickled her lips, and she smiled.

"Thank you," she whispered.

"For what?" he asked. "Overreacting?"

"For caring," she said.

He tensed.

"Don't worry," she said. "I know you're just being a good partner…" But she wasn't thinking of the partnership they had in the ranch. She thought instead of the partnership that Elise and Liam had, and that Sadie and Lem had: a marriage. "Uh, partnership in the Four Corners," she said. "That's what I meant…"

He nodded. And his gaze, with his dark eyes so very intense, dropped to her lips. Then he leaned forward and kissed her back.

She forgot about everything except the sensation of his mouth on hers. She could have kept on kissing him forever if someone hadn't suddenly cleared their throat, causing them to jerk apart.

She was glad the wagon had stopped because she might have fallen off otherwise, with how quickly he released her. Then he scrambled off the back. But he didn't rush off. He held his hand out to her, to help her down. But when she put hers in his, she noticed that his hand was shaking just like she was shaking.

What in the world was happening between them?

And why?

This wasn't part of her plan for her future. This was the exact opposite of what she'd said she wanted. She didn't want anyone in her life but her babies.

And her business partners.

She didn't want a life partner.

FRANKIE DIDN'T KNOW what to think of the kiss she'd just witnessed. At first she'd been too stunned to do anything but stop and stare. She hadn't even known anyone had been on the wagon but Trish.

When she'd hopped on the tractor for the trial run, only Trish and the kittens had been riding back there. But when she stopped the tractor and came around to help Trish down, she'd found that her cousin was no longer alone.

Brett had joined her.

And they looked like they were really together. What in the world was going on with them?

They broke apart the minute she cleared her throat. Maybe she shouldn't have done that. Maybe she should have just walked away.

But this wasn't like Blake and Maci, who she loved together. Or Elise and Liam, who were perfect together.

This was Trish and Brett.

Brett, who Frankie had once thought would never forgive Trish for not being there for her dad when he got hurt and then for his funeral.

But he must have forgiven her if he was kissing her.

Or maybe he hadn't.

But even if he had, this wasn't a good idea. Trish was newly divorced and very pregnant. And Brett wasn't much better with kids than Frankie was.

She couldn't believe these two people, of any two people she knew, would be able to make a relationship work. And if it didn't, the fallout would make life at the ranch messy for everyone.

The only more unlikely pair Frankie could imagine would be her and Nolan Stokes.

CHAPTER EIGHTEEN

"WHAT WERE YOU THINKING?" Once Trish left the yard where Frankie had parked the tractor and wagon, she and Brett hurled that same question at each other.

Instead of answering her, Brett rushed on, "Why would you let her ride on the back of the wagon like that? She could have fallen off and hurt herself and the babies!"

The color receded from Frankie's face while his was probably flushed since his skin was hot. He'd been hot since he'd run for the wagon and then wrapped his arms around Trish.

"That was dangerous." To be honest, he wasn't certain if he was talking about the wagon ride or what he'd done, wrapping his arms around Trish and then kissing her like he had.

"I made certain to go really slow," Frankie said in her defense.

"But there are no sides or back on the wagon," he pointed out. "She still could have fallen off."

Frankie nodded. "Yeah, that was stupid."

Guilt rushed through him for upsetting her. "We'll fix it," he said. "Even though I don't think hayrides are a good idea."

"That's not how it looked a minute ago," she said. "Now, tell me what you were thinking."

He shook his head and admitted, "I wasn't."

She smacked his shoulder now. "That was stupid, too," she said. "Trish just got divorced. She's pregnant and vulnerable. She shouldn't be getting involved with *anyone* right now—*you*, least of all."

His pride stung, he had to ask, "Why me, least of all?"

"You and I aren't like Blake and Maci and Liam and Elise. We're not looking for a *relationship*." She grimaced when she uttered the last word like it left a nasty taste in her mouth. "And we're certainly not looking to have *children*." She shuddered when she uttered that word, like just the thought gave her chills.

Truthfully, it gave him some, too. And Trish was about to have children, not just one like Lucy but two. Two infants who would be totally dependent on someone.

He already felt as though he had too many people dependent on him, dependent on him to be strong, to be stoic, to get things done.

"It's best for people like us to stay uninvolved," she said. "Instead of risking someone getting hurt."

He wasn't sure if that someone would be Trish or him, though. She had kissed him first and more than once. But his father had raised him to be a gentleman, so he wouldn't share that with anyone.

"I know. You're right," he told Frankie.

"Of course I am," she replied. "And just think of the mess you could cause if you two keep up with this…whatever it is."

Like Frankie, he couldn't think of a word to describe the attraction he felt for Trish Dempsey. Or maybe he just didn't want to put a name to it.

"The estate has finally been settled," Frankie continued. "We're all working well together with this partnership. You don't want to undo all of that for…"

Love?

He gasped as the thought popped into his head. Of course this wasn't love. He didn't even know what love was. He'd dated before, but he'd never been in a serious relationship, one that he had imagined going anywhere. And this one certainly couldn't lead to marriage.

Trish had made it clear she would never marry again, in case it didn't work out and her kids had to suffer the consequences. Which made sense.

She had to put her kids first.

And Brett…

He had to put the ranch and his family first, like he'd been doing all these years. He nodded at Frankie. "You're right. I don't know what that was…" He pointed toward the wagon where he and Trish had kissed just a short while ago. He could still taste her on his lips, still smell the scent of hay in her soft hair. But he could never risk a repeat of that.

While he'd been worried about her falling off the wagon, he was scared to death now that he was the one falling hard for Trish Dempsey.

THE MINUTE BRETT helped her off the wagon, Trish had headed straight for the house. She needed to press a cold cloth against her face to cool off her embarrassment and her attraction to the cowboy.

What was wrong with her?

Why was she forgetting the vows she'd made to herself during her divorce? She was never going to depend on another person, never going to link her life up with someone she might lose. Or with someone she might not have ever really had.

She couldn't risk it. Not for herself and definitely not for her babies.

She didn't want them to grow up feeling like the rope in the tug-of-war between adults. She didn't want them to get so frayed from the struggle that they forgot who they were and what they wanted because they were trying to make miserable people happy.

She could not risk their childhood becoming the nightmare that hers had been. Except when she'd been here at the ranch.

At the Four Corners, she'd been so happy. And she was again, now that she was back. The camps were coming together. She just needed a few more activities that the kids would enjoy. And the hayride was a good one.

But Brett, as usual, was probably right about liability issues. She would need to add sides to the wagon and a gate across the back. She would ask the contractors working on the bunkhouse if they could take care of that, too.

After taking a shower to wash off the hay and the embarrassment of Frankie catching them kissing, she went back outside to find Brett already working on the wagon. Tears stung her eyes.

He was so sweet that it wasn't fair. Even when he didn't like what she was doing on the ranch, he helped her with it. Was that just who he was? Or did he have a reason for being so nice to her?

Did he care about her like she was beginning to care for him?

That was dangerous for both of them. Neither wanted a relationship. He'd explained his reasons, and she'd explained hers.

It wasn't worth the risk.

But he was just so kind.

"You didn't have to do this," she said. "I would have asked the contractor."

He tensed, then turned toward her. "I wasn't sure. Thought you might start swinging the hammer yourself." He clenched a hammer in one of his hands.

She chuckled and shook her head. "Not with the ache I already have in my side."

He dropped the hammer and moved closer to her. "Are you okay?"

She nodded. "Just the ligament-stretching thing that made me think I was having the babies early." She patted her belly. "They're just trying to get more room in there." Meanwhile, she felt like if she stretched any more, she might break. And not just physically…

Emotionally, she'd already been through so much that if she let her heart stretch to include Brett, she was afraid that it might burst.

"Uh, what did Frankie say to you?" she wondered aloud.

He chuckled. "Coward. You took off."

She chuckled, too. "Guilty." Then her smile slipped away. "I saw the look on her face. She was pretty appalled." Or had she been jealous? Frankie and Brett were very close. But Trish had figured that it was a familial, sister-brother relationship they shared. Maybe because they were so much alike, both determined to stay single.

He rubbed his hand along his jaw, making her remember how her lips had tingled when she'd moved her mouth across it. She'd started that kiss, but she'd let him take the heat for it from Frankie.

He sighed. "She warned me not to take advantage of you."

Trish felt more like the one taking advantage of Brett. She'd kissed him the first time. And she kept letting him help her even though she knew he wasn't a fan of any of her plans for the ranch.

He continued, "She pointed out that you're recently divorced, pregnant and very vulnerable."

"Oh," she said. "I don't know whether that's sweet, or if I should be offended."

"She was being protective," Brett said. "She loves you."

"She loves you, too," Trish said. "And maybe she knows that you wouldn't be happy with me, with an instant family."

But part of her, her heart, wished that he could be happy with her, with them. However, she was all too aware of what happened when two people wanted vastly different things. There was no way to compromise on whether or not to have children, especially since hers would be here soon.

She'd left her husband because he'd lied about what he wanted and had tried to manipulate her into changing her mind. At least Brett had been honest with her. She was the one who wasn't being entirely honest with him and with herself. Because while she'd been convinced she wanted to raise her kids alone, she could imagine how it would be to raise them with someone else. As long as that person was as in love and as committed as she was.

Maybe she needed to be committed to even entertain the idea of marriage again so soon after ending one.

"She doesn't want either of us getting hurt," Brett agreed. "She also doesn't want things to be awkward in the partnership of the Four Corners."

"It won't be," Trish said. "And that—" *kissing* "—won't happen again."

Was that a flash of regret she caught passing through his dark eyes? Had he glanced at her mouth like she found herself looking at his?

She forced herself to look away. She'd already caused enough problems with the ranch. She would make certain to keep her attraction to Brett from affecting anyone else. If only she could stop it from affecting herself…

BLAKE WAS GOING to have to propose soon. He hated leaving Maci so much that he kept coming home late to the Four Corners. But usually when he came home, he found Brett still awake, like he was now, poring over something in Frank Dempsey's den.

"What are you working on?" he asked his older brother.

Brett jumped as if startled. He must not have heard Blake drive up and walk into the house. He rolled his shoulders, but the burdens he carried on them kept them looking tense like Brett's face was. Dark circles rimmed his dark eyes. He replied, "Just looking over some of the quotes for liability insurance for the camps, making sure they cover the petting zoo and hayrides."

"Hayrides?" Blake repeated. "That sounds like fun."

"Yeah, fun," Brett said sarcastically.

"You are really struggling with this new venture," Blake remarked. But despite how much Brett hated Trish's plans for the ranch, he hadn't fought them. He hadn't even tried to get the others to vote against her.

Brett just grunted.

"Did you realize that it could be lucrative?" Blake asked him.

"Lucrative?" He sounded skeptical now.

Blake nodded. "Yeah, Elise was telling us the other night at dinner how much daycare costs. And summer camps are even more expensive. Trish's plans will definitely support themselves and then some."

Brett's mouth dropped open a bit. "Really…"

So he hadn't known that she was going to make the ranch money, but he hadn't fought spending money on her plans. "What's going on with you?" Blake asked him. "You're working pretty much around the clock nowadays, skipping meals and skipping sleep, too."

"You've done that yourself," Brett reminded him. "And pretty recently, too."

Blake chuckled. "Yeah, but I was falling in love and didn't know how Maci and I were going to be able to make it work."

"Figure it out yet?" Brett asked, but his grin proved he was teasing.

"Yeah," Blake replied with a grin of his own. He felt like grinning all the time now. "And I can't wait to propose."

"Surprised you haven't already," Brett replied.

"I didn't want to rush Maci," he said. "I wanted to make sure the will was settled, so that she didn't have to worry about taking Trish's lawyer on in court and defending how she'd written up Frank's last wishes."

"She wrote them exactly as he wanted them," Brett said.

Blake had wondered if Frank had told his older brother what he'd wanted. Clearly, he had.

"The estate is settled," Brett said, then sighed. "So guess you will be proposing soon."

Blake nodded. "I have to find a ring that she will like—"

"Ask Dad for Mom's," Brett suggested.

Blake's heart flipped for a second with the thought. "That would be great, but you're the oldest son. You should get it."

Brett shook his head. "For what? I don't ever intend to get married."

"Still?"

Brett tensed. "What do you mean *still*? What do you think has changed?"

Trish. His brother had been different since her arrival at the ranch. And he was working himself ragged like Blake had himself when he was struggling to figure out how to make his love with Maci last.

Blake had finally realized that there was no struggle. A love like theirs, as strong as it was, would withstand any conflict. Any legal ones like the will being contested. And if health tested them like it had his parents, he knew they would take care of each other.

"Uh, I just thought that with Liam and me and Livvy all falling in love that you would realize it isn't as risky as you think it is."

Brett shuddered. "Still not a chance I'm willing to take. I decided long ago to focus only on the ranch. I'll be the 24/7 person, so you and Liam can focus on your wives and families."

Blake's heart swelled with love for his big brother. No wonder he had always idolized him and Liam had as well. "That's not fair, you know. Just because you're the oldest, it doesn't mean you have to take care of everyone else."

Brett shook his head. "That's not it at all. I love the ranch. It's all I've ever wanted and all I will ever want. So ask Dad for Mom's ring. I think Maci would love it."

"Once I ask her," Blake said, "I'm going to have a question for you, too."

Brett tensed again.

"I can't imagine anyone else being my best man," he said. All their lives Brett had been his best friend.

Brett blinked. "Liam might be offended."

"Liam would expect me to ask you, too," Blake said. Their younger brother knew how close they were and had often been jealous of that closeness until he'd fallen for Elise.

And now Blake had fallen for Maci.

But Brett was still all alone. Like Dad.

Maybe Grandma and Grandpa were getting to him, but Blake had the sudden urge to matchmake. He wanted his older brother to be as happy as he was, as Liam and Livvy were, too. But Brett was stubborn, so stubborn that he might prefer being alone to ever changing his mind about love.

CHAPTER NINETEEN

AFTER HIS LATE-NIGHT conversation with Blake, Brett wanted to make sure that their dad gave their mom's ring to his younger brother instead of holding on to it for him. So after tending to the cattle the next morning, he made the drive into Willow Creek.

He found his dad alone in the building that had once been a cigar shop. Maci must have been working from home after her late night with his brother. Well, his dad wasn't completely alone; Smokey, the kitten, lay upside down on his desk, her eyes rolled back in her head with just a touch of the green showing. He chuckled. "Someone's asleep on the job already," he said.

His dad rubbed the little furry belly that faced him. "Yeah, she had a wild night shredding the toilet paper roll, so she had to take a nap," he said. Then he pointed at Brett. "Looks like you had a wild night, too, son."

Brett chuckled. "I wasn't shredding a toilet paper roll."

"That's good," Bob said with a smile that quickly slid away again. "Looks like you weren't sleeping, though."

"You look a little tired yourself," Brett replied with concern. He suspected that it wasn't just the kitten's antics that had kept his father awake.

Bob yawned and nodded. "Yes, I'm getting old."

Brett shook his head. "No, Dad. You're not old. Now, Grandpa…"

Bob laughed. "Don't let him hear you say that. Even though we just celebrated his eighty-first birthday, he doesn't seem a day older to me than he ever did."

"He was always Old Man Lemmon," Brett said, recalling his childhood in Willow Creek.

"Thanks to Sadie," Bob said.

"Thanks to Sadie is why he doesn't seem to be aging," Brett said. "They seem really happy." So was it possible to survive loss and mend a broken heart enough that it could love again?

Obviously, it had been possible for Lem and Sadie. But his dad looked every bit as lonely and tired as he had since his wife had died. Then he petted the kitten again and a smile curved his lips. "Yeah, they are very happy," Bob agreed. "And I'm happy for them."

"What about you?" Brett asked.

Bob tensed. "What do you mean?"

"Are you happy, Dad?"

Bob's head bobbed in a quick, almost nervous nod. "Of course. Of course, I am."

"Really?" Brett was skeptical.

"Yeah, I have a beautiful new granddaughter," he said. "And a new daughter-in-law, and soon I will have a wonderful son-in-law, too. All of the family, really, is doing so well."

"That's the family," Brett pointed out. "What about *you*?"

Bob's face flushed with color, and he narrowed his eyes as he stared across his desk at Brett. "What's going on with you? With all these questions?"

Brett sighed. "I just worry about you," he admitted. "You've been so sad since Mom died."

His dad nodded. "Yes, I have been. But it's getting better. It actually has really helped being back in Willow Creek and getting close to my family again."

"We would have never stopped being close if you had let us know what was going on with Mom," Brett said.

"I know that," Bob said. "But to tell you about her illness..." He sighed. "It wasn't my decision to make."

"So you would have reached out had Mom let you?"

Bob sighed now. "I'm not blaming your mother. And I actually don't know what I would have done then. Now... I think a little differently."

"If you knew how it would end, would you have done it all over again?"

Bob's forehead furrowed with confusion. "What are you talking about?"

"Falling for Mom, only to lose her like you did, would you do it over again if you'd known?"

Bob shuddered. "Losing her was hard. But I would still do it even if just to have you and your brothers and sister."

Not for the love? That was a question that Brett couldn't bring himself to ask; it was too personal, even for a child to ask a parent.

"You're in a strange mood today," Bob said. "Did you drive all the way into town to ask me all these philosophical questions?"

Brett chuckled. "No. I didn't even know I would ask them." But he couldn't help wondering what his dad thought now of marriage and loss. Of the risk…

"So why did you make the trip?"

"I came to talk to you about Mom's engagement ring."

Bob gasped, his dark eyes going wide. "You want her ring? I didn't even know you were seeing anyone."

"I'm not." But the woman he saw every time he closed his eyes popped into his mind again. Trish with her soft curls, her beautiful eyes and face.

"Then why do you want the ring?"

"I don't want it," Brett said. "I want you to

know that you can give it to Blake—that he's going to ask you for it."

"Oh…" Bob nodded. "That makes sense."

"More sense than me ever needing that ring," he muttered.

"What? Why do you think that?"

Brett shrugged. "Marriage isn't for me."

"Why not?"

"I've seen too much suffering because of it," he admitted. "You, Grandpa, Frank Dempsey…" He shook his head. "It's just not worth it."

Bob frowned. "I don't agree."

"Because of us, of me and my siblings, you feel the need to say that," Brett said, and he was only partially teasing now.

"Love is scary," Bob said. "It's hard. But if you ever let yourself fall for someone, you would realize that it's worth it."

A sudden yearning in his chest, in his heart, took Brett by surprise. But he shook his head. "No. Not for me." Once again Trish popped into his mind. "And it's not fear. I made the decision long ago to focus only on the ranch. Ranching is hard work, long hours, and I don't want to split my time between it and a family. And I don't want my brothers' relationships to suffer for the ranch. So when Blake asks, you can give him the ring."

"You're sure?" Bob asked. "You are the oldest, and your mother said before she passed that it should go to you."

His mother had never really known him very well. She hadn't understood how hard it had been on him to move away from Willow Creek to the big city. She'd never understood how badly he'd wanted to move back west. And she certainly hadn't realized that he wasn't the one who would carry on whatever family tradition she might have been hoping to start.

"I'm sure," he said.

But in his head, along with the image of Trish, he heard a familiar voice whispering, "Liar…" But that voice wasn't hers; it was his.

TRISH WASN'T SURE exactly why she'd chosen today to visit the cemetery, but she stood now at her father's gravesite, staring down at the tombstone that Maci had chosen for him: *Beloved father, uncle, friend and rancher.*

Father had come first. Was that Maci's choice? Or had it been yet another of his last wishes that, as executor of his estate, she had carried out for him?

Trish would have thought that he would put rancher first. Because of her mother's lie, she'd believed that he'd put the ranch before her. But now she knew the truth.

"Ah, Dad, I am so very sorry," she murmured. "If I could have come to see you while you were in the hospital, I would have. But I was so afraid I was going to lose these babies if I did. I want to bring your grandchildren into the world, and I figured you would want that, too. I'll raise them on the ranch like I wish I had been raised full-time."

The only way she could ensure that they were raised full-time in any one place was to have them on her own. No shared custody with anyone.

Maybe that was why she'd chosen today to visit his grave, after she and Brett had kissed on the hayride wagon. She'd needed to remind herself of how much her dad had suffered, of how much he'd lost when he'd divorced and only been granted limited visitation with her.

He'd nearly lost the ranch, too. He would have lost it had Brett Lemmon not helped rescue it just as he kept rescuing her. She'd gone over the books herself, so she knew that was a fact, not just Maci, Frankie and his brothers singing Brett's praises.

He had sacrificed so much to keep the ranch going, and he'd vowed to always put it first in his life, before love and marriage and children. It might matter even more to him than it did to her. But like her, the other heirs cared about the Four Corners, too.

"You did the right thing, Dad, with your will," she said. While her lawyer probably still doubted it, Trish had no more doubts, except that maybe the others deserved their share more than she did. "I will respect your wishes."

In order to do that she had to make sure that she didn't mess up the partnership she shared with

Brett and the others. She had to make sure that it didn't get awkward and weird because of her attraction to the bachelor cowboy.

She couldn't kiss him again. And she had to keep her distance from him. Maybe she was mourning that decision almost as much as she was mourning her father.

"I miss you so much, Daddy," she whispered, her throat burning with the sobs that were threatening to bubble up and out. Some tears slipped down her cheeks.

Then an arm slid around her shoulders and a tissue was pressed into her hand. Blinded by the tears, she hadn't seen him walk up to join her, but she felt Brett in every tingly nerve ending.

"How do you always know?" she murmured.

"What?"

How did he always know when she needed him? But she couldn't ask him that question because then she would be admitting that she needed him. And she didn't want to admit that, even to herself.

"How did you know I was here?"

"I didn't," he said. "I swear I'm not stalking you. I came into town to talk to my dad, and any time that I come into Willow Creek, I stop by here to talk to Frank, too."

"Of course you do." Because he was good and loyal and kind. And it wasn't fair, not to her heart that was fighting so hard to keep him out.

"I was surprised to see you here," he said.

She sniffed back the tears that kept trailing down her face. "Because I'm a horrible daughter and you didn't think I even knew where his gravesite was?"

His arm around her gave her a gentle squeeze. "No, Trish."

"I had to ask Frankie," she admitted. "I am a horrible daughter."

"When Frank had his accident, you'd just gone through IVF with a high-risk pregnancy," he said. "You couldn't travel then or for his funeral. And you were going through your divorce, too. You had your reasons to stay away."

"Then," she said. "But I should have visited him before the accident. I should have come home years ago."

"You were married."

"And miserable," she said. "And too proud to let my dad see that he was right, that I never should have married Harold."

"Stop beating yourself up," Brett said. "Frank was too proud and stubborn, too. He could have gone to see you. He should have been at your wedding no matter what he thought of your husband-to-be. He let you down, Trish."

At that, the sobs that had been burning her throat slipped out, making her tremble as the tears poured from her.

Brett closed both arms around her and held her against his chest while she cried on his shoulder.

How did he always know what she needed? Not just him this time but his words; they released the heavy pressure of the guilt she'd been carrying for years.

"It wasn't all on you, Trish," Brett said, as he rubbed her back and touched her hair. "Your dad was the parent. He should have made the first effort. He should have made certain that you were okay all these years because you weren't."

She held so tightly to him now, not wanting to let him go. He'd given her a lifeline, something to hold on to so that she didn't drown in her grief. Maybe that was the real reason she hadn't come home when he'd gotten hurt and then died. She'd felt so guilty that she knew she would have lost it and probably her babies, too. The grief and the guilt would have destroyed her.

"Shh…" he murmured as he stroked her hair now.

Finally, the sobs subsided, and a sigh slipped out of her lips, a ragged one of relief. "I can't believe you're saying all these things…"

"Why not?" he asked.

"My dad was your best friend," she said. "You've told me that. Everyone's told me that."

"Just because we were friends doesn't mean I can't admit when he was wrong," Brett said. "Or when I was wrong. And I was wrong about you."

She wanted to ask if that was all he'd been wrong about, or was he wrong to think that love wasn't worth the risk? Had he changed his mind about that?

But even if he had, she couldn't. She had her babies to worry about, their future to secure.

BOB CLOSED THE office early, shortly after Brett's visit, actually. He didn't have any appointments that day and Maci didn't either or she wouldn't have been working from home. He was going to have to hire a new assistant soon. So he should discuss that with his business partner, Katie O'Brien Haven. But that discussion wasn't the real reason he drove out to Ranch Haven.

His conversation with Brett had unsettled him so much that he needed perspective and advice. The minute he parked, he rushed up the front steps and opened the door and walked in as he'd been told to do so many times before. "Hello?" he called out.

The kids were at school so the house was almost eerily quiet. Even the twin babies were curiously quiet.

"Hello?"

Was everyone gone or just busy working the ranch?

He walked down the wide center hall to the enormous kitchen that was the heart of Ranch Haven. The long center island had some pans of bread rising on it but there was nobody in the room. Nobody sat at the long dining table that stretched between the hearth of the big brick fireplace and the interior wall. The French doors on the other side of the table were open to the patio. And that was where he found Sadie and Lem, sitting at one of the small iron tables, their heads close together as they studied the screen of a tablet.

Relief coursed through him at the sight of them both looking so spry and happy. “There you two are,” he said as he walked out to join them. He leaned down and kissed Sadie’s leathery cheek. She spent so much time in the sun. Then he walked over and kissed his dad’s, and his snowy white beard was soft against Bob’s face.

His dad squeezed the hand he’d rested on his shoulder. “What a wonderful surprise,” he said with so much happiness.

Bob felt the familiar flash of guilt for all the years he’d stubbornly pushed his father away.

“What brings you out to the ranch?” Sadie asked.

She was so insightful that she would know he had a reason; she probably even had a pretty good idea what that was.

“I’m worried I screwed up my kids,” he admitted as he dropped onto one of the chairs around the table.

“Nonsense,” Lem said. “Your children are perfect. They’re *my* grandchildren.”

“And mine,” Sadie said. “And they are perfect.”

He grinned with pleasure at their praise. "Yeah, they are pretty perfect."

"But…?" Lem prodded him.

"Brett is just so determined to stay single," he said.

"You're sure about that?" Sadie asked.

He nodded. "He came to see me today to tell me to give his mother's ring to Blake to give to Maci. And his mother wanted him to have it."

"Oh…" Lem let out a sigh of disappointment.

But Sadie looked skeptical. "That doesn't mean he'll stay single," she said. "In fact…"

"What?" both he and Lem asked when she trailed off.

She shrugged. "It's almost like he wants to get rid of the ring to get rid of the temptation to use it."

"For whom?" Bob asked. "He's not even dating anyone."

"Dating, no," Sadie agreed. "But I think he's interested in Trish Dempsey."

"She's pregnant with twins," Bob said.

Sadie smiled. "Yes, and beautiful and sweet."

"I've met her," Bob said. "She's not what I was expecting." Not after everything she'd put his sons and her cousin and Maci through. "But really?"

Sadie shrugged. "I don't know for sure."

He narrowed his eyes and looked at his father. "Are you two scheming?"

"Your kids have made that unnecessary," Sadie

said. "They have a way of finding their soulmate on their own. Look at Liam and Elise and Blake and Maci..."

"But you helped set up Livvy and Colton," he reminded them.

"Well, your daughter had just ended a horrible relationship, and Colton is stubborn like his father," Sadie said.

"And his grandmother," Lem added, but he winked at his wife.

"Trish Dempsey just ended a horrible marriage," he said. At least that was what Maci had told him. "So she's not looking for romance. And I don't believe Brett is either." He sighed. "I'm afraid I set a bad example. That because I haven't started dating, they think their mother's death destroyed me."

"Did it?" his father asked.

He shook his head and admitted, "No. It just made me think..." About all the mistakes he'd made. But he was afraid that he was still making them. Maybe the only way to stop would be to go back and correct some of the mistakes he had made.

CHAPTER TWENTY

ONCE SHE'D CALMED DOWN, Brett had left Trish back at the cemetery alone. He felt like she might have needed a little more time with her father. And maybe with herself and her thoughts.

He'd needed some time and distance away from her, too. Seeing how upset she'd been, he'd gotten angry. Not with her but with Frank. His friend had definitely made mistakes with his daughter. He'd let his pride and stubbornness keep them apart.

That pride and stubbornness were two traits that Brett had in common with Frank, and which had helped them to understand each other so well. But what did that mean for Brett? Would he miss out on things because he was too stubborn to change his mind once he'd made it up?

He needed to think about that with a clear head. And he never had a clear head around Trish. He needed to get back to the Four Corners and on the back of his horse. A ride in the fresh air might clear his mind.

But when he arrived at the ranch, he found an

unfamiliar vehicle parked in it. It wasn't as big as the lawyer's Hummer, but it was a long black town car. A limousine at the Four Corners? It looked even more out of place than the Hummer had.

Everyone else must have been out working the ranch or away because the town car was running. Once he jumped out of his truck, the chauffeur stepped out and opened the back door.

A man came out first. He was probably only ten or fifteen years older than Brett, but he had a lot of silver in his hair and lines in his face. He reached in and helped out a woman. She was slim and blonde with a face stretched taut, but she was definitely older than the man.

"Where is my daughter?" she demanded of him.

He arched an eyebrow. "Excuse me?"

"Where is Patricia?"

He glanced back toward the road, but he was really hoping that Trish was taking her time in town. He didn't want her coming back to deal with her mother after how emotional she'd been at her father's grave. It would be too much for her.

"She's not here," he said. "So you have no reason to be."

"What did you do to her?" her mother asked, as if he'd murdered the woman that he…

He what?

He couldn't finish that thought. He wouldn't let himself.

"Trish is fine," he said. Or at least he hoped she was. He cursed himself now for leaving her alone.

"Where is she?" the man asked. "She's my wife."

"Ex-wife," he automatically corrected him.

And the man's pale face flushed. "That was a mistake. She must have realized that by now."

Brett laughed at the man's arrogance. He reminded Brett way too much of the neurosurgeon Livvy had dated. "She knows her only mistake was in marrying you in the first place," he told him.

The guy clenched his hand into a fist, and Brett braced himself for a blow. But the guy didn't swing.

"And who are you to Patricia?" her mother asked.

"Her partner," Brett said.

Her mother snorted. "She knows better than to fall for a ranch hand ever again."

"He's not a ranch hand, Aunt Belinda," Frankie said. She must have come from the barn because she'd walked up without anyone noticing.

Belinda looked Frankie up and down, and her mouth twisted into a sneer. "I am not your aunt," she said. "And he is not Patricia's partner."

"You're right about us," Frankie said. "And I am grateful we're no longer related. But you're wrong about Brett. He is Trish's partner, and he's mine, too."

Trish's mother gasped as if horrified.

"You're thinking the wrong kind of partner,"

Brett said, taking pity on the uptight woman. "Frankie, Trish, my brothers and I are all equal partners in the Four Corners now."

"Well, I'll have you know that we will be taking legal action to change that."

Dust billowed as a truck barreled down the drive toward them. It stopped abruptly behind his, and Trish clamored out. He stepped closer to her mother and ex, trying to shield her from them. Dealing with them was the last thing she needed right now. And he was worried about her talking to them in the state she'd been in when he'd seen her last.

Frankie had thought she was vulnerable before, but she was especially vulnerable now. Before she'd needed protection against him; now she needed it from him.

"Go in the house," he told her. "Frankie and I will get rid of the trespassers. I'll call the sheriff if they won't leave."

"Call the sheriff," her mother said. "You should be arrested for the con you pulled on my daughter and on my gullible ex-husband."

"Stop!"

TRISH UTTERED THE one word like she had the day that Nolan Stokes had been fighting with her partners. And like on that day, everyone fell silent with shock for a moment. Her shouting had to be even more of a shock for Harold and her mother than it had been for the others.

"My father was not gullible," Trish said first. Her heart still felt raw from her visit to his grave. She glanced at Brett. "He was stubborn and proud but not stupid."

"Still idolizing your daddy," her mother remarked bitterly.

"No," Trish said. "I see him clearly for who he was." She stepped around Brett, who'd tried wedging himself between her and the visitors. "And I see the two of you very clearly, too." She had no doubt about why they'd shown up here.

"So you've come to your senses," Harold said. "You're ready to come home."

She snorted. "You don't want me back. You don't want them." She patted her belly. "You're only here because you're afraid of my mother and you're going to do whatever she tells you to do so you keep your job." She lifted her chin and studied her beautiful mother. "And I get it, Harold, because I think I was afraid of her, too. I never wanted to disappoint her, but it was all I ever seemed to do."

"Never more so than now," Belinda said. She gestured at Trish's belly. "You did this to yourself…and then you insisted on that messy divorce."

"It was only messy because you kept telling Harold to fight me," she said.

"But you hired that fancy lawyer, Nolan Stokes," Belinda said. "Now I know how you were able to afford him. He knew you were due to inherit the Four Corners soon."

"He started the divorce proceedings before Dad died," Trish pointed out. "He didn't know."

"But your dad died before the divorce was final," Harold said, "so you cheated me out of my share."

Trish snorted. "You weren't in my father's will. He didn't want me to marry you, and he was right. And he was right to split up the ranch like he did, too."

"We'll see about that," Belinda said. "As a former deed owner, I should have had the rights of survivorship. This should be mine."

"Former," Trish said. "You're not on the deed now. The five of us are." She gestured at Frankie and Brett, who'd been curiously quiet. "It's done. There's nothing the two of you can do to get your greedy hands on it. So you better leave, or I will have Brett call the sheriff to cite you for trespassing. Sheriff Cassidy is his cousin, so he would be happy to do that."

"What happened to you, Patricia?" her mother asked, her voice sharp with disapproval.

Trish smiled. "I'm not afraid of you anymore, Mother. I don't care what you think of me."

"And this man…" Her mother shook a perfectly

manicured finger in Brett's direction. "A ranch hand—"

"He's not a ranch hand," Trish said. "He's my partner."

"He's like your father."

"Yes," Trish agreed. "A hardworking, honorable man."

Her mother shook her head. "No. He's not. And you're not honorable either, Patricia. How you handled the divorce is despicable. Fraud even. Harold and I will be taking you to court."

Finally, her mother turned and stiffly folded herself back into the limo. Harold quickly followed her like the lapdog he was. The chauffeur slammed the door behind them and shot an apologetic glance at her before getting into the driver's seat. He backed slowly past them and their vehicles and back onto the road.

As the limo drove off, all the tension drained from Trish's body.

"Wow!" Frankie exclaimed. "You were fierce, Trish."

She smiled. "Yes."

"You really were," Brett said. "You didn't need us at all."

She only wished that were true, but she was very afraid that she needed him much too much.

"THAT VISIT WAS sure a surprise," Sadie said with a smile as Bob drove off. Lem stood next to her on the porch staring after his son with such love and yearning. She squeezed his hand. "You can't worry about the years you lost," she reminded him. "Just about the time you have now."

He nodded. "You are so wise."

"That's not exactly what you used to call me," she said. "Wisecracker. Wisea—"

He chuckled. "You can't worry about the years you lost…"

"No, we can't," she said.

He sighed. "We can worry about now, though," he said. "And I'm worried about Bob."

"And he's worried about Brett," Sadie said. "Do you think we should be doing some scheming?"

"You aren't already?" he asked.

She chuckled. He knew her so well. "I was thinking about having another party."

"My birthday is over," he said. "And yours was months ago. What will we celebrate?"

"Whom," she said. "Whom will we celebrate…"

"You obviously have some idea."

"Of course." She patted his arm, then she leaned down and nuzzled her cheek against his soft white beard. "Don't worry. We'll make sure that there is no reason for anyone to worry about anyone…" But a little flutter of nerves passed through her stomach. She hoped that she wasn't making her husband a promise she couldn't keep.

CHAPTER TWENTY-ONE

TRISH NEVER FAILED to surprise Brett. He'd thought she would be so emotionally fragile after visiting her father's grave that she wouldn't be able to deal with her mother and her ex-husband. Maybe part of him had even worried that they would manipulate her again like they once had, and that she might wind up leaving with them. That was why he'd tried standing between them and her.

He hadn't wanted her to leave. The very thought of it had made his chest ache like his heart was being ripped out. She belonged here. But her mother had never seen that, and so he'd worried…

But she hadn't needed his protection. Or Frankie's. She'd handled the visitors on her own. Just as Frankie had said, she'd been fierce and fearless.

Or so he'd thought, but he saw a flicker of something cross her face as she turned to head into the house. "Are you okay?" he asked.

She nodded. "Yes, but we need to tell everyone else what just happened."

"We should take an ad out in the paper," Frankie said. "I wish I had taken a video of you telling them off. You were amazing."

Trish smiled, but it didn't quite reach her eyes. "I still don't trust them," she said. "And we need to tell the others what happened."

"We'll get everyone together," Brett assured her. "Why don't you lie down for a while? Take a nap." He didn't like the way she kept rubbing her belly. Was she having contractions and just assuming that they were false?

"I'm not tired," she said.

"I don't think I could have handled going that round with your mother," Frankie said, "and I'm not pregnant. Brett's right. You should take it easy for a bit. Watch your blood pressure."

She uttered a groan of frustration.

"We know you're tough as nails," Brett assured her. "But you visited your father's grave today and then came back for this..."

"Oh, that's right," Frankie said. "I knew I should have gone with you." She glanced at Brett. "Did you go?"

"We just ran into each other there," he said. *Like it was fate or something.* Usually a thought that fanciful wouldn't have entered his head. But there was something about Trish that had him feeling it was all inevitable, that no matter what he'd planned for his life, it was going in another direction, one he'd never envisioned for himself.

"That must have been hard, Trish, and then coming home to those two…" Frankie shook her head, and her big eyes were full of admiration for her cousin.

Brett was in awe, too. "It was a lot, Trish, and as tough as you are, you're also carrying two babies. You need to make sure that you don't overdo it, for their sakes. I know they're the most important thing to you."

Clearly, the babies had meant nothing to her mother, which had infuriated Brett. After seeing them on that monitor and feeling them kick from time to time, they were so real to him and already had their own little personalities. The girl was going to be feisty like her aunt Frankie and her mom while the boy was going to be the quieter, more contemplative one. Kind of like him…

But these weren't his kids. And instead of feeling relieved about that, he felt oddly disappointed. He already cared about them.

But their grandmother wanted nothing to do with them. She'd been disapproving of everything Trish had done that mattered to her. He couldn't imagine how tough her childhood must have been with that woman as her mother. No wonder the ranch had become so important for her; it hadn't been just fresh air and animals and fun times with friends, like she'd said. It had been her sanctuary away from disapproval and criticism.

Trish let out another sigh, but this was one of

resignation. "Okay. I will lie down for a little while. But make sure that everyone is here for dinner, so we can talk."

He nodded. "I'll do that for you." He would do anything for her, he suddenly realized. But she didn't want that, and she didn't need that. She really could take care of herself and her babies. And once again, instead of feeling relief, he felt disappointed that she didn't need him.

As she walked toward the house, some of the tension eased from him. She hadn't left with her family like he'd momentarily feared. But he couldn't help but feel like he was still losing her somehow. Maybe just to herself.

BRETT KEPT HIS PROMISE, not that she'd had any doubt he would. Just as she'd told her mother, he was an honorable man. He made sure that everybody was at dinner that night. He'd even asked Elise to pick up pizzas on her way home, which she had happily done.

They all sat around the big round table in the kitchen, eating pizza and drinking soda. Joking and laughing. As Trish looked from smiling face to smiling face, her heart swelled with love and appreciation for all of them.

While Lucy and Elise had moved in after her dad died, the others had been here with him. Had kept him company. Had made him so happy that he'd wanted them to stay here even after he was gone.

She knew that now. And she wanted to make sure that wish was honored no matter what.

"The pizza party was a great idea," Elise told Brett.

"It wasn't my idea," he said. "Trish wanted everyone to be here for dinner."

"More plans for the ranch?" Liam asked hopefully. "Maybe we can stage kiddie rodeos. I'm sure my big brother can find a liability policy to cover those."

Brett groaned, and Liam and Blake laughed.

"I could train them to become rodeo riders," Liam continued. "I'm sure I can get Caleb Haven to sign up."

"I'm sure he would prefer his uncle Dusty to teach him," Blake said, but he grinned as if he was teasing his brother.

"I would, too," Liam agreed. Then he glanced back at Trish. "I'm sorry. What are your plans? I'm sure it's something great."

He was so sweet. She used to wish she had a younger brother. She'd felt like she had sisters in Frankie and Maci, but she'd really wanted a brother. And she would have been lucky to get someone like Liam.

She shook her head. "That's not why I wanted you all here."

"What is it?" Elise asked with concern.

"Her mom and ex-husband showed up today," Frankie said, her voice sharp with resentment.

Maci gasped. "Are you all right?"

She nodded.

"She was fierce." Frankie praised her like she had earlier.

Brett didn't agree this time. He just sat in his chair, his body tense as if he was bracing himself for her to continue.

So she told them the rest. About the accusations of fraud and the threats to go after the ranch.

"Can they go after it?" Blake asked Maci.

She sighed. "They can try."

And knowing her mother and Harold, Trish had no doubt that they would.

"I should have invited Nolan to this meeting, too," she said.

Frankie sucked in a breath. "He isn't family, and you don't need him anymore. You have Maci."

"I understand," Maci said. "He represented you in the divorce. And they could even go after him over that. He should be informed."

Frankie groaned. "Let me know when he'll be here, and I will make sure that I am somewhere, anywhere, else."

Trish wondered about that. The estate was settled, so why was Frankie still here and not back on the road?

The ranch was probably in her blood, too, like it had been in Trish's dad's and like it was in Trish's. She loved it here. But if there was any chance that her mother or her ex could get their hands on a share of her share, she would rather give it up to the others. To the people her father had really wanted to inherit and stay here.

But she hoped it wouldn't come to that, that between Maci and Nolan, they could make sure that Trish's father's wishes were granted.

She glanced around the table then and she wondered for the first time if her father might have had other intentions. Everybody talked about how Sadie and Lem liked to matchmake.

Could her father have intended something similar? Blake and Maci were together, but that was more in spite of the will than because of it. Could he have wanted her and Frankie with Brett and Liam?

Elise hadn't met Liam until after Trish's dad died. She couldn't imagine Liam with anyone but Elise. They were so in love. And Brett and Frankie were so much like brother and sister.

But she and Brett…

They were definitely not like brother and sister. He wasn't family to her like Liam and Blake and the others felt like. But he wasn't exactly her friend either.

He was just her partner. And it would have to stay that way for both their sakes now. She had already caused too much drama at the ranch, and now it was about to ramp up again. She touched her belly where a little foot was insistently kicking.

They wanted out. They would be here soon.

And she wanted to raise them here on the ranch. She wanted to raise them without the drama, without the turmoil. But she wasn't sure how to make sure that she ensured their future without risking everyone else's.

NOLAN SHOULDN'T HAVE answered his phone, and he stared down at the cell in his palm as if it had betrayed him. But it wasn't as if he'd had to answer it. He'd been pretty sure who'd been calling because the persistent woman had kept trying to reach him at his office. Then she'd figured out where he lived.

And now she'd somehow learned his cell number. She was as resourceful as she was persistent and so he'd finally answered her call. Maybe he shouldn't have been avoiding her all this time. Maybe it was inevitable that it all come out anyway. All the secrets.

His cell rang again, and he swiped to accept. "Stokes."

"Nolan, it's Trish Dempsey."

For a second he'd thought it might have been *her* calling back, making sure that he would really keep his word. She didn't know him; he always kept his word.

But it was Trish.

"Haven't heard from you in a while," he said, and he sat up a little straighter in the chair in his home office. "Is everything okay?"

"No," she replied.

He sighed. "I don't want to say I told you so…" But he wasn't surprised that he could.

"It's not about the ranch," she said. "Well, it is about the ranch. But not in the way that you're probably thinking it is."

He smiled at her vagueness. "What are you talking about?"

"My mother and ex-husband showed up at the ranch today," she said. "They found out my father died, and they're claiming I defrauded them for not disclosing that during the divorce. They're going to try to get the ranch away from me and from the others." Her voice cracked in his phone. "We have to make sure they can't do that."

"They can't," he said.

"If there is any chance, though, I will do whatever I have to so that they don't get even a share of it," she said. "If I have to give up my share to the others, I will do that."

"Trish—"

"No, I'm serious," she said. "My mother getting her hands on this ranch again—" he could almost hear her shuddering over the phone "—that would be the ultimate betrayal of my father."

Nolan believed her father had betrayed her when he'd split her inheritance up with strangers. "Are the Lemmons making you think that you have to give up your share so that she doesn't get it?"

"No, of course not," she said. "They don't know that I would sign away my rights."

"And they don't have to know," he said. "There is no way that your mother or your ex-husband can get their hands on your inheritance."

"Are you sure?"

"Yes, and I would be happy to show you the laws about inheritance," he said.

"I need you to meet with my partners and Maci and assure all of us of that," she said.

Her partners.

She had just as fully embraced the Lemmons as her father had. What was the deal with them?

"I presume I will see you all this weekend at the party?" he said.

"What party? Where?" she asked.

He chuckled. Sadie March Haven was certainly living up to her legend with her persistence in tracking him down and making him promise to appear at her party. "At Ranch Haven," he said.

"You were invited to a party at Ranch Haven?" she asked. "What kind of party?"

"A welcome home party," he said. "For you, Trish."

Now her gasp rattled the phone.

"I must have ruined the surprise," he said, but he didn't feel guilty about it. There would be other surprises at this party. A lot of them.

CHAPTER TWENTY-TWO

WHILE TRISH HAD been on her phone with her lawyer, Grandma Sadie had called Brett with the invitation for the party at Ranch Haven for her.

A welcome-home-to-Willow-Creek party.

And, when Trish had ended her call with Nolan Stokes, she'd informed Brett that his grandmother had already invited her lawyer.

Why?

Was this one of her and Grandpa's matchmaking schemes? But if so, then the match they might be trying to make was between Trish and her lawyer?

A fierce jealousy caught Brett by surprise. He'd never felt anything like that before. The feeling continued to gnaw at him days later as he drove Trish out to Ranch Haven.

Or maybe he was just unnerved because Trish was. Despite her lawyer's assurances about her mom and ex-husband's threats, she'd been different since their visit. Quiet.

He missed her excitement over her camps and

the petting zoo. And he hated that she had dark circles beneath her beautiful eyes, like she hadn't been sleeping. He wished that he'd managed to get rid of Belinda and Harold before they'd upset her like this.

"You're not worried about this party, are you?" he asked as he made the turn onto the long driveway that led back to the enormous two-story house with the wings that Sadie had built onto it years ago.

"I don't understand why they would throw me a welcome home party," she said like she had a few days ago when her lawyer had told her about it. "I've only met them once. And after my parents divorced, I didn't live here…just those summers and holidays I spent at the Four Corners."

He shrugged. "I don't know, either. Grandma sure seems to like parties, or at least she likes getting all of her family together."

"But I'm not family," Trish said.

He chuckled. "I think Grandma and Grandpa tend to make everyone they meet part of the family."

"Through matchmaking?"

"Sadie has definitely been known to make some matches in her family," he said. "Is that what you're worried about?" Maybe he wasn't the only one with concerns about why her lawyer had been invited.

She glanced across the console at him. "I'm not

worried about that. I can't imagine they would want to set me up with anyone in their family."

"You have to stop putting yourself down," Brett said. "Everybody understands why you couldn't come back for your dad's funeral, and they also understand about the will."

"What about them?" she asked as she rubbed her belly.

"My family loves babies," he said. "Your pregnancy is another reason they would *love* to match you up with someone in the family." So maybe he didn't have to worry about them trying to match her up with the lawyer. But what about him?

He was the last Lemmon bachelor.

That realization should have scared him, but he didn't feel anything but relief that they probably wouldn't be trying to match her up with Stokes.

She emitted a wistful-sounding sigh. "Your family is so different from mine."

"That's a good thing," he said.

"It is."

He reached across the console and touched her hand. "I'm sorry that I didn't step in more when your mother and ex visited. But you were handling it so well..." In the moment. But they had still affected her. Too much.

"You already step in so much to help me, Brett," she said, and she turned her hand over and entwined her fingers with his. "And I appreciate that, but I also appreciated that you trusted me to handle them myself that day."

He gently squeezed her fingers. "And you did. And Stokes told you that you don't have to worry about them getting part of the ranch. It's all good. Let's just enjoy your party."

He parked near the old schoolhouse Sadie had moved from town years ago when the city had been about to tear it down. There were already so many vehicles in the driveway that it was the closest he could park to the main house. He ran around the front of his truck to open the door for Trish and help her out. But she hesitated for a moment as she studied all the trucks and cars.

"How big is this party?" she asked, her voice nearly a whisper, as if she was worried someone might overhear her.

"These are probably just the vehicles of the people who live here," he said. "It's a big family." He remembered how overwhelmed he'd been on his first visit here and even on his last for his grandfather's birthday party.

Her light brown eyes widened with surprise. "And I thought we had a lot of people living at the Four Corners."

He laughed. "Not even close to Ranch Haven. This is a busy place. Loud. Full of kids and animals."

"Are you warning me?" she asked.

He nodded. "Are you up for this?"

She drew in a deep breath, then nodded. She put her hand in his, and as he helped her down from the truck, something swelled in his heart. "You look beautiful today," he said, the words just slipping out of him at how lovely she looked in her pale green dress and sandals.

"I didn't think I should wear my bibs to a party," she said. She touched her curls with her free hand. "And I made sure to get all the straw out of my hair."

With his free hand, he touched her soft curls. "I don't think you missed any."

She really was beautiful. So beautiful that she nearly took his breath away. He wanted to kiss her so badly that he leaned down a bit, his face so close to hers that he could smell the mint of her breath.

The way she stared up at him with her gaze intent on his mouth made him think that she might want him to kiss her. But they had both agreed, after their kiss on the hayride, that they couldn't risk their partnership getting awkward over this attraction. Because both had vowed to stay single, it couldn't lead to anything but disappointment and heartbreak.

But Brett had begun to rethink his vow. Liam was proving that he could work hard on the ranch and maintain his wife and child as priorities, too. He and his family were thriving. So it was possible to have it all like Liam.

Still, Trish wasn't likely to believe that, especially after that visit from her mom and her ex that had reminded her of how miserable her marriage had been. And he wasn't about to put any pressure on her now, not when she was already so stressed from their visit. Just because he'd changed his mind didn't mean that she would. Ever.

For a second, when Brett had helped her out of the truck, Trish had thought he might kiss her. And she'd really wanted him to kiss her.

But then he'd pulled back.

So maybe she'd just imagined the way he'd been looking at her. Or maybe not. He had called her beautiful. And because of the way he'd looked at her, she'd felt beautiful.

But now, as they neared the front door of the huge house, nerves clamored in her stomach. Was she overdressed? Underdressed?

She had no idea what to expect at Ranch Haven. And she was glad that after taking her hand to help her down from the truck, Brett kept holding it. She needed that connection to him, that support he always offered her whether he agreed with her or not.

Instead of pressing the doorbell, Brett just reached for the doorknob with his free hand and pushed the door open. "Grandma gets mad if we ring the bell," he said. "Only salespeople and strangers ring the bell."

She smiled. While she'd only met his grandparents briefly, she had been so impressed. She'd been so young when both sets of her grandparents passed that she didn't remember them. But people like Sadie and Lem would be unforgettable no matter how long their grandchildren and great-grandchildren had them.

She pressed her free hand to her belly where the babies were kicking and moving. She wouldn't be able to give them grandparents, let alone great-grandparents. Her mother had made it clear to her years ago that she would never be called Grandma and that she wouldn't help raise anyone else's kids. Raising her own had been difficult enough.

Trish couldn't remember being difficult; she'd always tried so hard to please her mom. She would never put that kind of pressure on her children.

"Are you okay?" Brett asked.

She realized that she hadn't moved yet; her feet were planted on the porch. Then a fluffy ball of black fur catapulted out of the house, jumping around her legs and Brett's. It snapped and growled, then latched on to the bottom of Brett's jeans.

Instead of being horrified, Brett laughed and reached down to scoop it up with one hand. "Meet Feisty," he said to Trish. The little dog pressed kisses to his chin. "She's fierce like her owner."

"She's Lem's dog now, the little traitor," Sadie said as she joined them. But Feisty jumped from

Brett's arms to hers when Sadie hugged him. Then the older woman hugged Trish, too, and she somehow wound up with the fluffy long-haired Chihuahua in her arms.

"Welcome to Ranch Haven," Sadie told her. "And welcome home to Willow Creek, my dear."

Trish could have pointed out that she'd never really lived in Willow Creek, and that she had moved here weeks ago. But she just smiled. "Thank you for this party," she said. "I was definitely not expecting one."

"We love a party at the ranch," Sadie said. "And there is no better way for you to meet all of the family." A trio of little boys ran down the hall then. One had pale blond hair, one sandy-brown hair and the third was a dark-haired toddler.

The one with the lightest hair stopped when he saw Brett and sighed. "You're not Billy the Kid."

"No, I'm not," Brett said with a smile. "But he and Elise and Lucy should be here soon."

"Baby," the toddler said with a wide smile.

"This is Caleb, Ian and little Jake," Sadie introduced her great-grandsons. "This is Miss Trish."

Little Jake pressed a hand against her stomach. "Baby," he said again.

Trish nodded as her heart warmed with affection for him. "Two babies," she told him.

"Aunt Melanie had two babies," Ian said. "They cry a lot."

"A lot," Caleb agreed.

Trish felt that pang of alarm she'd felt when Darlene had told her how difficult twins could be. Could she handle it alone?

Brett squeezed her hand, and she was surprised to find that he was still holding it through all the greetings. She noticed when Sadie noticed, and a big smile spread across the older woman's face.

"Miss Elise is coming?" Ian asked. "She isn't out saving kids?"

"Not today," Brett replied.

"What about you?" Ian asked Trish. "Do you save kids, too?"

She shook her head.

"Miss Trish is starting a camp at the Four Corners," Brett said.

She glanced at him with surprise that he would bring it up.

He continued, "She's converting our old bunkhouse into a big cabin. And she has a petting zoo with all kinds of animals, even a pet skunk, and she's going to offer hayrides."

"Wow!" Caleb said. "I want to go to camp."

"Me, too!" Ian exclaimed.

"Me, too!" little Jake mimicked the older boys.

"I guess Elise is right," Brett said. "Your camps are going to make us a fortune."

Trish chuckled. "And we didn't even have to offer the rodeo riding classes."

"What?" Caleb exclaimed. "Rodeo riding classes? Sign me up!"

"Me, too!" Ian exclaimed.

"Me, too!" Jake echoed.

Trish gave Brett a guilty look and shrugged. "Whoops..."

"Can't imagine what the liability insurance will cost for that," Brett muttered.

Trish laughed.

Sadie laughed, too. "Now, come back to the kitchen, you two. Trish needs to meet everyone else before the other guests arrive."

"And she needs to get some chocolate chip cookies before Caleb eats them all," Ian said. "Aunt Melanie said that when her babies were in her belly they really liked chocolate chip cookies."

Trish was glad that she had Brett to hang on to as she met person after person and child after child. She would never remember all the names, but she would remember how kind and welcoming everyone was even though they'd never met her and must have heard about what she'd done in regards to her father's will. But like Brett had assured her, they must have understood and didn't judge her for any of the choices she'd made. The Haven family was more accepting of her than her own mother was.

Her heart warmed with appreciation for all of them. Then her partners from the Four Corners showed up, and her heart swelled with more love for them. They were all so kind and funny and special to her.

Frankie and Maci had always been her sisters, but now Liam and Blake were her brothers. And Elise was another sister and Lucy her niece. She had to make sure that nothing happened to the Four Corners because of her, because that was their home even more than it had ever been hers.

BOB WASN'T SURPRISED that there was another party at Ranch Haven. His dad and stepmother loved throwing them. He was surprised, when he started wading through all the people in the house, to find Sue Lancaster among them. She'd dipped out onto the patio where he'd headed for relative peace from the chaos in the kitchen.

"Uh, hello, Sue," he greeted her. "I didn't know you knew Trish Dempsey."

Sue shrugged. "I only met her once at the hospital. I'm not sure why I was invited. I guess it's because I often watch Bailey Ann."

Sadie's grandson Dr. Collin Cassidy and his wife Genevieve had adopted Bailey Ann. The little girl had had a heart transplant not that long ago. "That's sweet of you to watch her," he said.

"She's a sweet girl," Sue said with a smile. That smile transformed her from the usually tense-looking older woman she was to the carefree teenager she'd once been.

He sucked in a breath at how lovely she was. "You haven't changed a bit," he murmured.

She touched her hair that was a silvery white

instead of the pale blond it once had been. "I've changed a lot, Bob." The tension was back in her face and body.

He sighed with disappointment. He knew that he'd messed up with her years ago, but he'd never figured out how. Or he just couldn't remember after their last disastrous date because he couldn't remember much about that date at all. "I'm sorry," he murmured. He was sorry for whatever he'd done that had upset her. And he was even sorrier that she might have changed because of it.

CHAPTER TWENTY-THREE

BRETT STUCK CLOSE to Trish to make sure that she wasn't overwhelmed with all the people and noise like he usually was. Like his dad was. He'd seen him escape to the patio a short while ago.

That was where Brett usually went, too. But not today. Trish was meeting so many new people and he wanted to be there to support her. To answer any questions she might have and to make sure that nobody judged her.

But she kept looking around, and he felt that unfamiliar jab of jealousy again when he realized who she was looking for. "No sign of Stokes yet," he mumbled.

She shook her head. "He said he would be here."

"Can you trust him?" he asked, and he wasn't asking out of jealousy now. He understood why she needed to talk to her lawyer in person. The man had assured her that the ranch was safe, but Brett knew Trish needed some proof from her lawyer to relieve the fear Brett had seen in her since her mother's visit.

"I thought I could," Trish said. "But I've trusted the wrong people before."

Like her own mother and her ex-husband. He wanted her to know that he wasn't like them.

"You can trust me, Trish," he promised. "I would never lie to you or try to manipulate you."

He only wanted to support her. And it wasn't because she was pregnant and vulnerable like Frankie had said; it was because she was Trish. She was strong and creative and sweet. And he'd fallen for her and for the babies she carried. He wasn't sure when it had happened, and he certainly hadn't wanted to.

But he had, even though he knew that she wasn't ready for a relationship so soon after her divorce. He had to accept that she might never be ready.

But just as he'd vowed to help his brothers run the ranch and protect their relationships, they could do the same for him. If Trish was ever ready, Brett figured he just might be able to make a relationship work without anyone or anything suffering. Not even him.

TRISH WONDERED ABOUT Brett's sudden intensity. Did he think she still had doubts about him and his brothers? That she still wondered if they could be the con artists that Nolan had made them out to be?

She'd seen with her own eyes how hard they

worked on the ranch. And in the books, she'd seen how little they'd been paid for all that hard work. They were good men who'd helped out her father, not because they knew they would be in the will, but because they were just good men. Selfless and honest and so willing to help anyone and everyone.

Brett had been so helpful to her in bringing her plans for the ranch to fruition. She'd even caught him feeding and caring for the petting zoo animals that he'd helped her pick out. He seemed particularly drawn to the skunk, maybe because it couldn't protect itself anymore. And Brett was just naturally protective of everyone around him. Of his siblings. And of her.

He was being protective of her at this party, too, sticking close to her side, introducing her to everyone and making sure that they were nice to her.

She knew that he was protecting her. She didn't need his protection, though, because everyone was so friendly and warm. But she did appreciate how close he stuck to her. He looked so handsome today in dark jeans, a white Western shirt and his black cowboy hat and boots. Her heart fluttered every time she looked at him, and her skin tingled from how he held her hand.

Other people had noticed. Sadie wasn't the only one who'd caught their hand-holding and smiled. Lem had hugged them both, and she'd heard some of the others murmur, "Sadie strikes again."

Sadie had had nothing to do with Trish's feelings for Brett. They were all because of him, because he was such a good man. She'd been determined to only love her babies and put them first. But she couldn't imagine Brett ever hurting them or anyone else.

Not even her.

He was too selfless to do that; he always put everyone else before himself. It would have been impossible for her not to fall for a man like that. But knowing how willing he was to make sacrifices for everyone else—that was the last thing she wanted him to do for her. She had to make sure that the ranch was safe for him because he'd made it clear over and over how he intended to always put that and his family first.

"I know I can trust you," she assured him. She could also love him, if it wasn't so soon after her divorce. But had she ever had a real marriage?

Harold wasn't who he'd pretended to be when they'd started dating, so she hadn't ever felt as close to him as she already did with Brett. Most of her marriage, they'd lived separate lives. She'd gotten married to start the family she'd always wished she'd had, a family like the Havens—full of love and affection and acceptance. But she'd been more alone in her marriage than she'd ever been. So no, it wouldn't be too soon for her to fall for someone else when that someone was a man like Brett, who was genuine and dependable and honorable.

Tears stung her eyes as emotion overwhelmed her.

She did love him. She loved him so much that she would give up her share of the Four Corners if there was any chance that Harold and her mother could get a piece of it.

"Where is Nolan?" she muttered. She needed him to assure her that the ranch was safe.

"Nolan?" a female voice repeated.

Trish was surprised to see the ER nurse standing next to her in the kitchen. "Sue, right?" she greeted her. She'd only met the woman once, so she didn't think she was here to welcome Trish home to Willow Creek. Was she related to the Havens as most of the town seemed to be either by blood or marriage?

She noticed the woman's ring finger was bare. And then Bob, Brett's dad, appeared behind her. His face was flushed, and so was hers, like they'd either been arguing or they were just embarrassed.

"Uh, welcome back to Willow Creek," Sue said. "I just wanted to say that before I left..." She looked anxious to get out of there.

Trish could see how it might be overwhelming to be around so many people and kids. But as an ER nurse, the woman would be used to chaos.

"I'm glad you came," Trish said, although she was also confused.

"Look who else finally strolled in..." Frankie remarked. Like Brett, she'd been keeping close to Trish, probably being as protective as he was. "The sleazeball lawyer..."

"He is a not a sleazeball," Trish said, automatically coming to Nolan's defense.

But it was Sue's reaction that stunned her. All the color drained from the woman's face as she stared at the man who'd walked into the kitchen.

He was staring back at her—at her and at Bob. Nolan's eyes weren't just similar to Sue's; they were exactly the same. They had to be related.

"Oh, no..." Sue whispered.

Trish found herself touching the woman's arm, steadying her like Sue had done for her when she'd tried to get dressed at the hospital. The poor woman looked like she was about to pass out from shock.

But how was seeing Nolan Stokes a shock to her?

NOLAN HAD BRACED himself for this, for all eyes to focus on him the minute he walked into the house of the formidable Sadie Haven. He was used to that kind of attention. Sometimes he even commanded it. At least in a courtroom.

But one gaze unsettled him.

Or maybe two.

Frankie Dempsey stared at him with her usual contempt, and for some reason that bugged him.

It bugged him how little she thought of him, and maybe that bugged him because for some strange reason he found himself thinking about her. All too often.

But the gaze that unsettled him the most came from eyes that looked exactly like his and like his children's eyes. He was glad that he hadn't brought the kids like Sadie had urged him to.

He didn't want his children here for this, though he would have to explain everything to them soon. But first, he had to explain it to everyone else.

Trish was his client, and hopefully also a friend since he had so few. So he addressed her first, "Welcome back to Willow Creek, Trish." He leaned down and kissed her cheek. And both Frankie Dempsey and Brett Lemmon sucked in a breath like he'd slapped them.

So Brett was jealous.

He grinned.

And Frankie?

She certainly wasn't jealous of him. She couldn't stand him. But she had no idea…

Nobody did.

"I'd like to speak with you," Trish said softly, "with my partners…like I told you on the phone a few days ago."

He nodded. "Looks like your partners are all here." Sticking close to her like Brett and Frankie were. There was a crowd of people around them, too.

Including the woman with his eyes and the man who stood just behind her looking confused.

Did he really not know?

"As I told you on the phone, Trish, you don't have to worry," he said. "Your mother signed away her claim to the ranch long ago in exchange for a big check from your father. She can't touch the Four Corners."

"And Harold?"

He shook his head. "He can't either. Even if you hadn't been divorced before you claimed your inheritance, a spouse doesn't automatically share an inheritance. Your share of the ranch is yours alone. So you don't have to sign away or give up your inheritance to protect the ranch and your—" he stared at all of them "*—partners.*"

Frankie and Brett whirled toward her. "You were willing to do that?" Frankie asked while Brett just looked stunned and something else.

In love…?

Nolan actually felt a flash of pity for him. Love had brought Nolan nothing but pain.

He turned back to that other couple now, the woman with his eyes and the man standing behind her. "Hey, Mom, Dad," he greeted them.

And now everyone gasped while the woman got even paler and started to shake. He raised his voice even louder like he did in a courtroom to project. "Seems like I'm the only one who knows this, so let me share a deep, dark secret. My parents gave me up for adoption when I was born. They are Sue Lancaster and Bob Lemmon."

From the look of complete shock on Bob Lemmon's face, Nolan finally believed that his biological father had had no idea that he had another son.

Sue shook her head as tears filled her eyes, the eyes she'd genetically passed onto him and he onto his children. "I wish you hadn't done this..." Tears trailed down her face. "Not like this..."

He'd only met her twice. The first time had been nearly a year ago when he'd finally decided to figure out why he'd been given up for adoption, why nobody had wanted to keep him. First his biological parents, then his wife.

He hadn't told Sue his name then, or anything about himself. He'd wanted answers, not to answer any questions himself. And then, several weeks ago, when Sadie Haven Lemmon had started digging around about him, he thought he'd better give his biological mother a heads-up that her secret was probably going to come out.

"I gave you the chance to tell him if he hadn't known," he reminded her.

"But I didn't know if he knew or not..." she whispered.

"I didn't know," Bob said. "I had no idea..." He kept shaking his head like he still didn't believe it.

"I paid your assistant to get something with your DNA on it," Nolan admitted. "I can show you the results if you need proof that I'm your son. Your oldest son." He glanced at Brett then to see how he was taking the news that he wasn't the firstborn anymore.

Brett looked as stunned as his father. Not upset or mad. Just surprised.

The only person who looked mad was Frankie Dempsey. But that would probably be the way she always looked at him. She shook her head. "This was a real jerk move even for you, Stokes," she said.

And then he finally saw himself how she was seeing him, as someone who'd snuck around and stirred up trouble and had now caused a big scene at a party for her very pregnant cousin.

He'd been so hurt and angry over his wife leaving not just him but their children, too, that he hadn't been thinking clearly. His kids' pain had affected him most, and he'd blamed himself for it, for the reason they'd been abandoned. Something had to be wrong with him or with the people who'd brought him into this world. And he'd let his anger build, not with his wife, but with his biological parents, with Sue Lancaster and with Bob Lemmon.

But now that he could see more clearly and see what he'd done, he had to admit that Frankie Dempsey was right. He was a jerk.

No wonder his wife had left him and that he had no friends and family. Except he did have family…

Nearly everyone in this house was related to him by blood or marriage. And now he had probably just alienated every single one of them just as he had Frankie Dempsey.

Yet, for some reason, alienating her seemed to bother him most of all.

CHAPTER TWENTY-FOUR

BRETT COULDN'T FIGURE out what was the biggest shock. Finding out that he had an older brother or the fact that Trish had been willing to give up her share of the ranch to protect it from her mother and her ex.

Blake and Liam had both offered to do that at some point in the course of the will being contested. But then they had both felt a bit strange to be inheriting at all since they hadn't worked at the ranch as long as he had. Trish, on the other hand…

He knew how much the ranch meant to her. That it was the place where she'd made her happiest memories and it was the place where she wanted to raise her children. She wanted to give them the childhood she'd wished she'd had. And she wanted to share that experience with other kids through her camps.

She didn't just love the ranch; it was everything to her. Her safe space from her mother, from criticism and pain. And she'd been willing to give it up to keep it safe.

"Are you okay?" she whispered to him.

He shook his head. He wasn't okay. He was so in love with her that he could barely breathe, let alone think. She was the kindest, most generous person he'd ever met. And he didn't want to lose her.

So he just kept hanging on to her, their fingers entwined. She kept him anchored and calm as the revelations kept coming. He was more worried about his dad than he was himself. It was clear Bob had had no idea he'd fathered a child with his prom date all those years ago.

And then, after dropping that bomb on all of them, Nolan Stokes just turned around and walked out of the room. Someone rushed out after him. Maybe Frankie.

Sadie and Lem might have, too.

He couldn't see them, though. He saw only Trish as she turned toward him and rose on her tiptoes. With her free hand, she touched his jaw that he hadn't even realized he was clenching.

"Are you okay?" she asked again. "I am so sorry. I had no idea..."

Neither had he. He'd never been in love before, but he was now. And he finally understood why his brothers had risked their hearts like they had. It wasn't as if he had a choice, though.

Trish, and her babies, had stolen his heart without him even realizing he was losing it. And now he had to make sure that he didn't lose her, too. He didn't want her to sign off her share and leave the Four Corners, because then there would never be the chance of her falling in love with him, too. Of her trusting him with not just her heart but with her children as well.

But Nolan had offered his assurances, and Brett had a feeling that the man spoke the truth. It might not be pretty, that truth, but he wasn't going to lie.

So Trish's share of the ranch should be safe.

And Nolan Stokes was Brett's older brother.

TRISH WAS USED to Brett supporting her, but now she was the one trying to support him. He looked like his legs had been kicked out from under him. All the Lemmons and even the Havens looked that way: totally shocked.

"I'm sorry," she apologized to all of them like she just had to Brett. "I had no idea what Nolan's connection was to all of you."

But now it made sense why he'd sought her out and warned her about the Lemmons. He was holding a grudge against them. He must have thought that they'd rejected him when he was a baby. But it was clear that they had had no idea he even existed. Sue was the only one who'd known. Not Bob and certainly none of his family.

"You don't need to apologize," Brett said. "Of course you didn't know..." And there he was again, her white knight rushing to her rescue, defending her even from herself.

Was it any wonder that she'd fallen for him?

But she couldn't tell him that, not now when he had to be reeling, as everyone clearly was, over Nolan Stokes's shocking revelation. All she could do was be here for him as he'd been for her since she'd shown up at the Four Corners late that night so many weeks ago.

Had she fallen for him then? At first sight?

Or had she fallen for him when he'd caught her on the stairs in the bunkhouse? Or when he'd carried her to his truck and into the ER when she'd thought she was in labor? Or had it been when he wrapped his arms around her on the wagon?

She didn't know the exact moment that she'd fallen, but she knew that she was definitely in love. Real love. The kind she'd never felt before.

The kind that might actually last…if she could take that risk. Would Brett be willing to take it, too? Or was he already overwhelmed with everything that was going on?

And how determined was he to stick to his original vow of putting the ranch first, before himself, before marriage and children?

Could he come to love not just her but her babies as well? She couldn't be with someone who wouldn't be able to love them as much as she did. She knew all too well how much it hurt to have a parent who didn't unconditionally care about you.

As hard as she'd fallen for Brett, she had to keep her feelings to herself if he was still determined to stay single and childless. She couldn't make things any more awkward than they already were at the moment.

BOB PROBABLY SHOULD have raced after Nolan Stokes, the son he hadn't known he had, as Nolan rushed out of the house. But he hadn't been able to move yet then. He'd been utterly frozen with shock. But now, as Sue started to push through the people on her way out the door, he could move. And he chased after her.

"Where are you going?" he asked her as he caught up to her on the front porch.

She shook her head, tears flowing freely down her face. "I can't..."

"Sue, I didn't know," he said. "Why didn't you tell me?"

She shook her head again.

"Please," he said. "You owe me an explanation."

She turned on him then, her pale eyes ice cold. "I owe you?"

"You didn't tell me you were pregnant."

"Yes, I did," she said.

He shook his head, but she didn't seem to notice as she continued, "And that was hard to do with the way that you avoided me after the prom. You got what you wanted and then just never called again. You left for college without so much as a goodbye." She stared at him, fury written all over her features.

Heat rushed to his face. "I acted that way because I was embarrassed," he admitted. "I didn't know the punch was spiked at prom. I got so drunk that I don't remember anything about that night."

She narrowed her eyes and studied his face as if she didn't believe him.

And now, knowing what he'd forgotten, he could understand her skepticism. "Really," he vowed. "It's all a blank. And I felt so bad about that that I was too embarrassed to try to talk to you again. I knew I blew it with you. And I didn't know how to undo it."

"You could have called me," she said. "Or at least called me back when I tried to get ahold of you at college. I had to get your number from your dad."

Guilt washed over him now. He'd been mad at his dad for giving her his number because he'd figured that Lem was trying to set him up with a Willow Creek girl so that Bob would come home. And by that time, he'd met his wife-to-be, too. So he hadn't called Sue back.

Things had felt safer with his wife. His feelings hadn't been as overwhelming as they'd been with Sue.

"I'm sorry I didn't call you back," he said. "I didn't know why you were calling. And since we never talked, how did you think I knew that you were pregnant?"

"I sent you a letter," she said. "It was never returned to me, so I figured you read it."

He shook his head. "No..." But now something from those days came back to him. The day that the girl he'd been dating had suddenly asked about Sue Lancaster. He'd wondered how she knew about his first crush, the beautiful blue-eyed girl he'd fallen for in high school.

Had she seen the letter? Had she seen it before he had and never showed it to him? They'd been in and out of each other's dorms then.

"You never saw the letter?"

He shook his head. "No. I had no idea, Sue. I swear I would have come back if I'd known. I would have been there for you."

She shuddered. "Nobody was. I was already away at college when I realized I was pregnant, and my parents wouldn't let me come home. They told me that the best thing I could do for the baby I was carrying was to give him up, so a mature, established, happy couple could raise him."

"Did they?" he wondered aloud.

She shrugged. "I don't know. Nolan won't answer any of my questions about himself. He just seems so angry." Her voice cracked with sobs.

Bob closed his arms around her, holding her trembling body. "I am so sorry, Sue." He hated that she'd had to go through her pregnancy alone, with no support from her parents and especially with no support from him.

If only he'd known…

"Me, too," she murmured as her arms closed around him. "Me, too."

He'd messed everything up so badly, and apparently not just with her but with the son he hadn't known he had. Now he understood why Nolan had hired his assistant to spy on him. He'd wanted to know if his dad was the deadbeat he'd thought he was. And he'd wanted to know for certain if Bob was his dad. Getting that confirmation hadn't brought the man any peace, though. He was still so angry with him.

Rightfully so.

Bob would have to figure out a way to fix this.

"So you really don't remember anything from that night?" she asked as she stepped back from him again.

His arms fell to his sides, and he shook his head. Then he clarified, "Except how beautiful you looked. I remember picking you up at your house and the blue dress you wore and the corsage I found had a flower that exactly matched the color of your eyes."

Those eyes stared at him now with such shock—and something else, something he used to see in them all those years ago.

CHAPTER TWENTY-FIVE

AN UNCOMFORTABLE FEW days had passed since Trish's welcome-back-to-Willow-Creek party. Nobody knew what to think of having another sibling they hadn't known about, so they mostly avoided the subject.

And so far they'd avoided Nolan, too.

Brett was tempted to reach out to him, but the man seemed so angry and bitter. And Brett didn't understand why. It wasn't as if his dad had made a choice to give him up; he hadn't even known about him. His dad had come by the Four Corners to make that all clear to them.

Brett should try to point that out to Nolan. But he wasn't a lawyer like him. He didn't know how to effectively argue with a man like that, who was so well-known for his courtroom victories, to get through to him. Their father had even admitted to being too intimidated to try to talk to Nolan yet.

So Brett focused on what he could control. The ranch. He worked with the cattle, getting orders ready for the new wholesaler. And he worked on

Trish's camps. The bunkhouse was finally done and ready according to the contractor. But Brett wanted to make sure that it was clean before he showed it to Trish. He was mopping up the dust from the polished floor when he heard the door creak open.

"There you are," Trish said with a smile.

"You should leave," he told her, as he tried to step closer to her to block her view of the nearly finished space. There were things he wanted to do before she saw it, like clean it and maybe put up some streamers and balloons.

She gasped as her smile faltered. "Leave?"

"Just go away for a little bit," he urged her. Just long enough for him to make the place look as special as it was to her and to him.

"You don't want me here?" she asked, her voice cracking slightly.

"Just let me clean up the dust and dirt the contractors left," he said. "I want you to see your dream come true without any distractions. Well, except maybe for some balloons and streamers." And a cake. Or cookies. Maybe he should have reached out to Grandma Sadie, so she could have thrown a party for the camp.

"Oh..." Tears glistened in her eyes.

The sight of the tears struck him like a blow, and he dropped the mop to reach out to her. "What did you think I meant?"

"For me to the leave the ranch," she said.

He shook his head. "No, no, I never want that to happen," he assured her. "I never want you to leave..." *Me*. That was what he really wanted to say. And that he loved her. But was that fair? Wasn't she still vulnerable from her divorce and her pregnancy? The last thing he wanted to do was take advantage of her. Or burden her with feelings that she couldn't return. That wouldn't be fair.

But he couldn't help loving her. "I still can't believe you were willing to give up your share of the inheritance," he said. "That you, of all people, would have signed away your share of the ranch."

"I didn't want my mother or my ex to get their hands on it," she said. "That would have destroyed my father."

"It would have destroyed you, too," he said. "You love this place so much, Trish." He touched her stomach through her overalls. "And you want to raise your children here." He could imagine them running around the place. In his mind, they would look like her, with her wild curls and her pale brown eyes. And the little girl would be leading the way, confident and brave, while her brother trailed behind her.

"It's safe," she said. "Nolan said the judge immediately dismissed the claim my mother and Harold tried to make."

"So they carried through on their threat," he said. "They really tried to get a piece of it." She had been so right about them. She had also talked to his brother.

"Yes," she replied. "But the judge said they had no valid argument to dispute ownership. My mother had signed off the deed years ago, and Harold had no right to my inheritance from my father even when we were married."

He blew out a breath of relief, grateful to the judge for shutting them down and to his brother for helping her. No matter how Nolan had handled things, he had had Trish's best interests at heart. He wasn't the snake that Frankie believed he was.

"That's good," he said as he squeezed her shoulders. "You've got everything you want, Trish."

"No."

He stepped back then and gestured around the bunkhouse with its pool table and ping-pong table and long dining table where the kids would eat and do crafts. She'd thought of everything. He just wished he'd had time to finish cleaning and staging it for her.

"No," she repeated. "I don't have everything."

He peered around the space again. "I don't see anything you missed. The hay wagon is good to go. And Liam has been working with the animals so that they'll be good with all the kids. I can't think of anything you don't have."

"You," she said, her voice soft. "You, Brett, I don't have you."

His heart seemed to stop beating for a second

before it resumed at a frantic pace. Was she saying that she wanted him? Was it possible that she'd fallen for him, too?

BRETT LOOKED AS stunned as he had when he'd found out he had an older brother. His mouth was slightly open, and his dark eyes were wide with shock.

"You," she repeated. "I want you, Brett. But I know we agreed that we wouldn't make our partnership personal or messy. And I know that you are determined to stay single and focus only on the ranch. But I can't keep it inside any longer. I can't not tell you how I feel." Her love was just too big, too overwhelming for her not to express it. "But I don't expect you to return my feelings. I know that you have no interest in marriage or children—"

He gasped as if he was just remembering to breathe. "You have me, Trish," he said. "You had me from the minute I met you after midnight in the driveway. And those babies had me from the minute I saw them on that ultrasound screen, moving around, the little girl kicking while the little boy sucked his thumb. I can't wait for them to come into the world, into *our* world. I can't wait to hold them and love them and protect them."

"Really?" She couldn't believe it. She wanted to so badly because this was the father she wanted for her children. But she knew that he was telling the truth because Brett Lemmon didn't lie. And he couldn't help himself from helping others. He was such a white knight. Her white knight. And he would be a fiercely protective, loving father for their babies.

"I love you," he said, and he grinned slightly. "I didn't want to..."

She smiled, too. "I know you really wanted to hate me."

"You're not possible to hate," he said. "You're too sweet, too genuine, too loving to resist. I couldn't help but fall for you and for the babies that are so much a part of you, of that enormous heart of yours."

"It's not all too much?" she asked. "You were so determined to put the ranch first, before marriage and kids."

He shook his head. "It's just right, Trish. Between the two of us, working side by side, we can handle anything. Nothing will suffer. Not the ranch, and definitely not these babies." He touched her stomach.

She trusted him. She knew Brett Lemmon was a man of his word. So she threw her arms around his shoulders to pull his head down for her kiss.

But he resisted. "Trish, I don't want to rush you. You just got divorced. And you're pregnant. And you were determined to raise your babies alone, to not share them with anyone."

She snorted. "We both know you wouldn't let me do anything alone. None of my partners will." Just as they all helped with Lucy, she knew they would all help her with the twins. "But I don't love you because I want your help," she said. "I love you because you give your help to me even when you don't want what I want."

"I just want you to be happy," he said.

"I know, and that's why I love you so much," she said. "It wouldn't matter if I'd been divorced for three years or three months. That was never a real marriage anyway."

"So it isn't too soon?" he asked, his dark eyes brightening with hope.

She shook her head. "I love you now, and I will always love you," she assured him.

"I love you," he said, "and I will always love you." Finally, he lowered his head and kissed her, gently and deeply, with all the love he'd just professed to her.

He felt the babies shift inside her stomach.

Chuckling, he touched her belly. "And I love them, too. I can't wait to meet them."

She felt a sudden rushing sensation and then a sharp pain. "I don't think you're going to have to wait long. They're coming." She knew this wasn't false labor, because her water had just broken on his freshly mopped floor. Fortunately, it wasn't too soon now for them to come. It was actually perfect timing.

Because now they would come into the world with a mother and a father who both loved them very much.

FOR THE FIRST time in a long time, Lem Lemmon had been feeling his age. Not so much physically—he and Feisty had just finished their morning walk—as mentally. He just couldn't wrap his mind around Nolan Stokes's big revelation at the ranch a few days ago. Sadie had invited the lawyer to the party to find out why he'd spied on their family, and his explanation had been a shock to say the least.

Lem had another grandson and apparently three more great-grandchildren. He couldn't wait to meet them all and get to know them. To love them.

"He'll come around," Sadie promised when Lem's call to Nolan once again went to voicemail. She reached across the patio table and squeezed his hand. "He's just proud and stubborn."

"He's definitely a Lemmon then," Lem said with a chuckle. Eventually, they did all come around.

Sadie chuckled, too. "Yes, he is. Good-looking just like his grandpa."

He grinned at her. "Are you sweet-talking me, woman?"

"I know, not my style," she admitted.

She was more likely to call him an old fool than good-looking, but insults had once been their love language, or at least that was how Lem chose to look at their past—when he bothered to look at it at all. There was so much going on in their present, and despite their ages, they had so much to look forward to in the future.

His cell rang and he quickly swiped the screen, hoping that Nolan was finally returning his call.

"Grandpa, it's Brett."

He felt a faint stab of disappointment that it wasn't Nolan. But Sadie was right; he would come around eventually. Sadie was always right.

"Hello, grandson," Lem greeted him, his heart filling with love.

"Grandpa, Trish and I are on our way to the hospital," Brett said, and he sounded breathless.

Then a low groan emanated from the speaker of Lem's cell.

"The babies are coming," Trish said.

"Our babies are coming!" Brett said.

Tears stung Lem's eyes while Sadie clapped her hands in excitement. "We're on our way!" she called out. "You two hang in there."

"We're going to be us four soon," Brett said. "A family in every way." He clicked off the call then.

Lem smiled at Sadie. "We didn't have to do any scheming this time either. Those two fell in love on their own."

Sadie cocked her head. "I think they had a little help."

"What did you do?" he asked.

She shook her head. "Not me. I was thinking about Trish's father and the way he drew up that will. He treated your grandsons like they were his sons. He wanted them to be."

Lem nodded. "Yes, that makes sense."

"Of course," Sadie said as she kissed him. "Who wouldn't want a Lemmon?"

Lem had a feeling that there was a Lemmon who didn't necessarily want to be a Lemmon, let alone have one. But he would deal with Nolan later.

"Let me drive to the hospital," he said. "I can't wait to get there to hold those babies." And he also wanted to be there for Brett and Trish and to celebrate them being a couple now. A family.

Because family was most important.

And hours later when the babies entered the world, it was clear that Brett understood that so very well. He sat next to Trish in her hospital bed with a twin cradled in each of his arms. She leaned over to kiss the head of the baby boy who pressed his little mittened fist against his mouth. And Brett leaned over to kiss her head. There was so much love in his dark eyes.

So much love for Trish and for their babies.

* * * * *